Fireballs

FIREBALLS

Dan Binchy

St. Martin's Press
New York

For my darling Joy,
our four children, and a rather special Gran

Library of Congress Cataloging-in-Publication Data

Binchy, Dan.
Fireballs / Dan Binchy.
p.   cm.
"A Thomas Dunne book."
ISBN 0-312-10984-9
1. Country life—Ireland—Fiction.   2. Villages—Ireland—Fiction.
I. Title.
PR6052.I7726F57   1994
823'.914—dc20   94-7141   CIP

First published in Great Britain by Century.

First U.S. Edition: August 1994
10 9 8 7 6 5 4 3 2 1

—————

MICK FLANNERY STARED in exasperation at the pile of post lying scattered on the hall floor beneath the letter box, and jabbed at it with his toe. He was a large, middle-aged man with a weight problem that even a well-cut suit could not conceal. That morning, as usual, he had arranged his hair so that it hid most of the bald patch at the back of his head. Pink jowls hung drooping from his cheekbones, like slabs of raw beef in a butcher's shop, giving him the look of a St Bernard which has developed a taste for the barrels of brandy it carries. Florid at the best of times, his complexion now took on a darker hue.

The post was impossible to ignore, even though he was already late setting off for Dublin. And most of the envelopes were of the brown, windowed variety.

Mick bent, muttering an oath, and selected one at random. Slitting it open with his thumbnail, he held the offending bill at arm's-length and bawled, 'For the love of Jaysus, Maggie, I thought you'd paid this thing ages ago. Now the shaggers are threatening to cut us off!' He waved the Final Demand in the general direction of the kitchen and his invisible wife.

When this evoked no response, he raised his voice even more and declaimed, 'Can't you see the headlines in the *Clarion* already: *"No light for our Euro MP. Mick Flannery to be kept in the dark for not paying his bills!"* Just what I need with this shaggin' election coming up!'

Maggie Flannery appeared in the kitchen doorway, wiping her hands on her apron. A tall, thin woman with a tired face, she surveyed her husband with raised eyebrows – a warning that if he wanted an argument, she was more than ready for one.

In all the years she had been married to Mick, Maggie had known few pleasures. Her greatest solace was the Church, an institution for which her husband showed scant respect – otherwise why would he always be womanising and drinking? Of course Mick went to Mass and all that – what politician could afford not to? – but she knew in her heart that it was nothing more than a cruel fraud. When he marched up the aisle each Sunday morning, a massive prayerbook clutched in one hand, to him it was merely another public function, like opening a new factory or presenting the prizes at the home-baking competition. He would stride up to the very front row, herself bobbing like a cork in his wake, kneel down, make the Sign of the Cross with a dramatic flourish, then bury his face in his hands for the rest of the service. With this bogus display of piety, Mick Flannery was advertising the fact that, at considerable inconvenience to himself, he had assembled his loyal followers and brought them here to this place of worship – so would the priest mind getting a move on with saying the Mass, as every minute of the day, even a Sunday, was precious to a Member of the European Parliament!

Michael and Margaret Flannery had not slept together since their last child was born. Their marriage had long been a succession of uneasy truces shattered by blazing rows. This she blamed on his philandering, while he attributed it to her religious mania. Yet they were careful to project the image of a normal couple, a vital ingredient for anyone seeking elected office in rural Ireland. Maggie Flannery always joined her husband on the election platforms, sitting demurely in the background. She liked to think her presence lent these farcical occasions a certain respectability. At night she prayed that God and His Blessed Mother would forgive her for such hypocrisy.

There was nothing out of the ordinary about the flare-up this morning: Mick was always short of money, however much he earned. Yet suddenly, today, Maggie decided that enough was enough. She'd reached the end of her tether. After nearly thirty years of strain, something finally snapped.

She fixed Mick with a glare of raw hatred and hissed: 'That's no more than I'd expect from an old windbag like yourself. If you ever gave me enough money I'd have paid that bill, and a lot more like it. Instead, you waste every penny you get from Brussels either drinking your skull off or chasing women half your age. 'Twould be far more in your line to be out knocking on doors and asking dacent people for their vote!'

This unexpected attack, and the home truths in her accusations, left Mick temporarily speechless. Then his flushed cheeks went purple with rage.

'Well, bejaysus, if that's what you think,' he spluttered, 'then all I can say is that I pity you – and the rest of the gossiping old busybodies down at the Legion of Mary. I'd have thought the lot of you would have been too taken up with praying and hymn-singing to bother with a sinner like me. Thanks be to God I don't have to rely on a few silly old bitches togged out like the shaggin' Ku Klux Klan to get myself elected . . .'

But Maggie Flannery was not going to let him run away with the argument. 'Maybe you do and maybe you don't,' she interrupted heavily. 'Only time will tell. But how can you be sure of anyone at all voting for you this time? Maybe that brazen hussy of a bank manager's wife you're always sniffing around will give you her Number One – from what I hear, she may have given it to you several times already. But don't mind about the likes of her, because the rest of us have copped on to your antics by now. And about time too, after years of putting up with your lies and broken promises. The only thing you ever did for the people of Brulagh was to get the Leisure Centre built, and even then you had the nerve to call it after yourself. "The Flannery Leisure Centre!" my left foot!'

Her mockery echoed round the front hall as Mick tried to regroup his forces.

But she was off again. 'Do you really believe,' she jeered, 'that you can buy votes by throwing away even more money on a . . . on a *shrine* to yourself?' Then Maggie paused dramatically before delivering her parting shot. 'Though if you ask me, it's more likely to be your tombstone. You're dead as a doornail this time round, Mick – and I'm the only one honest enough to tell you to your face!'

And on this tender, loving note, she swept back into the kitchen, slamming the door in his face.

As it turned out, these were the last words husband and wife were to exchange for several weeks to come.

2

OVER AT THE parochial house, it was almost evening before the priest got round to opening his mail.

Now he leaned back in his swivel chair, stretched luxuriantly like a cat, sighed deeply and held one particular letter out before him. Typed in red at the top was: *'For the attention of Father Jeremiah O'Sullivan, P.P. To be read at all Masses on the Sunday after next.'*

It was a Pastoral Letter from the Bishop. As with all correspondence from His Grace, it was neatly typed up by his secretary – which was just as well, because the episcopal handwriting resembled those Etruscan tomb inscriptions that even now defied the best attempts to decipher them. Previous epistles of this nature had often, because of their inordinate length, to be extended over two Sundays. In an unspoken pact with his flock, Father Jerry gave them advance warning of these double-headers. Rather than digest their Bishop's teaching on faith and morals, many of the congregation took their custom elsewhere.

Having first skimmed through it quickly to get the gist of what was in the vast, barren wasteland of His Grace's mind, the priest then went through it again more carefully.

As might have been expected, His Grace was inveighing against the evils of modernity. Today's drug culture was contrasted unfavourably with the happier times of the past. It was not surprising that the precise time and location of this Golden Age were left deliberately vague. Suffice to say that it was an age of dancing to traditional music at every crossroads. Applecheeked maidens in modest attire performed sedate jigs and reels with sturdy fellows, strong of limb and pure of heart. Bodily contact of any sort was unthinkable and the only refreshment on tap was pure water from the well. Sadly, in His Grace's view, after such a promising beginning, things had rapidly gone downhill.

The primrose path to perdition was traced in some detail down through the centuries, skidding to a grinding halt some seventeen pages later in the present squalor of discos and rock concerts, where even the most revolting excesses of mind and body had overnight become the accepted norm. In common with many others in this sleepy corner of Southern Ireland, it seemed the shock of the new had dawned on the Bishop thirty years too late. The Faithful were solemnly warned to abjure such dens of iniquity. To expose oneself to such occasions of sin would inevitably lead to unwanted pregnancies, drug abuse and an unhealthy dependence on the demon drink.

The last paragraph of the episcopal meanderings struck a discordant (if more commercial) note – being a timely reminder that the annual collection for the Foreign Missions would be taken up that very day. Those among the Faithful who found themselves unable to venture forth to preach the one, true faith to a pagan world, could do the next best thing by contributing generously to this deserving cause.

Father Jerry filed the letter carefully in a plastic folder marked PULPIT. There it shared space with advance notices of bingo sessions, whist drives and details of the new Flower Arrangement Classes to be held in the Flannery Leisure Centre. He wondered if it should be read out over two Sundays, or whether he should get it over with in one reading. More importantly, should his flock be warned in advance of such a marathon?

He was still undecided as he rummaged in the drawers of his desk for another file. Bulging with documents, this one was marked in black felt tip WAYS AND MEANS. With a start he realised that a meeting of that same committee was due to begin in less than five minutes. He picked it up, first placing his pipe in his coat pocket, and made for the front door. As he reached it, he called towards the kitchen: 'Julia May, I'm off to a meeting in Dr Buckley's. Leave the door on the latch in case I'm late, will you?'

Not waiting for a reply, he closed the door behind him and strode briskly down the short avenue that led to the street. It was almost dark and the last fleeting slivers of orange and gold were disappearing behind the dark mass of Mount Brulagh as he let himself through the open door of the surgery.

The dining room was already crowded. A large mahogany table monopolised over half the floorspace. It was littered with pencils, glasses, notepads promoting medication of one sort or another, and two gigantic ashtrays advertising some nasty fortified wine. The Doc was busy pouring a drink for a tall, elegant woman in her mid-twenties. She had long black hair cascading over her shoulders and she was speaking in the languid drawl of a genuine blue-blooded aristocrat. Her smart black trousers and perfectly cut red jacket managed to exude just the right blend of old money and good taste. Though he couldn't quite catch what she was saying, Father Jerry had no doubt about it that it would be brief and to the point.

Lady Aphra, only daughter of the Eleventh Earl of Gallerick and wife of an American called Luke Divareli, was someone who believed in speaking her mind. In the ordinary course of events, she wouldn't have been seen dead within a mile of a GAA meeting. The Gaelic Athletic Association had been formed to wean the native Irish away from rugby and cricket, the pastimes of Aphra's forebears, and encourage them to play 'national' games such as Hurley and Gaelic football. From such modest aspirations had sprung a claustrophobic monopoly that banned its members from playing 'foreign' games. Until quite recently, to attend a soccer match – or any other 'foreign' game – was to incur an automatic suspension from the Association. The fact that Aphra's breeding and background set her poles apart from the GAA and its supporters was, in itself, the clearest warning that this was to be no ordinary meeting.

When Father Jerry arrived, the Doc broke off from talking to Aphra and shot him an inquiring glance. The priest nodded and was rewarded with what appeared to be a glass vase of Irish whiskey. As the Doc handed it to him, he guided the priest to a quiet corner of the room.

'Wait till you hear what her Ladyship has in store for us. I'd better not tell you or you might drop dead from the shock . . .' He broke off here to glance at his watch. '. . . You'd better get this thing started, otherwise we'll be here all bloody night. Do you want me to round them up?'

Father Jerry nodded and made his way to the table as the

Doc bawled: 'Come on now, take your seats and we'll make a start!'

Putting on his public face, the priest looked serious as he intoned, in the same voice as he used to say Mass, that the Hon. Sec. would now read the Minutes of the inaugural meeting of the Ways and Means Committee of St Fintan's GAA Club.

This was done by Bernie, a pleasant lady in her fifty-somethings, who had long carried a torch for the Doc and took the thankless task of Honorary Secretary to every organisation of which he was a member.

'Thank you, Bernie,' Father Jerry said sedately. 'Could we have a proposer and a seconder for the adoption of the Minutes? Good. Now, as you are all aware, this committee was set up to devise ways and means to correct the alarming trend that has been creeping into the balance sheet of St Fintan's. If allowed to continue, this would inevitably result in a most embarrassing financial situation developing in the not-too-distant future . . .'

As he spoke, Father Jerry reflected, not for the first time, on the twist of fate that had sent him to this quiet backwater of Brulagh to mastermind, not the saving of souls as his priestly vocation might have suggested, but the improvement in the financial health of a sports club. Spiritual care had been replaced by fiscal management, and this applied equally to any of a dozen similar organisations. Apart from saying Mass, administering to the sick and dying and giving Absolution to the ever-dwindling number who made their way to Confession, he might as well have been a social worker. What annoyed him most about this was the fact that he was quite content with his lot. Once, before illness had halted his career, Jerry O'Sullivan had been troubleshooter-cum-errand boy for no less than the Vatican Diplomatic Corps. They, however, without a moment's hesitation, had put him out to grass the moment his health broke down, assigning him to the tiny parish of Brulagh. The priest hadn't been back to Ireland in over a quarter of a century, and was appalled at the prospect of spending the rest of his life in a dreary backwater.

Only recently, it had begun to dawn on Father Jerry that for the first time in his busy life he had found true peace. He could even chuckle inwardly at the fact that the avuncular voice now advocating fiscal rectitude had once, however unwittingly, helped

7

the notorious Archbishop Marcinkus and his cronies play merry hell with the Vatican finances.

'. . . You were therefore charged with devising some strategy to arrest, if not correct, this drift towards bankruptcy,' he summed up now to the waiting group. 'This meeting has been called to hear the result of your deliberations.'

A silence greeted his introduction. The name 'Aphra' was mumbled from several directions until it became clear that it was she who had been selected, as if by acclamation, to acquaint the Reverend Chairman with the findings of the Ways and Means Committee. Getting to her feet, Lady Aphra cut an impressive figure; with long fingers tapering to perfectly manicured nails of deepest red, she crushed out a half-finished cigarette in the ashtray. With a look of cool superiority, she took in her audience: the black-clad priest sucking on his pipe, the Doc in his crumpled tweeds and poor Bernie in her twinset that must have been rejected by Oxfam.

In a well-bred drawl, Aphra brought the committee up to date by guiding them through the various ideas that a succession of meetings had generated. The merits of sponsored walks, whist drives, raffles and non-stop draws had all been endlessly discussed. Listening to her, Father Jerry was thankful that she did not resort to her usual unladylike expletives when it came to detailing matters that were so obviously considered beneath her. All these stratagems, Aphra explained with ill-concealed impatience, were merely stopgaps that might well staunch the losses – but only for as long as the members were prepared to work night and day organising such events. Then, she insisted as her composure began to slip, they would be back where they bloody well started! She paused and looked round the expectant faces. Some were nodding in agreement at what she had said, while others were wisely biding their time until she had explained quite what it was she had in mind.

Aphra coughed to clear her throat before she came to the Doc's hobbyhorse. It was something proposed and rejected at every meeting, and with every new defeat he looked more like an elderly spaniel that has just had its bone confiscated.

'Dr Buckley has suggested that we stage a monster Céilí!' she said in a voice loaded with irony.

This evoked an assortment of knowing smiles, eyes raised to heaven in exasperation, and even some half-smothered guffaws. Despite the presence of some support for the idea, Aphra decided to knock the Céili firmly on the head once and for all by detailing its many drawbacks. There wasn't any hall large enough in which to stage such an event, therefore it would have to be held outdoors. That meant the summertime. Avoiding the period when the followers of such events might be away on holiday brought one into September. The problem here was that September was the month when both GAA All Irelands – hurling *and* Gaelic football – were staged. Supporters of both Céilis and the GAA tended to be one and the same people, so it was reasonable to assume that they would be unable – or unwilling – to pay the ticket price it would be necessary to charge if the monster Céili were to cover its expenses. Furthermore, no one could see such an event generating enough money to make such a one-off exercise worthwhile. She smiled triumphantly at the end of her demolition and even the Doc had to nod glumly in agreement: the Céili had been well and truly scuppered.

Aphra was prepared to be generous in victory. 'Now the only good thing about the Céili,' she pointed out, 'was that if everything had come together, it would have solved our financial problems at a single stroke . . .' Here she paused, eyeing the company glacially as she lit a fresh cigarette. 'Therefore, instead of a Céili – which, I think we are now agreed, won't make any serious money – I propose . . .'

She paused briefly, exhaling the smoke with obvious relish, '. . . That we stage a Rock Concert!'

3

ANOTHER DIFFICULT MEETING was taking place some hundred miles away in Dublin. The Office of the Taoiseach was a large, wood-panelled room with enormous windows looking out on a courtyard. At intervals along the walls hung the portraits of former leaders. These were a mixed bunch, but no more different from each other than the two men deep in conversation below them.

The smaller of the two, Patrick Mullarkey, was none other than the current Irish Prime Minister. His delicate fingers were steepled beneath his nose, a sure sign that he wished the meeting to end. If Mick Flannery, newly arrived from Brulagh, and seated on a corner of the huge desk with his stomach straining to escape the confines of a rumpled white shirt, was aware of this then he chose to ignore it. He was waiting impatiently for Mullarkey to finish so that he could get a word in edgeways.

'So there you have it,' Mullarkey concluded. 'The Friendly Sons of St Patrick want a heavyweight to lead their Parade on Paddy's Day. I can't go as I've things to look after here – and let's face it, Mick, they don't come much heavier than yourself.'

Mick Flannery shot the speaker a searching look. It was true his girth had expanded since the time of his winning those four All-Ireland medals, but not by *that* much, surely? There wasn't a trace of a smirk, however, on Mullarkey's boyish face. The Prime Minister patterned himself on the late JFK – right down to the toothy grin and blow-dried fringe. In Mick's opinion, this was the only possible explanation for the midget's meteoric rise to the top.

'. . . so naturally I said to myself, Mick's the only man for the job! Our Ambassador tells me that the New York GAA board want to put you in their Hall of Fame.'

When Mullarkey had broken this news at yesterday's cabinet

meeting, it had been greeted with a mixture of disbelief and unbridled hilarity. The politest comment was to the effect that the Chamber of Horrors would have been far more appropriate. There was no disputing the fact that Michael J. Flannery was a legend in his own lifetime because of his feats on the hurling field over thirty years ago. Since then his exploits in beds and bars at home and abroad had created an altogether different legend. The only possible reason for the portly figure across the desk from Mullarkey still being alive was that as a player, he had been the fittest man on the team.

The Prime Minister smiled to himself as he remembered the old days back in Brulagh when Mick was the local TD. TD was the Irish equivalent of a Member of Parliament. At that time Mullarkey was a struggling Junior Adviser attached to the Department of Agriculture. Even then he had coveted Mick's seat in the Dail, something that sparked off a lifelong enmity. In the bloodless coup that made Mick a Member of the European Parliament and allowed Pat to win the vacant seat in the Dail, the old scars did not heal as might have been expected. Mick had never helped Mullarkey in any way as he rose to the top of the political ladder. Quite the opposite, in fact.

Now the boot was on the other foot. Benign neglect of his constituents ensured that Mick's political star was on the wane. He had been damn lucky to be presented with a seat in the European Parliament due to the untimely death of its original occupant. Soon, however, Mick would have to face the music in the European Elections. Though this would not directly affect the Government majority – the next General Election not being due for three years – Mick and he sailed under the same party colours. By packing him off post-haste to America, Pat Mullarkey was throwing Mick a lifeline. The publicity gained by his leading the St. Patrick's Day Parade down Fifth Avenue could do his electoral prospects nothing but good. Being included in some ludicrous Hall of Fame wouldn't hurt either.

Mullarkey's concern to get Mick re-elected was not entirely altruistic. The greatest threat to Mick came from Noel McBride, a wiry little man who campaigned as 'the Farmers' Friend'. An arrogant but successful businessman, McBride's fingers were stuck in many profitable pies. He now proposed to apply his undoubted talents to improving the state of Irish agriculture – if only the farmers would vote for him, *en masse*. To this end, he had assumed the mantle of the Farmers' Friend.

Even now, McBride was busy spreading alarm and despondency among farmers who were already hopping mad at recent directives from Brussels. While these were aimed at reducing the enormous farm surpluses being stored in intervention, they were perceived by the sons of the soil as nothing short of a vicious attack on their very existence. A direct result was that a new party had sprung up from the seeds of this discontent – the United Farmers' Party. Their founder was fast proving himself to be a waspish orator with an impressive line in vitriolic invective – so much so, in fact, that he was expected to give Mick Flannery a good run for his money in the forthcoming elections for the European Parliament.

McBride was already making headlines by claiming that Government policy had plunged more farmers into bankruptcy than he had eaten hot dinners. Worse, still, the louse was warning that EC policies on agriculture would sound the death knell of the small farmer; he claimed that Mick Flannery's cavortings around Europe had done nothing to stop the rot. Sadly, such rantings appeared to find favour with the masses. If this were to result in Mick losing his seat, it would also be viewed in the media as a direct hit on the Mullarkey ship of state. A straw in the wind, the political pundits would claim and, at the very least, a clear indication that his political honeymoon was over. Indeed, Mullarkey was already slipping in the opinion polls and some callous hacks were muttering darkly about a 'heave'.

Mick Flannery broke in on Mullarkey's train of thought. 'What bloody Hall of Fame would that be?' he said.

Jerking back to consciousness, Mullarkey flicked through a bundle of files until he found the right one. 'The General Committee of the New York GAA are staging the award ceremony in the Gaelic Palace, no less. Try to turn up sober – and for God's sake, *don't* mention the North . . .'

The prospect of a drink-crazed Mick Flannery broadcasting his views on the delicate Northern situation over the American airwaves fell squarely into the kind of Category One Disaster that *could* force an unwelcome General Election. Raising a hand to forestall Mick's protest that such a thing could never happen, Mullarkey pressed on.

'. . . Because after all . . .' his voice assumed a honeyed note of persuasiveness '. . . you will be a kind of Ambassador at Large.'

Again Mick searched his face for any indication that he was referring to his girth but could find none.

'And this is something that might help you in your forthcoming campaign. "Responsible Statesman representing his country abroad, familiar figure in the corridors of power", that sort of thing.'

Mullarkey, whose private opinion of the electorate was unprintable, had to struggle to keep a straight face as he came out with this drivel. Even the most thoroughly brain-dead voter was aware that any close consultations Mick might engage in were conducted with the barmen and unattached ladies of whatever capital city he was currently infesting, in the pursuance of what he would, no doubt, refer to as his 'political duties'. Indeed, Mullarkey knew that it would take a lot more than a junket to New York to get Mick elected. In fact, Mullarkey was intrigued to know what Mick might have concealed up his sleeve to persuade an increasingly sceptical constituency to vote him in for another five years as their European Representative. He decided to ask Mick point blank what his plans were.

'By the way, did you have anything special in mind to hook them this time?' he ventured. 'The voters, I mean. I'm told the opposition are saying terrible things about you.'

Flannery seemed unconcerned.

'Yerrah don't pay any attention to those shaggers. They're only like fleas on a dog's back. To tell you nothing but God's honest truth, most of my time is taken with defending yourself. They're saying that what few farmers you didn't ruin with your advice in the old days, are now facing disaster due to your latest plan for agriculture. Needless to say, I'm nearly gone blue in the face from telling 'em that there's not a word of truth in it. But, as you know yourself, when it comes to sending the truth after a lie, you'd be better off pissing into the wind! Anyway, since you asked, I have this notion of making a coal port out of Brulagh.'

Mullarkey was out of his chair like a gaffed salmon. '*What?*'

'Don't jump out of your skin, for Jaysus sake. I only said a coal port. You know, like Swansea, Port Talbot, that kind of thing.'

'Christ, Mick, that's what I thought you said. Have you gone clean out of your mind? Even if the locals don't object to being choked to death with the dust, where in the name of all that's holy do you think you're going to find the coal? Sure there's hardly any turf left in the bog, not to mind coal. When we had that survey done a few years back before they closed the briquette factory, they came up with sweet damn all. You read the cursed thing yourself. It said in black and white that there was nothing there except rocks and bog. Now are you trying to tell me you've uncovered a coalmine?'

Mick made his voice sound as condescending as he could in replying. 'Calm down, Pat, or you'll do harm to yourself. I'm not telling you anything of the sort. All I'm saying is I have this contact who is in the coal business in Kentucky. His crowd are planning to ship coal over to Europe – Genoa I think – in bloody great big barges. An ocean-going tug tows about ten of 'em at a time. Then all they do is drop off one at Brulagh. They have discharging machinery on board so you just wait for the tide to rise and the barge discharges the coal onto the pier without any cranes, loaders or that kind of thing. Then it's moored offshore to be picked up by the tug with the empties coming back from Italy. Just like the milkman dropping off the bottles on your own doorstep, actually.'

'For God's sake, Mick, that bloody pier wouldn't carry a *lorry*load of coal, not to mind the contents of an ocean-going barge. You – of all people – should know that. God knows, you promised to get it fixed often enough!'

Mick shrugged off this barb. Indeed, the pier *had* played a central role in his campaigns down through the years. There was no good reason why it should not continue to do so, though he was damned if he would admit as much to the little bollix across the desk.

'Well, we'd have to spend a few quid on it all right, just to get it big enough to take a few thousand tons at a time. And maybe a bit of a road down to it for the lorries. At the moment it's hardly wide enough to take a wheelbarrow.'

'Where's the money going to come from?' Mullarkey spluttered. 'Brussels again?'

'Right the first time, Pat. All I need is an okay from the Department of the Environment – the one you used to run before they made you Taoiseach, remember?'

By now Mullarkey was close to apoplexy. 'Do you think for one moment I'm going to allow my Civil Servants to okay some crazy plan to cover my home town in coal dust just so that you can get yourself re-elected?'

Mick cut him off before he could say something he might regret. 'Easy Pat, easy! There's going to *be* no coal dust. You could eat your dinner off the stuff they mine in Kentucky. I'll go down there after New York and check it out myself. In the meantime, you surely don't want it said that you're standing in the way of three hundred jobs for your home town, now do you?'

4

THE THIN GRASS ribbon of fairway on Brulagh Golf Course tumbled down in a series of irregular plateaux to pull up short at a minuscule green whose flagstick peeped out coyly from behind yet another monstrous sand dune. Just to keep the ball in play required two or more blows of unerring accuracy. The slightest deviation from the straight and narrow spelled disaster. This gave the course a built-in failure system. As the heart beat faster, fear transmitted itself to the ball, which promptly assumed the flight pattern of a drunken snipe.

As for the green, it was a tiny oasis in a sea of tall dune grass that could have comfortably hidden a herd of elephant. It was tucked snug into the base of impressive earthworks that supported a ruined castle, once the lair of the McCarthy tribe. Now it was home to a clubhouse that commanded spectacular views of Mount Brulagh and the tiny harbour. By comparison, the village was a poor painting set in a magnificent frame. The drab buildings that lined its main street were a dull monochrome of greys ranging from the near-silver of the carved limestone steeple atop the church to the dark, almost black slate of the roofs. In between were the countless greyish tints that only unpainted concrete can provide. The magnificence of the rolling mountains and the restless Atlantic on either side served only to emphasise the dreariness of Brulagh village.

The threesome, comprising of Aphra's husband, Luke Divareli, the Doc and Father Jerry, paused at a gap in the dunes to refresh themselves with a view of the harbour. A stubby pier jutted into the water, with a freshly painted half-decker attached to it by an umbilical cord of blue nylon rope. A few smaller boats clustered round it as though seeking protection from the incoming tide. Luke Divareli turned to his playing partners.

'Can Mick really be serious about this coal thing?' he asked.

Rumours of Mick's latest hare-brained scheme had already been current in Brulagh for some time. The Doc shrugged, glancing furtively at Father Jerry in the hope that he would field the question. The priest, however, was otherwise engaged in trying to pitch his golfball over a towering sand dune.

'Hard to say,' Doc Buckley replied. 'You can never be quite sure of anything where Mick is concerned. Surely you must have heard all about some of his other crazy ideas for Brulagh? They always seem to crop up just before an election. Then, of course, when he gets re-elected, he forgets all about them. Your Orchid Club and this golf course were about the only things Mick was ever involved in that actually got off the ground. Even then, the hotel and the marina never got built.'

'No, they didn't.' Luke Divareli spoke more forcefully than usual. 'And what's more, I'm damn glad they didn't. Like I was saying to Aphra only yesterday, we've enough problems over at the Orchid Club as things are. I dont want to bellyache, seeing as how we're full till September, but it's what happens after that I worry about. Bookings between then and the start of the hunting season are light, almost nil in fact. That's why I'm right behind Aphra and this rock concert. It might fill the gap nicely.'

By now they had reached the green. Father Jerry was having an off day. His first putt steamed past the flagstick, coming to rest just short of the only bunker on the last hole, a deep mineshaft that gnawed its way hungrily into the side of the green as though taking a bite out of it.

The Doc did not let this pass without comment. 'Lucky it stopped where it did,' he grinned. 'The power of prayer, I suppose. If it finished up in that crater, we'd have to send the Gallerick pack in to flush you out of it!'

The priest let the jibe go, the better to concentrate on his next putt, but the Doc's remark was enough to get Luke going on one of his favourite hobbyhorses.

'Well, you'd have to be prepared for a long wait. Gally just won't listen when I tell him those blasted hounds are too damn slow. The guy just closes his ears and puts up the shutters. They're fine for scent and stamina but they just can't run fast enough. Last season, the visitors almost rode over them several times. Even allowing for the fact that some of the riders might have been complete novices, it still proves that the dogs need some new blood. But goddammit, that Gally's stubborn as a mule. Claims the dogs' bloodline goes back to Cromwell, for Chrissakes! Any time a stray pooch has the cheek to mate with one of the kennel bitches, he gets Harmon to drown the pups and shoot the father if he can find him . . .'

The Doc wondered whether Gally had ever considered asking Harmon the butler to do likewise to his outspoken American son-in-law. Probably not, he reflected, in view of the improvements Luke had wrought to Gallerick Hall. It could be argued that Luke had already instilled considerable speed into the Gallerick blood-line.

Luke was soldiering on regardless: 'Aphra's got stud-books going back to Methuselah. When I first suggested it, the whole family wanted to rip my head off and stuff it down my neck. When they cooled down some, they began to see the sense of it – all except Gally, that is. He goes around muttering to himself. I can't figure out which bugs the old guy the most – the idea that his beloved hounds are too slow, or that he should get in a few American stallion hounds. Now, to show he still hasn't forgiven me, he's digging his heels in and refusing to give us the back field for the rock concert. I sure hope Aphra can talk him out of it. It's a goddam nuisance 'cos she can't sign a contract with The Howling Dogs until she's sure of getting it.'

The field in question, situated at the rear of the country seat of the Eleventh Earl of Gallerick, was a giant natural amphitheatre of some sixty acres – big enough to hold fifty thousand fans. The possibility that Gally could object to them invading his back field did not seem as preposterous to either of his listeners as it did to the eager young American, currently engaged in sinking the winning putt.

'Game, set and match, I think, gentlemen,' said Luke smugly. 'Why don't we have a quick one in the lounge and go on to Sean's for a bite of lunch?'

Father Jerry demurred. 'I'll gladly take a drink off you – if only to reduce my losses. As for lunch, count me out. Julia May's expecting me.' His housekeeper ruled his roost with a rod of iron.

The tiny bar in the low clubhouse had two large windows. One framed the last green, with its ribbon of fairway ambling up to it through a canyon of towering sandhills topped with waving fringes of dune grass. It was an ever-changing palette of greens as sunlight sent shadows skittering frantically across the rolling landscape. A thin silver thread divided the flat green fields from the foothills of Mount Brulagh, looming purple and menacing against the freshly laundered sky. This was the river that skirted the Orchid Club on its winding journey to the sea. In the distance, another trio were plodding wearily towards the last green, impatient for the safe refuge of the bar and the welcome sound of ice clinking in tall glasses.

The second window trapped a seascape of breathtaking splendour. Beneath shrieking gulls and scudding clouds lay an endless necklace of deserted beach. Further off, tall black cliffs stood proud against the Atlantic that foamed white with rage at their base.

The cramped surroundings of the bar were deliberate. When the new golf course received the blessing of the villagers, it was largely because Luke had promised them that neither the Orchid Club nor the clubhouse would be an island where tourists flocked to spend their money with no benefit to Brulagh. The bar of the clubhouse, therefore, was more of an anteroom to the village where golfers could get their breath back before venturing further afield in search of food and drink. There were three other watering holes: Sean Flannery's Brulagh Inn, where they planned to lunch; Timothy Houlihan's establishment, confusingly called the Gallerick Arms Hotel, which was some distance outside the village and, of course, the Orchid Club.

At this point, Father Jerry paid over his losses, finished his drink in two quick gulps and was gone.

Luke remarked sadly at his departing back, 'Julia May's sure got that poor bastard by the balls!'

The Doc had not yet fully accustomed himself to Luke's unusually direct way of putting things, but he admired him too much to risk offence by reproving him. The young American had revitalised Brulagh in the short time that he had been there. When the ancestral home of the Gallericks caught fire, he married Gally's only daughter Aphra and rebuilt the tumbledown Manor, turning it into what was now the Orchid Club. Aphra was a perfect foil for the brash, tough American with her aristocratic ways, languid Oxbridge accent and purple language. Now that they had both thrown their weight behind the proposed rock concert, it would become virtually unstoppable. More's the pity, the Doc reflected sadly. The idea of it, compared to his cherished dream of a Céili, was sheer anathema. He paused for a moment. Luke was a straightforward enough sort who would give an honest answer to a question that had been troubling the Doc for some time, ever since the meeting of the Ways and Means Committee.

'What is the latest on the concert?' he inquired.

'Not a lot. Aphra has booked The Howling Dogs for a weekend in mid-September. My office called this morning to say that some guy, their Road Manager I think, is going to fly over here to take a look at the site. I told my wife to stall him till we get the go ahead from the Finance Committee and the field from her father.'

The Doc considered this. 'And will it get the go ahead, do you think?' he asked.

'Aphra thinks it will. Otherwise Mick Flannery will have to borrow the money from the bank. If the Committee agree, Aphra should be able to persuade Gally to loan the field. She can usually twist him round her little finger.'

'What happens if it rains? It often does, you know, around that time of year.'

'I guess we take out insurance to cover that.'

The Doc greeted this last remark with a noncommittal grunt. Luke was ruthless.

'Now pay up and look sweet,' the American commanded. 'Are you still on for lunch now that Father Jerry can't join us?'

The Doc handed over his four pounds as though they were drops of blood and then shrugged, 'Might as well salvage something from the wreckage, I suppose.'

The Eleventh Earl of Gallerick – a lanky, slightly stooped figure clad in crumpled tweeds and shod with sensible leather brogues, was striding briskly down the avenue with two gundogs and a golden labrador in tow. Approaching seventy, he still had a spring in his step, and a good head of hair, much of which curled upwards over his collar. His nose could best be described as aquiline. Furthermore, it had the purplish hue of one who enjoyed a drink –

or two. Larks were singing high above him and a solitary crow winged its way across the cloudless sky, twig in beak, to add to its nest high in one of the many giant oaks that dotted the rolling green carpet of parkland. Gally, as everyone called him, paused to admire his own nest. All traces of the recent fire had been removed; only the newer slates on the roof of the west wing indicated that major repairs had been undertaken to the stately pile. Thanks to the insurance money and Luke marrying Aphra, what might have been a major disaster had instead been transformed into a stroke of good fortune as significant as any in the long and chequered history of the Gallericks, who had lived here since the time of Cromwell.

The house itself was a perfect gem. Originally called Gallerick Hall, since the fire it had been renamed the Orchid Club, as befitted a luxurious retreat for the well-heeled. It was a long, low building whose recently restored roof was framed by battlements of cut stone. Huge windows were set in ornate frames sculpted expertly from the grey limestone. The huge porch – a later addition by an ancestor much taken with Plato – was a miniaturised replica of a Greek temple, complete with columns and friezes. Marble steps led up to it from the generous expanse of gravel hemmed in by sweeping, manicured lawns that rolled down to the lake. A pair of swans sailed serenely across its mirrored surface, every now and then shattering their reflection by pecking the still water in search of a tasty morsel. This caused ripples that wobbled the giant lily pads and rustled the tall stand of bulrushes by the far shore.

A lone heron circled lazily overhead, its giant wings barely moving. Gally approved of its economy of effort in staying aloft. It reflected almost perfectly his own attitude to life in general and the Orchid Club in particular. He would yield to no one in his affection for Aphra, his only daughter. When she had restored the dwindling family fortunes by falling in love with the Yank, there was no one happier for her than Gally. Luke Divareli was a splendid fellow once you got used to him. A bit precipitate and inclined to fly off the handle when his judgement was questioned, but no more so than the rest of his fellow countrymen currently infesting the Manor – or, as young Luke insisted that everyone referred to it – the Orchid Club.

21

It had to be conceded that the lad had a good business head on his shoulders. This was a quality singularly lacking in the Gallerick ancestry, with few exceptions. Before Luke appeared on the scene, dripping with dollars from some banking deal that no one seemed to want to talk about any more, the estate had been going to rack and ruin. Creditors, including that dreadful Tom Donnelly and his awful Allied Banks of Ireland, had been pressing hard for payment, and every scheme that Gally had dreamed up to keep the blighters at bay seemed doomed to failure. For example, his plan to raise pheasant and deer on a commercial basis was thwarted by the creatures effecting a well-timed break for freedom. All that bloody fellow Harmon's fault, of course, for not making sure the orchard wall was in good repair before locking the damn things in. Too late to do anything about that now and, as usual, everyone blamed him for the débâcle. Since the Great Escape, the nearby woods teemed with these two species, giving both pleasure and sport to the guests but only angst to His Lordship, who benefited not at all from their presence.

To his left, several sleek horses pranced behind the post-and-rail fences, pausing only to nuzzle the tiny foals that tottered uncertainly on their spindly legs. Amazing thing, Nature, His Lordship pondered. Who would have believed that those ugly, awkward quadrupeds would grow into chestnut beauties with muscles rippling under their glossy coats? Much the same had happened with his daughter. A gangly teenager with pigtails and thick glasses, she had turned overnight into a raven-haired siren. Further contemplation of the Mysteries of Nature were interrupted by a sharp voice belonging to the focus of his thoughts. The elegant figure of his only child was striding briskly towards him along the avenue.

'Morning, Father dear! Taking a breather from the pressures of a busy life?'

Gally ignored the barb. She and Luke were continually pestering him to mingle more with the guests. Indeed, his sole function in the Orchid Club was to greet the newcomers, make them feel at home and break bread with them when required. This went down particularly well with rich elderly Americans. The blue-rinse brigade liked nothing better than to regale their friends back home with stirring tales of sitting down to dinner with a real live 'Dook' in his own castle. The fact that he was an Earl, not a bloody Duke, and that Gallerick Hall wasn't a castle and never had been, seemed to bother the blighters not one whit.

Despite his fond thoughts, Gally had set out on this walk with the express purpose of avoiding his daughter. He knew she had been lying in wait for him, to elaborate on her latest brainwave – or that of her husband, more likely. Luke had been giving *him* a wide berth since he had baulked at the idea of using the big field for the Rock Concert.

Gally had raised his hand, stifling any further discussion on the subject by saying in a firm tone that brooked no argument: 'Luke, old chap, if you think for one moment that I'm going to allow a horde of unwashed, drug-crazed flower children to fornicate and defecate all over the back field, then you have another think coming! Then there's the noise – absolutely deafening! What would the rest of our guests think? No, there's absolutely no question about it whatsoever. The Rabid Mongrels or whatever they call themselves will play here over my dead body!'

Luke had changed the subject instantly. It seemed that bookings for the autumn period were a bit on the slack side and Luke was inviting him to suggest ways in which this might be remedied. Gally was forced to confess that nothing much came to mind. At this, young Luke nodded grimly as if he had expected as much, and left precipitately. Gally formed the impression that he had not heard the last of this rock concert nonsense.

Now Aphra had been pestering him for the past few days to host a pre-dinner cocktail party at which he would regale the guests with stirring tales of ancestral derring-do as he traipsed past the portraits of the long-dead Gallericks that lined the walls of the large dining room. Pleading that most of them did absolutely nothing save extract exorbitant rents from a sullen peasantry, only to squander the proceeds on slow horses and fast women, failed to dampen Aphra's enthusiasm for the ill-conceived project. When he spiritedly claimed that everything of the slightest interest that had occurred to the whole damn family would fit comfortably on the back of a postage stamp and would take approximately eleven seconds to recite in a slow, measured voice, she had just stamped her foot in a fit of pique.

'I might have known you would kick at doing your bit when it came to helping out with the guests. Your idea of entertaining them is to huddle in a corner of the bar with Colonel Thompson and old Daphne, like rhino round a waterhole, guzzling pink focking gins until they come out your ears. Don't you think Luke and I haven't noticed! Well, I would remind you, Father dear, that we are all equal shareholders in the Orchid Club. That being so, everybody – and I mean *everybody* – is expected to pull their weight. Now if you can't be bothered to draft out something interesting to say to the assembled multitude before dinner, then I'll do it for you. But you're going to learn the focking script off by heart and deliver it as if you had composed every word of it yourself!'

Now, it seemed, she was holding the threatened script in one hand as she walked towards him. Gally decided to adopt a conciliatory tone in response to his daughter's greeting.

'Good morning to you, Aphra my love. I was just taking a stroll and admiring the beauties of Nature when . . .' he began with as much grace as possible, but found he was wasting his sweetness on the desert air.

'Great, great,' she interrupted, 'but some other time, if you don't mind. I'm in something of a rush as it happens. There are seven focking investment bankers and their wives about to descend on us at any moment and their rooms haven't been cleaned up yet. Honestly, I despair of bloody Harmon sometimes. He's just informed me that the housekeeper had to dash off to her aunt's focking funeral. Of course Harmon, the senile old bat, couldn't bother his arse to tell me. Anyway, here's the speech . . .' she pressed it into his reluctant palm. 'It's full of just the sort of thing we need – all about the Nabob and the Hawk and the Legend of the Lake and so forth. They'll lap it up. Be damn sure you learn it off by heart. It's no focking good at all to drone on from a prepared script. Absolutely bore them to death in seconds, it would – almost as bad as saying the first focking thing that comes into your head. And above all, whatever else you do, stay sober. Under no circumstances take even one bloody drink before the "off". I want your solemn word on that!'

Gally nodded absently and glanced through the sheets of paper before protesting feebly. 'Aphra, you can't possibly expect me to deliver this. It's absolute drivel! Legend of the Lake, my backside!

Even the most completely braindead of our esteemed *clientèle* has heard a silly story like that before.' But once again he was cut off in midstream as he gestured at the offending documents.

'Change it yourself then, if you imagine you can do any better,' Aphra challenged. 'Just remember that Luke says it should have lots of snappy snuff about errant ancestors. That's what the punters want to hear – juicy bits about duels at dawn, bonking the serving wenches, being buried with their favourite horses and all that kind of thing. Not a cartload of boring old twaddle about a new roof being added in 1822 or stuff like that. Now, speaking of clapped-out old bores, you really must do something about Harmon.'

Gally always felt protective towards his butler. They had soldiered through many difficult times together. Even now they had a little joint venture going on that no one was supposed to know about. Could be worth a few quid for both of them in the years to come. And the beauty of it was that no one *would* get to know about it. Money for old rope – or old port, rather, he chuckled inwardly.

'What about him?' he said aloud. 'What's the poor blighter done now? Apart from forgetting to tell you about Bridie, that is.'

'No dammit, not just that! This is something far worse. He's been selling the guests your vintage port at fifty dollars a bottle . . .'

A cold hand gripped Gally's heart. Every time he came up with a nice little earner, fate decreed that it would be strangled at birth. Damage limitation must now be the order of the day. The slightest suggestion that he was involved in the scam to rip off the more gullible of their guests, and life would be made even more difficult for the Eleventh Earl of Gallerick than heretofore. His imagination conjured up dreadful visions of Aphra's revenge. Instead of just shooting the breeze over drinks for five minutes of pre-prandial enlightenment to a select bunch of citizens from The Land of the Free, he might easily end up hosting a medieval banquet attired in an Elizabethan ruff, baggy velvet pantaloons and hose, with buckled shoes and a floppy hat. It was not inconceivable that a thoroughly incensed Aphra might even expect him to pluck the strings of a lute while rendering *Greensleeves* in a reedy tenor.

'Absolutely impossible, my dear,' he assured her nervously.

'Couldn't possibly be my vintage port. All the bottles are numbered in their racks – I'd spot one missing right away. Anyway, who'd want the stuff? It has to be brought up from the cellar like a babe in arms lest the crust breaks before it's decanted. If the silly blighters took it back to America, it would be like drinking diesel oil with bits of Melba toast floating in it. Not that they'd notice the difference, I dare say!'

Aphra was livid with rage. 'There you go again. That sort of nonsense drives me absolutely focking mad! You really think we are so much smarter than our guests, don't you? I do wish you would get rid of the idea once and for all, then we could get down to the serious business of making a go of this place rather than having you sniggering in the corner like a focking schoolboy. Anyone who can afford the rates we charge here must be worth a packet. And are you trying to tell me that they made their money from behaving like fools? I suspect that you and Harmon think that the fact they're impressed with all this blue-blooded ancestry shit makes them complete focking idiots. Well, you both couldn't be more wrong!'

Gally thought to protest his innocence of this well-founded charge but he was swept aside by an impatient wave of his daughter's hand before he could get as much as a word in edgeways.

'Anyway,' she continued, 'I've just heard from Mr Grossheimer that Harmon sold him a bottle of your port. He wondered how he should pack it properly so that it wouldn't spoil on the flight back home I was so flabbergasted I told him I would consult you about it and let him know.'

Gally struggled valiantly to appear unconcerned at this latest thunderbolt. 'Very wise of you too, my dear, if I may say so. Why not let me handle the whole thing? There's obviously been some misunderstanding. More than likely it's a bottle of Johnny Slattery's paint-stripper he's talking about, and the pair of them just got their lines crossed. Happens all the time, y'know. Differences in culture and background, that sort of thing. Obviously there's been some mistake. Look, why don't you run along and sort out the rooms for those banker chappies and I'll have a quiet word with both Harmon and Gross-what's-his-name. You've more than enough on your hands as it is, without trying to cope with niggly little things like this.'

She seemed somewhat mollified by this, but gave a final admonishment. 'And don't think for a moment that you're going to wangle yourself out of giving the pre-dinner talk, Father. Change anything you like in the script, but do *please* remember what I said about keeping it short and snappy. It's the scandals and the legends they want, not the bloody architectural guff that'll bore them absolutely rigid. Okay?'

He brushed her cheek with his lips in farewell. Watching her stride purposefully towards the house, his mind raced furiously as he sought to retrieve the situation *à propos* Mister Bloody Grossheimer. The blasted bottle that Aphra referred to was supposed to be their test run, as it were. Harmon had purchased several cases of low-grade port from a Portuguese trawler that had tied up at the pier last week. Grossheimer, and indeed many of his fellow countrymen, had been fulsome in their praise of the Gallerick port. It had to be admitted that old Harmon put on a bloody good show for them when the last of the dinner plates had been cleared away. Dressed up to the nines in full butler's regalia, he would bring up from the cellar an unlabelled bottle, covered in dust and cobwebs. With much pomp and circumstance, he would decant it in front of a guttering candle, taking great care to keep the white blob of paint uppermost at all times. Gally would explain in sepulchral tones that the blob was to indicate which way up the bottle had been stored so that the noble crust inside the bottle would not be shattered until the very last moment of decanting. This never failed to impress, especially when Gally added fifty years or so to the vintage port's true age.

The decanting ceremony over, Harmon would proffer the first tasting sip to Gally, who would swirl it around his palate and nod sagely to give it his imprimatur. Then, each guest would get a thimbleful. The lack of a label coupled with the distinctive white blob made it inevitable that some guests would approach Harmon discreetly in the hope that he might procure a souvenir bottle or two for them, no questions asked. When Harmon mentioned this to Gally, they hit on the idea of doctoring up cheap bottles by steaming off the labels, daubing a blob of white paint on the glass shoulders of the bottles and leaving them under the straw in the kennels for some time so as to give them the appearance of age. There could be no question of selling the genuine article on the quiet since the stocks of vintage port were carefully monitored at all times. It was a bottle of Iberian Infuriator that Grossheimer had been sold, and now the problem would be to retrieve it before the scam was exposed.

As he walked back disconsolately along the avenue, the Eleventh Earl of Gallerick barely glanced at the scene that had so entranced him minutes earlier. The swans still wet their beaks in the water. Indeed, they had been joined by a waterhen and her young who were paddling furiously to keep up with their mother. The heron still flapped around the treetops and the lone crow was involved in a domestic dispute with its mate as to the precise placement of the last twig. All this now went unnoticed by Gally, who was racking his brain in an attempt to find some way to fireproof himself from the wrath that was to come, should Aphra discover the truth. With a sigh he decided that if all came to all, he would disclaim any knowledge of the offending bottle, thereby consigning the frail carcase of Harmon to the wolves.

His Lordship's final thought on the matter was that if such should come to pass, his sympathies would lie mainly with the wolves.

5

CHARLEY HALPIN, CHIEF Reporter on the *Clarion*, was en-sconced in the snug of the Brulagh Inn. He was a small man of middle age who spoke in a sing-song accent that strangers thought was part of an elaborate joke. It was only on closer inspection they discovered that Charley spoke like that all the time. Next to him on the wooden bench sat a lanky figure with a running nose. This was wiped with a sleeve just before the droplet was fully formed. The owner of the offending nose wore grimy dungarees that vanished into a pair of rubber wellington boots, encrusted with something brown that hopefully was mud. At first sight he appeared to be addressing an empty pint glass rather than the tubby reporter beside him.

'D'ya know what I'm goin' to tell you, Charley me boy, and 'tisn't one word of a lie?'

Familiar with this mode of address, the reporter from the *Clarion* recognised it as a rhetorical question not requiring a reply. Apart from journalism, his other income came from distributing Johnny Slattery's poteen for a commission of two pounds a bottle – which was the reason for their meeting in the privacy of the snug. Of late, production had dropped significantly and Charley wanted to know why. Already his regular customers were suffering from separation anxiety on a scale hitherto unknown. He inched his glass out of Johnny's spittle range and prepared himself for a succession of untruths from the moist lips of the bootlegger.

'That shagger of a new Sergeant has my heart scalded. I thought old Gus was bad but bejaysus he was an innocent child compared to this bastard. Of course, what else would you expect from a mountainy man?'

The fact that Johnny – living as he did high up on the barren slopes of Mount Brulagh – fell squarely into this category himself had evidently escaped his notice. He spoke with such vehemence that Charley deemed it prudent to shift his glass even further downrange. With Johnny in full spate, the door of the snug opened and they were joined by a third party. This took the form of an elderly man in a heavy tweed sportscoat with a pair of *pince nez* perched precariously on the tip of his bulbous nose. He was small, brick-red of face and almost completely round. From under a moustache – its ends artfully twirled upwards – he greeted them in the plummiest accent this side of the Khyber Pass.

'Hell-e-o-w chaps! Anyone care for the other half? Sean, give these two splendid fellows whatever they're having and the usual poison for myself.' Colonel Thompson had been in the village barely five minutes before initiating Sean, the eldest son of Mick Flannery and landlord of the Brulagh Inn, into the arcane rites of the Pink Gin. Some time ago he had bought Ballyglen, a Period residence two miles outside Brulagh and beside a lake teeming with fish. He had quickly become a familiar figure at the Inn, with his customised cocktail recipes. *'Six drops – no more, no less – of angostura bitters in the glass. Then swirl around vigorously so that a thin film of the precious liquid adheres to the inside of the glass. This is* immediately *followed by six hard shakes to get any excess of the damn stuff out. Absolutely bally lethal, just use it for the colour. Then bung in the gin, erring if one must on the side of generosity. Add tapwater to taste, and Hey Presto! One Pink Gin!'*

On discovering the existence of poteen, Colonel Thompson had displayed the ingenuity of his forebears who had founded an Empire on which the sun never set by adapting to the customs of the natives. As he so elegantly put it; 'In the case of our friend Johnny's gut-rot, a generous dollop of Rose's Lime Juice to kill off some of that dreadful liquorice taste.' The Colonel was a miracle of inventiveness where the doctoring of drinks was concerned. Now, blissfully unaware that he was barging in on what was meant to be a very private meeting, he was just getting into his stride, having drained his glass in one gulp.

'One of the grea-a-at things about this country, y'know, is the size of your measures. Here a large one really is . . . large!' At this moment the landlord reappeared, to be greeted as if his absence had been of several hours' duration, rather than seconds.

'Oh Sean, there you are, old chap. Thought for a moment you

had disappeared off the face of the earth, never more to be seen by the eye of man, woman or child. The same again for my two friends here and I suppose I had better try another one of those. Bottoms up, lads, and Caheeraca to the two of you!'

Johnny winked at Charley Halpin and then raised his glass in salute, echoing the toast. 'Caheeraca, Colonel!'

For a split second Charley Halpin was mystified. Then he remembered with an inner chuckle that when the Colonel first set foot in the Brulagh Inn, he asked Johnny the Irish word for 'Cheers'. With the Colonel's braying Sandhurst accent this sounded like 'chairs', which Johnny readily translated as *cathaoireaca*. By now it was too late to correct the misunderstanding and it had become a familiar joke among the regulars at the bar.

'Now, Johnny old chap, there's no need to introduce me to your friend. We already do business with each other, isn't that so, Charley my boy? At least, we bally well used to until he tells me that the well has . . . er, dried up somewhat. Can this really be true, old man? I *do* hope not. I have an old friend, a very old friend, coming over at the weekend. I've been telling him about your *premier cru*, the first run or the "pure drop" or whatever you chaps call it. The poor blighter's tongue is hanging out for some. The old boy will be most terribly disappointed.'

His captive audience were growing increasingly restive at this public airing of their production problems. To stem the flow, Johnny interrupted, 'Yerrah 'twill be all right, Colonel. I'll give Charley here enough to get you over the weekend.'

'That's fine – my chap will be delighted,' the Colonel brayed happily. 'He wants to explore the wetland round here, y'see. Quite daft, if you ask me, even if he is my brother-in-law. Spends all his time pottering around bogs and dreaming up wild schemes for getting money and God only knows what else out of them. Just back from a stint in Finland, actually. Supposed to be writing up a report or somethng of his rambles among the reindeer. Anyway, he's staying with me, hence the need for extra supplies for the garrison. He's absolutely bonkers about bogs . . .' Then he added hastily while sucking another three inches out of his Pink Gin '. . . speaking of which, Johnny, I'm told that you've got a bog that you hardly use.'

'Yeah, I suppose I have. What about it?'

'Well – how should I put it? Derek, that's his name by the way, would like to look over it.' At this point the Colonel lifted his glass to forestall any objections Johnny might raise to the suggestion before being fully acquainted with the facts of the case. 'Not to remove any turf or anything like that, in case you're worried about that sort of thing. I think he just wants to conduct tests of some sort or other on the soil. God knows why. Acidity and all that sort of scientific nonsense, y'know. Anyway, he wants me to get hold of a stretch of bog and they tell me you're the man to see about that sort of thing. Is that correct?'

Johnny nodded, brightening visibly. It was a relief that his moonshining activities were no longer being broadcast far and wide. Better still, this madman apparently wanted to lease the few acres of useless bog that had failed to provide him with as much as a single sod of dry turf for the past few years. His brain whirred furiously as he tried to calculate the most the old fart was likely to part with in rent for the thirty acres. There was no market to go by, since no one in their sober senses would take a present of a bog, much less pay good money to rent one. He soon decided on a hundred pounds as a strong opening position from which to beat a hasty retreat should the old warrior show signs of imminent apoplexy.

Indeed, those signs were already much in evidence. The Colonel's complexion was taking on the appearance of an explosion in a tomato cannery at sunset as he inquired, 'How big is it, old chap?'

'Oh, around the thirty acres, at the very least. And may God Himself strike me dead on the ground this very minute if it doesn't yield the finest of turf for miles around. In a fire there's a flame off it that would warm the cockles of an Eskimo!'

This was indeed risking the wrath of The Almighty. The last cartload of soggy turf he had drawn out of that cursed bog was still stacked more or less neatly in clamps against the gable end of his thatched cottage, perched high on the inhospitable slopes of Mount Brulagh.

A deep silence descended on the snug during which both parties reviewed their positions. Charley Halpin stared hard at the ceiling, trying to keep a straight face. When the colonel broke the *impasse*, he did so in a manner that almost resulted in both men falling off the wooden bench with the shock.

'What would you say to a thousand pounds?' he asked. 'That'd be for a year's rent, starting from today. You would have to show me where the damn thing is, of course. One part of the blasted heath looks exactly the same as the next as far as I'm concerned.'

When Johnny had recovered, he remembered to purse his lips as though considering the offer. His brain whirred like clockwork as he debated with himself whether to grab this incredible sum before the Colonel changed his mind, or to risk holding out for more. In the end wiser counsels prevailed as Johnny strove to inject a note of reluctance into his answer.

'Well, to tell you nothing but God's honest truth, Colonel, if the times weren't so bad, I wouldn't even consider your offer. But what with my poor aunt not being well in herself these past few months and the business nearly destroyed by the law, I've little choice in the matter, I suppose. Normally I'd be inclined to ask a bit more but seein' as how my piece of the bog is goin' to a dacent man like yourself, I couldn't bring meself to be too hard on you, now could I? So what we'll do is this. We'll have one more drink here to seal the deal, then I'll bring you out to see the place for yourself and show you the boundaries. Afterwards you'll get the papers drawn up for a year's rent and I'll sign 'em when they're ready. Then as soon as I've got the money, you're free to do as you please. Now does that sound fair and square, Colonel?'

The Colonel beamed happily. 'Couldn't be fairer, Johnny old boy. Why don't I write you out the cheque this very minute! Who'll I make it out to?'

'Cash, if you don't mind.'

'Cash it is, my friend. 'Not *Johnny* Cash, I suppose . . .' a noise like a geyser erupting proved to be the Colonel laughing uproariously at his own witticism. '. . . like the long-haired blighters that young filly, Aphra, is trying to inflict on us, eh what? The Baying Hounds or whatever the blazes they call themselves! Why in the name of all that's holy she wants to inflict an absolute shower like that on us is beyond belief. Still, that's the female of the species for you, is it not? Dangerouser than the male, I always say.'

Seeing the look of bewilderment on the faces of his listeners, he rapidly changed tack and reverted to matters of more immediate concern. 'Oh, never mind about all that. Here's the cheque. Sean, we'll have the same again, then we're off to see the bog!'

As they were leaving, they downed the next round like lightning. At the door, Johnny drew the Colonel to one side.

'By the way, Colonel, would ya mind cashin' the cheque for me in the bank? Donnelly the Manager and meself aren't the best of friends just at the minute! If I cashed it meself, nothin' would please the miserable bastard better than to take a good skelp out of it for his oul' bank. The less that hoor knows about me the happier I'd be and that's not one word of a lie.'

Their departure left the Doc and Charley Halpin the sole customers of the Brulagh Inn. Five minutes earlier, Luke had left quietly to return to the Orchid Club. Charley ambled over towards him and sat down, uninvited.

'Well, Doc, how are things?'

With a sigh the Doc replied, 'Okay, I suppose.' The Doc could have done without the interruption as he was draining the last of his coffee. Charley Halpin did nothing whatsoever for his digestion – especially when he was in pursuit of information, as seemed to be the case just now.

'Tell me this, Doc, and tell me no more. Is herself really serious about this rock concert business?'

The Doc was irritated by the sing-song accent and the un-disguised curiosity that lay beneath it.

'How the hell would I know? I've only been sitting on the bloody committee for the past thirty years or so. Why should anybody tell me if St Fintan's is staging a rock concert – or an organised orgy, for that matter? Not that there's much of a difference between the two, if you ask me. Why don't you ask herself, as you call Lady Aphra?'

'For the simple reason that she'd ate the head off me, that's the why! Jaysus that one's got a tongue on her like barbed wire.'

They lapsed into silence, each preoccupied with his own thoughts. The Doc had known Charley Halpin for a long time, but could never warm to the little man. Though they were both close friends of Mick Flannery, they were not especially friendly with each other. The Doc, who disliked hypocrisy in any form, could not get used to Charley writing glowing accounts of unsuccessful poteen raids conducted by the new Sergeant when he, himself, was the sole distributor for the gut-rot. Not that the Doc was above using a drop of it himself – but only as an embrocation, for external use only, either on himself or his horse after a good day's hunting. There was nothing better to get the ache out of tired bones – human or animal.

As for actually drinking the stuff, he occasionally did that too. Johnny Slattery paid his medical bills in poteen. Since his elderly aunt required regular visits, the basement of Doc's house held several cases of the 'pure drop'. To make it more palatable, the Doc put sloes, punctured with pinpricks, into a few of the bottles and let them stand for a year or more. That way he had a reasonably tasty liqueur which he used as a winter nightcap. Nevertheless, the supply far exceeded the demand and storage would soon become a problem. As if reading his thoughts, Charley interrupted before the Doc finished whatever he was about to say.

'Tell me, Doc. Is there any chance at all you'd have the odd auld spare bottle you might sell me? There's a fierce shortage at the moment and Johnny tells me that you must have a fair stockpile of it by now.'

Another silence descended on the table. The Doc was in no hurry to reply. It might even be fun to feign total ignorance and ask Charley to spell out exactly what he meant by 'spare bottles'. Then again, such indulgence might be foolish if it were to result in the little man taking offence and stalking off in high dudgeon without making an offer for what was, in effect, an unsaleable commodity. The attractions of converting Johnny's bartered medical bills into ready cash were many, especially when Charley was the prospective purchaser. Discretion would have to be guaranteed, though, as it would hardly do for word to get out that a medical practitioner was hawking moonshine liquor to the general public in times of scarcity. The Doc decided to test the market.

'That might be true,' he nodded. 'Now tell me what a bottle of the very best of it might be fetching nowadays?'

Without hesitation Charley answered: 'Four pounds a bottle.'

'Oh, I could never leave it go for that,' the other man demurred. 'Didn't I hear your friend, the Colonel, not five minutes ago complaining that he couldn't lay hands on a drop of it for love or money? Ah no, Charley me boyo, you'd have to do a lot better than that!'

'A fiver so, and that's my last word. Sure I'll hardly have anything for myself out of it at that!'

After further haggling, a price of six pounds a bottle was agreed, with Charley arranging to collect the goods that night. The Doc felt obliged to seal the deal in time-honoured fashion.

'Will you have one for the road?' he asked. 'I must be getting back to the surgery.'

Surprisingly, Charley declined. 'No, thanks. I've to meet Mick Flannery here in a few minutes.'

'Goodbye so. You'll call for that after dark, of course? Remember, six pounds a bottle was what we agreed!'

Charley nodded glumly as he watched the Doc go out the door.

Just at that moment, further down the road, Mick was at home, once more flicking through the late-morning post that had just dropped through his letter box. He picked out an envelope with American stamps, addressed to *Michael J. Flannery, Esq., Member of the European Parliament.* To this was appended his home address. Mick slit it open and saw that it was from the previous owner of the Brulagh Inn – a proper bastard if ever there was one – who rejoiced in the name of O'Shea and who had left the country rather hurriedly a couple of years ago.

O'Shea, as Mick now tried to picture him in his mind's eye, had been a small fiery man who fell out with everyone. Like the Bourbons, O'Shea learned nothing and forgot nothing. While this did little to endear him to his customerrs, his was the only hostelry for miles around, therefore it prospered, despite the best efforts of its owner.

Reading the spidery scrawl, Mick wondered what could have prompted such a miserable excrescence to put pen to paper. All soon became clear. O'Shea, it seemed, was connected with the people responsible for elevating Mick to the New York Hall of Fame. This, in itself, was something of a surprise because O'Shea's attitude to Mick had been one of ill-disguised hatred. This gave the letter something of a false ring as its tone was unmistakably wheedling. It began by congratulating Mick on the signal honour that had been bestowed on him by associations like the GAA, the

Friendly Sons of St Patrick and the Ancient Order of Hibernians. Of more immediate interest, it offered to set up a series of media interviews that would focus on Mick's career to date. This was just what Mick needed – a platform on which he could parade his past achievements as a hurler and a dedicated politician of international repute. What was the thing Charley said he needed most to win the next election? A sense of. . . ? Dammit, it just wouldn't come to him though it was on the tip of his tongue.

Not that it really mattered, Mick reminded himself, since he would be seeing the tubby journalist in a few minutes from now. Unusually, this was at the request of Charley – who had acted as his faithful conduit to the seething masses for three decades. Ordinarily it was Mick who summoned the *Clarion* reporter when he had something of importance that he wished to impart to the public at large. This was usually a timely reminder to the readers that, due to the ceaseless efforts of Mick Flannery in the corridors of Brussels, some new manifestation of EC generosity was about to be bestowed on them.

If it came to pass, then they were told about it again, accompanied by *paeans* of praise for the tireless exertions of their representative in Europe. As a final reminder, some time later an unattributed item would appear in the paper to the effect that residents of the area in which the work had been done were so overcome with gratitude that they had requested space in the columns to express their public thanks to Mick. By way of recompense, any item gleaned by Mick in the corridors of power that might be considered of national importance was always fed to Charley in the first instance. He would then sell the scoop to the other media hacks in the same way that he distributed Johnny Slattery's mountain dew.

Stuffing O'Shea's letter in his pocket, Mick looked at his watch and saw that he would have to hurry to catch the post. From a display stand outside the supermarket he selected a picture postcard of a donkey with panniers of turf across its back. The animal was accompanied by an elderly farmer smoking a pipe and wearing a cap that looked as if it could only be removed by physical force. It was unclear as to who was leading whom. Of greater importance, however, was that it was festooned with shamrocks of a particularly bilious shade of green.

37

O'Shea had become addicted to these during his stay in Brulagh, to such an extent that he used them as a motif throughout his bar. They were to be found in carpets, curtains, wallpaper, even the wrought-iron shutter that, when lowered, indicated the bar was closed; it too incorporated a profusion of the national emblem. A further infestation of the weed threatened to engulf the garish neon sign outside the bar, even going so far as to entwine the Celtic script which proclaimed the legend *O'Shea's Shamrock Lounge*. Mick was convinced that O'Shea would have used the shamrock motif on the toilet paper if a manufacturer could have been found to comply with his wishes.

On the back of the card he carefully transcribed O'Shea's address from the letter in his pocket. In the space reserved for the message, he wrote: '*Look forward to appearing on any media shows you can arrange. Will be in NY from March 10th to March 19th inc. See you then. Best wishes, Mick Flannery.*'

He dropped it into the postbox outside what used to be Mullarkey's Supermarket. As well as selling the usual groceries, it also did a thriving business in Aran Sweaters and tee shirts festooned with enough shamrocks and harps to gladden even O'Shea's heart. Thinking again of O'Shea sent a shiver of apprehension through Mick as he wondered uneasily at the sudden show of friendliness evinced in the letter. Well, he thought to himself, the die is cast; he slid the card into the mouth of the letter-box and heard it flutter to the bottom. Without a backward glance, he quickened his step so as not to be late for Charley Halpin.

He was glad to see they had the pub to themselves. He ordered two pints from his daughter-in-law and waited for her to drift out of range before addressing Charley.

'Hope I didn't keep you waiting long. I had to send a postcard and you'll never guess to who?'

'Awright, I give up. Tell me.'

'O'Shea, that's who.'

'Jaysus Christ, I thought the only thing you'd send that miserable bastard was a bullet. Not that it would ever get through that thick hide of his. What in the name of Jaysus are you doin' writing to the likes of him, anyway? All those shaggin' Irish-Americans are mad as hatters. You've only got to see their carry-on on Paddy's Day to know I'm not tellin' one word of a lie. Banners, bands, bagpipes and girls in short dresses throwing sticks in the air and driving what men are in the crowd mad from trying to get a look at their knickers . . .'

Mick decided it was time to break into this diatribe that might otherwise continue past nightfall. He hadn't been aware of the tubby reporter's deep-rooted antipathy to his fellow countrymen who had made a new life for themselves in The Land of the Free. But this was beside the point; he needed Charley's help in the forthcoming election, not his opinion of Drum Majorettes' underwear.

'Charley – forget about knickers for a moment. You said you wanted to see me about something?'

'Oh, that's right Mick, so I did. It's about this coal business. Are you really serious about it, or is it just another election gimmick?'

Mick looked around hastily to make sure there was no one within earshot. Then, in a tone more of sadness than anger he replied: 'Will you not be talking like that? If anyone heard you they'd make a meal out of it. Of course it's not just a shaggin' gimmick! Look – I've the details here . . .'

He pulled out a sheet of paper crammed with single-spaced typescript and pock-marked with white correcting fluid. The letter from O'Shea also fell out on the table.

'Take a look at that when you've got the time, then go off and write something about it. You know, the usual thing – new industry for Brulagh, jobs galore, prosperity just around the corner . . . all thanks to myself, of course.'

'Okay, I'll read it and then I'll call you to fill me in on the details – like how you're going to get round the dust all over the place and heaps of coal on a pier that's already on its last legs.'

'Christ Almighty, can't you read the shaggin' thing first before jumping the gun! There'll be no dust and we're getting a new pier. What the hell are you laughing at?'

Charley was spluttering into his pint, the laughter erupting inside him like molten lava. He could barely get the words out through the paroxysms of mirth.

'Yerrah go on outa that, Mick! I'm damned if I'm going to run that one again. As long as I've known you, you've been telling the punters that they're going to get a new pier. If you try it this time, they'll laugh themselves into a permanent state of hiccups, so they will. You're going to have to come up with something better than that to fool them this time, me boyo.'

'No one's trying to fool anyone, for Jaysus' sake!' Flannery was unamused. 'This coal thing is the genuine article. These two guys in Kentucky are starting to ship coal by a string of barges to Italy. They'll just drop off one of them at Brulagh Harbour, making us the coal depot of the south. Dead simple – can't fail.'

'Does Pat Mullarkey know about this?'

'Yeah, I told him about it.'

'And?'

There was a pregnant pause as Mick tried to parry the thrust.

'And what, Charley?'

The little man's accent became even more sing-song when he grew agitated. 'And what did our great leader say about his home town being turned into a giant slag-heap?'

Mick could hide his exasperation no longer. 'There'll be no fucking slag heaps! As for Pat, when I mentioned the jobs he shut up about the coal dust. Especially since the money is coming from the EC and not out of the Exchequer – though to listen to the miserable little bollix you'd think that he was payin' for it out of his own arse pocket. I wouldn't mind but the same man wouldn't give you the steam off his . . .'

Charley cut in with the key question. 'Are you sure about the EC money?'

'You leave that to me. Anyway, it's only a million or so. All that's needed is a new pier and a bit of a road.'

'Bit of a road, be damned! They'll have to build a whole new highway from the far side of the mountain right down to the pier. That's six miles at the very least!'

Mick was getting crosser by the minute. 'What's got into you, Charley? Can't you leave the details to me? You just write it up like always and I'll do the explaining when the time comes.'

The little man shook his head vehemently. 'No good, Mick. They just won't swallow it this time. While you've been away in Brussels I've been watching the changes round here. People are not like they were before. Now they're becoming more sophisticated. About what they eat and drink. How they spend their free time. And last but not least, who they vote for. It just isn't enough to tell them "Trust me and all will be well" any more.'

They glared at each other for a moment before Charley continued, this time in a more placatory tone, 'Look, Mick, we've been friends a long time. That's why I'm sticking my neck out by telling you all this. 'Twould be far easier for me to keep my mouth shut, say nothing and write a Mickey-Mouse piece about your coal thing. The trouble is that no one's going to believe it unless you come up with the goods. You're going to have to do better than that scrap of paper there with a lot of high falutin' plans in it.'

Mick raised his hands as though to fend off a blow. 'Okay, okay, I get the message. What I haven't told you yet is that I'm off to America next week. I meant to keep it quiet until I had the whole thing signed, sealed and delivered, but time's getting short and I really need you to write up about me in America. It's just the kind of thing we both need.'

Charley noticed the 'we' but let it pass. 'If you want a write-up, you'd better tell me all about the American trip here and now.'

This Mick proceeded to do in considerable detail. He mentioned the Hall of Fame Awards, handed over O'Shea's letter and explained that he would be travelling by private jet from New York to Louisville, Kentucky after the St Patrick's Day Parade. He could see the reporter brightening by the minute. This was grist to his mill, something the little man could really get his teeth into, not some dull election manifesto crammed with vague promises that no one would bother to read, much less believe.

By the time Mick had finished the litany of things that would happen in America, Charley's eyes were glistening. His voice had become almost Welsh with excitement. He promised that not only would he keep his readers abreast of Mick's triumphant progress in the New World, but that he could be relied upon to gild the lily. Readers of the *Clarion* would be led to believe that Mick was the central figure in the St Patrick's Day festivities.

Indeed, by the time they had finished digesting Charley's purple prose, the only question left in their minds would be how the previous two hundred or so Parades had managed *without* the presence of one Michael J. Flannery!

6

'I NOW DECLARE open this meeting of the St Fintan's GAA Club Finance Committee. As you will see by the sheet of paper before you, there are only two items on the agenda. The first is to decide on the rock concert, and the second is our old friend, Any Other Business. First I will call on Bernie, to read out the Minutes of our last meeting. Are you ready, Bernie?'

The Doc's admirer nodded curtly, cleared her throat nervously, adjusted a pair of horn-rimmed glasses and began to read the Minutes in a dull monotone. Anyone wishing to catch what she was saying would have had to strain their ears.

When she stopped, as abruptly as she had started, Father Jerry abandoned his efforts to relight his pipe and said mildly, 'Thank you, Bernie. Does anybody have anything to add to, or correct, in the Minutes?' The briefest of pauses was followed by, 'No? In that case I propose that they be adopted. Can I have a seconder to that? Thank you, Mossy.'

This was a ritual as formalised as a Papal Blessing. Mossy O'Connor sat on the Committee just to make up the required number. Long before now, it had been explained to him that he was not expected to contribute anything to the proceedings except his presence. In return he would receive two Stand Tickets, rarer than diamonds, for the All-Ireland finals. These Mossy sold to the highest bidder, claiming that he preferred to watch the games on TV. Before retiring, he had been Pat Mullarkey's superior in the Department of Agriculture (Advisory Section). In those days they had been at daggers drawn, but now that his *protégé* had achieved the highest political honours in the land, he regaled drinkers in the Brulagh Inn with tales of how he had put Pat right on matters agricultural. Of late, however, he found himself retracting much of this in the light of his erstwhile pupil's current policies.

Father Jerry pressed ahead while Mossy, his duty done, drifted off into a dreamless slumber. From time to time he would shake himself into wakefulness, only to allow the delightful drowsiness to engulf him yet again.

'Right so, let's set the ball rolling by asking our President, Mick Flannery, to give us his views on whether it is a good idea of St Fintan's GAA Club to stage a rock concert . . .'

As Mick cleared his throat, the priest raised his hand to indicate that he hadn't quite finished.

'Just before he does, however, it would not do to let the occasion pass without congratulating him on his elevation to the New York GAA Hall of Fame. I'm sure all of us here would agree that it is no less than a fitting reward for a lifetime of service to the game he loves so well!'

A smattering of applause rippled round the table, and Mossy was heard to mumble, 'I second that!' before slipping once more into oblivion.

Mick shoved back his chair, tried to button his jacket then abandoned the effort as being more trouble than it was worth. Stubbing out a half-smoked cigarette, he drained his glass and addressed the assembly in tones of some familiarity.

'Very Reverend Chairman, I'd like to thank you for those kind words about me and the Hall of Fame. When I tell the New York lads about the grand stadium we have here in Brulagh, I'm sure they'll be bursting to arrange a fixture with us. Indeed, if Bernie could write out an invitation on behalf of the Club, I could take it over with me. Anyway, back to the business in hand. As regards the rock concert, I'm all for it. I see from the projections worked out by Aphra's committee that if we get a crowd of twenty thousand or so, we break even. Pat Mullarkey has promised to do the opening ceremony so that will guarantee plenty of media coverage. Aphra says the last concert what's-their-names did here in Ireland drew nearly a hundred thousand but, of course, that was just outside Dublin. I suppose if we did a third of that, 'tis the most we could expect. At a tenner a ticket, that's coming up to a quarter of a million for the Club after expenses, just about what we need for the next phase of the development plan. Which means, by the way, that we won't have to go cap in hand to our friendly Donnelly at the bank. For me, that's as good a reason as any to go ahead with the concert.' With that, he sat down, lit a fresh cigarette and looked around, almost defiantly, to see what reaction he would get.

The Doc got up from his chair and placed a bottle of whiskey at Mick's elbow with the comment, 'The water's next to you – if you need it!'

Now that he was standing he was easy prey for Father Jerry: 'Well, Dr Buckley? Since you're up, why don't you give us your thoughts on the subject?'

The Doc hesitated for a moment, caught out by the sudden invitation. He knew that Father Jerry was against the rock concert as much as he was, but now he would have to speak first.

'First of all I'd like to set Mick's mind at rest about Mr Donnelly. I've just sent him to hospital in the ambulance.'

This was greeted by a variety of reactions. Mick's muttered, 'Nothing trivial, I hope!' was drowned out by Father Jerry's more charitable, 'What ails the poor man at all?'

The Doc could not disclose the fact that Donnelly had been admitted to an expensive Nursing Home where, it was hoped, he could be weaned off his recent addiction to drinking neat vodka before breakfast. Instead he tried to avoid further questions.

'Put it this way, there's nothing seriously wrong with him,' he said matter-of-factly. 'All the same, no one will be going cap in hand to him for quite a while. Now, as far as the rock concert is concerned, I have to admit that I'm dead against it. To me the very notion that any GAA Club, much less our very own St Fintan's, should even consider staging something as outlandish as a rock concert is incredible.'

With that he sat down, apparently reluctant to amplify his thoughts any further. Since they coincided with Father Jerry's views on the matter, however, the Doc was not going to escape as lightly as that. The words of the Pastoral Letter echoed painfully inside the Priest's head: *'The day cannot be far off when a kindly God will seek vengeance on His people for the sins they have committed in His name. The immorality that occurs in discos and at open-air concerts must surely rival the worst excesses of Sodom and Gomorrah* . . . and much more along these lines. If the Doc thought for a moment that he was going to escape with this mild rebuke to those who sought to promote the damn concert, then he was sorely mistaken. As a neutral Chairman, Father Jerry could not seem to be laying about him with the Bishop's crozier. For one thing, Aphra, being Church of Ireland, was not a member of his flock. Anything he might say could well be construed as an unwarranted intrusion by the Church of Rome into something that did not concern it. Far better, Father Jerry concluded, to get the Doc to make the running.

'I would be failing in my duty as Chairman, Doctor,' he said smoothly, 'if I didn't ask you to expand further on your reasons for finding it so "incredible"?'

The Doc snorted irritably and rose to his feet once more.

'All right, I'll tell you why! Who needs a mob of hooligans descending on us, and what guarantee have we that they won't put Brulagh to the torch?'

Father Jerry beamed encouragingly at his words.

'I hear Aphra is trying to get her father to give the big field for somewhere to put on the damn thing,' the Doc continued. 'Looks like we're here just to rubberstamp something that has already been decided. Though when and by whom I don't know. I want it to go on record . . .' he paused to give Bernie a chance to catch up on her note-taking '. . . that I'm against the whole idea. It flies in the face of everything the GAA stands for – our national heritage, for instance. Heritage my . . .' he sought a part of his anatomy likely to cause the least offence '. . . foot! Do you mean to tell me that you're serious about inviting a bunch of has-beens with a string of drug convictions longer than my . . .' tension heightened as they waited to hear which appendage he would select this time '. . . arm, backed up by half-naked women groaning as though they've got a pain in their bellies?'

Dropping his voice an octave, he continued: 'I want our Club's finances to be put on a sound basis as much as anyone, but this bloody rock concert is no way to go about it! There are too many things that could go wrong – crowd trouble, people getting injured, maybe even killed, in the crush. It's happened before, you know. And another thing – who's going to guarantee that it won't flog rain? If that happened, we'd have to cancel the whole bloody thing at the last minute. Then who's going to pay The Rabid Pups – or whatever the hell they call themselves – not to mention their gang of floozies?'

Father Jerry nodded vigorously, making it obvious that he agreed with every syllable uttered by the Doc. Then Mick Flannery was on his feet again.

'With respect, Reverend Chairman, if the feeling of the meeting is against the concert, then we obviously can't go ahead with it. But I think that on reflection, the Doc will see that it's the quickest way to raise money. We could be running bingo sessions, raffles and sponsored walks till the cows come home and we still wouldn't have raised the price of the first bag of cement! So I now propose that we don't take a vote at all. If some people feel . . .' and here he grinned cheerfully at the Doc and Father Jerry '. . . that they haven't been properly briefed on the details, then we'll have to put that right first. Would you agree with me?' Mick surveyed the faces around the table, seeing he had struck a chord.

Father Jerry sighed, knowing he had no option but to put it to a vote. 'All those in favour of postponing the decision on staging the rock concert please raise their hands.'

As he spoke, he was already composing a brief note to his Bishop. It would baldly state that due to his relentless efforts, the Committee of St Fintan's GAA Club had been finally persuaded to reconsider – if not quite abandon – the idea of a rock concert. In the period before the next meeting, he would twist arms and use his powers of persuasion to swing the vote against the concert . . . He broke off this train of thought to count the hands. They were all raised in favour of adjourning the decision until the next meeting.

'That seems to be well and truly carried. Bernie, would you include the motion again in next month's agenda? Now, for Any Other Business, there is a notification here from the Central Council of the GAA and . . .'

It was at this point that Mick Flannery begged to be excused for a while on the grounds that he had an urgent phone-call to make before lunchtime. In the sanctuary of the Doc's surgery across the hall, he hurriedly dialled the number of the Orchid Club. He wanted to bring Aphra up to date on what had just transpired.

7

JUST AS MICK was about to dial her number, the telephone on Aphra's desk rang. She picked it up and inquired with an throaty Oxbridge drawl: 'The Orchid Club. Can I help you?'

The *you* went on a bit longer than might have been expected, and it finished on a higher key than it had started. Her look of polite boredom vanished, however, when she realised it was Luke ringing from the Golf Club. 'Luke, dahling! What on earth are you ringing for at this time of day?'

Testily he explained in a brittle voice how the four visitors from a Japanese Trading House had brought golf on the course to a complete standstill. Despite buying two dozen golf balls each before driving off the first tee, they had run out of ammunition halfway round the course. Rather than wave through those playing behind them, as etiquette demanded, they had sat down to a leisurely picnic on the ninth green, unheeding of enraged cries of 'Fore' from those held up behind. Every so often they would break off from happily munching to record the occasion for posterity, snapping each other taking elaborate practice swings that sent divots of the precious green flying skywards.

Matters were not improved by their benignly yelling, 'Fore!' back at the enraged mob of impatient golfers in the ever-lengthening queue, assuming that the word was a form of friendly greeting, rather than a peremptory demand to get the hell out of the way.

By the time Luke arrived to sort things out, an ugly scene was in the offing. Waving the seething golfers through like a traffic cop, Luke quickly took the four Japanese businessmen aside and demanded an explanation. They confessed that this was their first time ever on a golf course; when they'd lost all their golf balls in the rough, they had decided to take a picnic.

Up to now, their golfing experience had been confined to striking balls off a multi-storeyed driving range in the Ginza Golf Centre. The numbers beside their names referred not to their golf handicaps, but to the floor from which they practised night after night. Beginners started on the fourteenth floor and worked their way down to ground level as they became more proficient. Sadly this bore no relation to playing conditions on a genuine golf course.

Aphra was all sympathy. Since those Japanese had arrived, she had scarcely seen Luke. Now she knew why.

'Oh my dahling, how absolutely dreadful! The sooner we have a driving range and par three course for people like that the better.'

'That's for sure. Have you mentioned the back field to Gally yet?'

'Not yet, but what you've just told me will give me the perfect opportunity. I'll tell him it's absolutely vital that he make it available for the rock concert. Then, with the proceeds from the concert, the bloody GAA can build their own golf facility to cater for idiots like those silly Japs. If we don't do something quickly, our regular golfers will walk out *en masse*. Hard to blame them if they're going to be delayed for five hours every focking day!'

Luke cut in, 'Must rush, honey. Gotta go and humour those guys held up out on the course. Life ain't gonna be worth livin' round here for a while, that's for sure.'

On that cheerful note, he hung up.

Mick arranged to meet the Doc for a drink later that night. By then he had got through to Aphra and told her about the meeting. The Brulagh Inn served not just as a pub but also the social and political nerve centre of the village. Mick and the Doc went into a huddle at the end of the bar counter.

'What was that you were saying earlier about Donnelly being rushed off to hospital?' Mick inquired. 'Like I said before, nothing trivial, I hope.'

The Doc shot him a reproachful look. 'Ah, don't be like that. Donnelly's not the worst of them.'

'Well sure as hell he's not the best of them, anyway! What's wrong with the hoor? I bet it's writer's cramp from sending shagging letters to the likes of myself . . .'

48

He broke off to mimic the Bank Manager's high-pitched voice: ' "*It has come to the notice of Allied Banks of Ireland that your account is overdrawn by seven pence. It is imperative that you furnish me, by return, with firm proposals to rectify this intolerable situation at the earliest possible moment!*" '

The Doc laughed dutifully, wondering to himself at Mick's sudden interest in the whereabouts of the banker. Suddenly he remembered that Mick and Donnelly's wife Josephine had once been an item. But that was ages ago – surely it couldn't still be going on? Most unlikely, he concluded. It would have been difficult for Mick to break wind without half the village knowing, never mind conducting a clandestine affair with such a public *persona* as Josephine Donnelly.

'That shagger is no more a bloody Bank Manager than I am,' continued Mick. 'More of a fucking hit man for the Mafia, if you ask me. Anyway, are you going to tell me what ails him?'

'I really shouldn't be telling you this, but knowing you, you're going to find out sooner or later. He's checked into a nursing home for a complete rest. While he's there, he'll get a thorough checkup.'

Mick unleashed a happy guffaw and spluttered, 'Checkup my arse. What you're really saying is that he's gone to dry out. You've sent the miserable bastard into dry dock, isn't that it? Well, I hope to God they keep him there. Hell isn't half hot enough for that hoor!'

The Doc preserved a discreet silence in the face of this onslaught so Mick pressed on regardless.

'Isn't that what you said would happen to myself if I didn't pack in the drink?'

Eyeing the pint of Guinness and whiskey chaser in front of Mick, as well as the cigarette clenched in his fist, the Doc could not resist the opportunity.

'Yeah, the same sort of thing. Only in your case it will be to the church, not the nursing home that we'll be taking you. I'm glad to see you're taking my advice about the drink and the fags to heart, as usual.'

'Yerrah, knock it off. A man's got to die of something, some time. I'd rather die of doing what I like than drop dead of overwork, worry or something of that sort.'

The Doc was about to point out that there was little fear of either claiming him but Mick had already got up. He made for the telephone at the far end of the bar and wrapped his hand around the mouthpiece to give added privacy to what he was about to say. He beat a tattoo with his fingers on the bar counter as he waited impatiently for the phone to be picked up at the other end.

'Hello . . .' he formed a mental picture of Josephine Donnelly, the generously proportioned blonde wife of the banker with whom he had been conducting a sporadic affair for some time. 'Mick Flannery here.'

'What a nice surprise . . .' Mick tried to decide whether she was being genuine or just teasing him. At times she took genuine pleasure in mocking him, sometimes as a prelude to making passionate love. This was something very much on his mind right now. 'Where are you phoning from?' she asked silkily.

'Sean's place. I just heard this minute about Tom being rushed off to hospital and I was ringing to find out if he was all right, that's all.' Not perhaps the most convincing of lies, but it would have to suffice in the absence of anything better. He felt a pleasant stirring in his loins as he imagined Josephine's full red lips pursing in amusement at such an unlikely pretext for the telephone call.

After a pause that seemed longer than eternity she replied, 'Why don't you drop in for a cup of coffee or something and I'll tell you all about it. The side door.'

Without waiting for his reply, she hung up with a silvery peal of laughter that Mick found almost as arousing as the '*or something*'.

Out on the street, Sergeant Johnson had taken up position in the shadows opposite the bank. Johnny Slattery and his partner in crime, Long Tom McCarthy, had gone into the pub earlier and should be emerging any moment now, as closing time approached. There was just a chance that they might check on the still before they went home – an unlikely chance, he admitted to himself as he shivered in the chilly night air – but nonetheless one he must take. He had tried everything else. Raids, swoops, searches with and without proper warrants had yielded little except a glimpse into the rather basic domestic arrangements of both men.

There was no moon tonight, just the stars. They sparkled high in the clear sky, the only unlit part of it being the dark mass of Mount Brulagh that loomed threateningly over the village. Kevin Johnson had cause to hate the mountain. His legs were scarred with scratches, some of them quite deep, that he had acquired from the many fruitless searches conducted through its wiry gorse and vicious briars. The sheep that eked out a miserable existence on its barren slopes were owned either by his quarry, Johnny Slattery, or Nora O'Brien, the young widow who lived on the farm next to him.

Of late, the Sergeant had become quite friendly with her. Nora was a placid woman in her late thirties with a rake of kids. Their friendship had blossomed since the time when he had first trailed Johnny through hill and dale in the hope that he would lead him to his illicit still. This consisted of an iron barrel, a portable gas cylinder and the 'worm' through which the evil-smelling wash was transformed, as if by magic, into one of the strongest liquors known to man . . .

In his enthusiasm for the chase, Sergeant Johnson had failed to notice the heavy mist rapidly descending on the mountain. Suddenly he was lost, more lost than he had ever been in his life. Crashing panic-stricken from slippery rock to prickly gorsebush cloaked in innocent-looking yellow flowers, he had finally stumbled on a small farmyard with a whitewashed cottage. The half-door was open, casting a welcome rectangle of yellow light onto the smooth cobblestones, glistening in the damp mist.

Inside, he had found Nora reciting the rosary with her children, their heads bowed as they knelt in prayer. In a clear voice she intoned, 'Hail Mary, full of Grace, the Lord is—' only to be swamped by a chorus of young voices responding with, 'Holy Mary, Mother of God, pray for us . . .' Their words trailed off as they became conscious of the dishevelled figure of Sergeant Johnson framed in the doorway. As the mantra of prayer faltered uncertainly, all of a sudden a hitherto-unnoticed body sitting by the open turf fire shattered the innocent *tableau* by leaping to its feet with a muffled oath.

'Bejaysus if it isn't the Sergeant himself. Tell us, what brings you to an out-of-the-way spot like this, at this hour of the night?'

It was none other than the Sergeant's quarry. His pursuer was not to know that Johnny had earlier been regaling the family with an account of how he had led the arm of the law a merry dance through some of the worst parts of the mountain. Only minutes before he had confidently predicted that if there were one shred of the Sergeant's uniform left by the time he got back to the Barracks, then it would be the greatest miracle since Maggie Flannery saw the statue moving down in the Grotto.* Nora had not been amused.

'*If* he gets back to the Barracks, you mean,' she pointed out sharply. 'It'll be dark shortly and there's a fog out there you could cut with a knife. He could fall and hurt himself – then he might die of the cold.'

'There's no fear of him dying of the cold,' Slattery had retorted sourly. 'I promise you that much! That hoor has a skin thick as any goat. If he has to spend the night out there, well and good. 'Twould be the best thing that ever happened to the shagger. Might give him a bit of sense rather than be chasin' the likes of meself all over the place and me only trying to scrape a dacent living.'

Nora had cut him short at this point by kneeling down and dedicating the rosary to the safe return of the young Sergeant. His dramatic entrance even before the prayers were finished left the children awestruck at the effectiveness of their pleas to the Almighty on his behalf.

Johnny's prediction concerning his uniform had not fully come to pass but the natty blue material with the silver buttons and massive buckle would never be serviceable again. To add to his misfortune, the peaked cap and one of the three white stripes that indicated his rank were missing.

Before he could catch his breath to reply to Johnny's impudent question the widow intervened: 'Take one look at the poor craythur! Get off those boots, Sergeant, and I'll fix you a basin of water for your poor feet.'

Eyeing Slattery suspiciously, the Sergeant entered and seated himself on the vacant stool by the fire. Meanwhile Nora added something from an old Rose's Lime Juice bottle to hot water in a basin. Whatever it was, it acted as a soothing balm to his throbbing feet. She poured more of the liquid onto a cloth and handed it to the Sergeant. 'When you've got some life back into your legs, go into the back room there and take off your pants. Then rub this into the cuts on your hands and legs. It'll stop them

* See *The Neon Madonna*.

going septic . . .' Then, as if to broaden the discussion she added, almost as an afterthought '. . . won't it, Johnny?'

His reply was a surly mumble, the essence of which was that he had to be 'off' followed by a vague reference to 'me aunt'. In a moment he was gone and the Sergeant did as he was told with the cloth. When he came back into the kitchen, his legs and hands burning from whatever had dampened the cloth, there was a steaming mug of tea waiting for him. He felt that some form of thanks, if not explanation, were in order.

'You're a great woman to be looking after me like this, with the kids to go to bed yet. Will your husband be home soon?'

This was greeted by an eerie silence, broken at last by the woman with an apparent *non sequitur*.

'You sit yourself down by the fire there and I'll get the children to bed.'

When she came back, she got straight to the point. 'I've no man this past few years. He hanged himself out in the barn when he got into trouble with the bank. Johnny wants me to marry him but I don't know whether 'tis myself or the farm he's really after. I suppose you were following him when you got lost?'

It was more of a statement than a question. The sergeant nodded.

'Well then, you'd be better employed trying to catch the Will o' the Wisp or the Banshee herself, so you would. That mountain is dangerous at the best of times. There are holes covered by furze and long grass. The sheep fall into them sometimes and that's the end of them. I'm in dread that one of the children will do the same though it hasn't happened yet, thanks be to God. I suppose you'll want to be off now?'

Again it was more of a statement than a question. He got up off the three-legged stool by the fire, stretched himself wearily and listened to her directions on how to return to the village. These were straightforward: follow the road downhill for three miles, taking care not to sprain an ankle in the potholes. He thanked her again and reluctantly made his way out the door. The slightest hint of invitation in her voice and he would have stayed the night. Maybe even forever.

Nora O'Brien was attractive in a homely way that reminded him of his own mother. And caring, too. He remembered the way she turned her back on him before pouring the poteen into the basin of warm water and later, steeping the cloth in it to spare his embarrassment.

The irony of the situation had not escaped him then, not even now as he gazed across the dimly-lit street at the door of the Brulagh Inn. There were some who might even consider it amusing that the Mountain Dew which he had acquired the scars of battle in trying to stamp out, should be the salve for those very wounds.

His further ponderings on the ironies of life were cut short by a movement in the dark alley that led to the side door of the bank – the one going up to the Donnellys' apartment. A figure was crouched against the door – could he be trying to force the lock? Kevin's eyes strained to pierce the gloom. It could easily be a drunk staggering home before closing time and relieving himself *en route*: Tom Donnelly and his wife were never done complaining of this practice and inquiring acidly what he proposed to do about it. But the door was opening now and the shadowy figure slipped inside. Why the hell hadn't the alarm gone off? Maybe the damn thing was on the blink again. Time and again he had warned the Donnellys to keep a constant check on the complicated electronic surveillance systems installed in every bank since a succession of IRA raids and hostage-takings had embarrassed the Government and the banks alike . . .

Indeed, before he was posted to this godforsaken spot, an unsuccessful bank raid had put Brulagh in the public eye for one hectic weekend. Like a lot of other things about the village, despite the attentions of the national media and the glare of publicity that should have illuminated every detail, however murky, of the incident, there were still a lot of things about the affair that were cloaked in secrecy. To the Sergeant's surprise, there were no files on what must have been the major, if not the *only* robbery attempt in the long history of the tiny village. The usual sources were not available to him for, not being a drinker, Sergeant Johnson didn't have access to the gossip of the bar counter. Thus he would never get the true facts about the siege of Rose Cottage and the affair of Maggie Flannery and the moving statue.

He was saved from making the difficult decision about whether to stay with his original mission of waylaying and trailing the two illegal distillers, or to investigate the stealthy figure that had just closed the door after him and disappeared into the bank, when a front door on his side of the street opened suddenly, throwing a shaft of light onto the pavement. Silhouetted against the glare were the familiar figures of the Doc and Charley Halpin. They were carrying large cardboard cartons out of the Doc's house and placing them with great care in the boot of Charley's motorcar – not carefully enough, however, to avoid the unmistakable clink of bottles. Kevin thought to stroll over and bid them goodnight, in order to find out what it was they were moving under cover of darkness, but some sixth sense told him to stay where he was in the shadows, and watch them for a while longer. He also wanted to remain in view of the bank, in case of further developments from that quarter.

As the last carton was being loaded, a bottle fell through the bottom of the box and shattered on the road, to the accompaniment of a chorus of, 'Oh Jaysus!' from Charley and the Doc. In the shadow of the car, something – quite possibly money – was being exchanged. Then the Doc went back inside the house and the car drove off hurriedly, with Charley Halpin at the wheel. The street returned to its former state of darkness. Sean Flannery still had five minutes to go before calling, 'Time, gentlemen – have ye no homes to go to?' – just long enough for the Sergeant to see what it was that had shattered on the road.

Approaching stealthily the spot where the car had been parked, he felt shards of glass crunch beneath his hobnailed boots. He stooped to investigate. A piece larger than the rest lay beside his boot. From its shape, it had obviously once been part of a bottle, and was sharp enough to pierce a tyre. Carefully, like a good citizen, he picked it up and was just about to drop it into a litter bin, when he noticed a tiny drop of liquid trapped in the curve of the broken glass. Putting it to his nose, the smell was unmistakable, so much so that it triggered off again the burning sensation in his hands and legs when he rubbed the cloth to his wounds that evening in the cottage up the mountain. Its aroma was that of the 'pure drop' – the very best of poteen. Beyond any reasonable doubt, it had been part of the consignment he had seen being loaded into the boot of Charley Halpin's car.

Kevin's mind raced feverishly. What the hell was going on? How could the Doc have a store of poteen in his house?

Moonshine was the very last thing any self-respecting General Practitioner would want to be associated with. If it could be proved that the Doc was involved in the illicit trade, he would be struck from the roll of his profession quicker than he could say Sergeant Johnson.

As for Charley Halpin, where did he fit in? Hadn't the very same man written glowing accounts of Garda efforts to stamp out the evil of illegally-distilled liquor? Two less likely people to be involved in what was referred to as *the business*, Sergeant Johnson's confused mind could not imagine. Anyway, he could never prove in open court that the glass had come from whatever it was that had been loaded into the back of Charley Halpin's car. As for the drop of poteen, it would have long since evaporated before he could get it back to the Barracks and seal it in a container as evidence for any future proceedings. Don't be ridiculous, he scolded himself. What legal proceedings? At the very most, all he had were suspicions and grounds for closer surveillance of the two unlikely suspects. And suspicions, as his Superintendent had drummed into him every time he had sought yet another search warrant in his quest to catch Johnny Slattery red-handed, were a horse of a different colour from hard evidence.

Reluctantly he turned his mind to the earlier incident of the shadowy figure in the alley. It was now a good twenty minutes since it had grabbed his attention. It must have been Tom Donnelly letting himself in after taking the air before going to bed. Still, Kevin supposed, he had better be sure, just in case. He would look a proper eejit if the bank had been robbed and he standing on duty not twenty yards away. It certainly wouldn't do much good to his prospects of promotion out of this dump – that was for sure and certain!

With nothing further to detain him outside the Doc's house, and the Brulagh Inn still showing no signs of calling it a night, he decided to check on the status of the side door leading to the bank. To his surprise, it was still off the latch. He pushed against it and it opened without protest. If the figure *had* been that of Donnelly, he would surely have closed the door after him before going to bed. Kevin felt in the pocket of his overcoat for the reassuring shape of the powerful torch he carried with him on his nocturnal prowls.

A scuffing sound came from somewhere above him. He groped

his way up the stairs in the dark, not daring to switch on the torch but holding it in his hand just the same. He might need it to defend himself against the intruder. There wasn't a light of any sort on in the house, but sounds of a struggle grew louder as he approached the closed door of the sitting room. The Sergeant could recall its layout from the time Donnelly and his blonde wife had invited him and several other local worthies in for a single glass of lukewarm sherry on Christmas morning.

He remembered an enormous couch and a lot of expensive leather armchairs scattered casually round the room. It was from the couch that the sounds were coming. Taking a deep breath, he approached it stealthily and switched the torch.

Its beam spotlighted two naked bodies in the final throes of lovemaking.

With a muffled oath Mick Flannery looked up from what he was doing.

The Sergeant struggled to find words adequate to meet the situation. There had been nothing in his training to prepare him for something like this. Josephine Donnelly was looking up at him expectantly, most of her nakedness covered by Mick's hefty torso.

As the Sergeant stumbled back down the stairs and let himself out, he gulped down great lungfuls of the cool night air. In his lonely bed above the Barracks, it took a long time for sleep to come. It might have been some consolation for him to know that it took Mick Flannery even longer.

8

O'SHEA HAD LEFT a message for him at the hotel just off Fifth Avenue. It contained a list of interviews, with the times and the addresses of the TV and radio stations. It also suggested that if Mick did not have any more pressing engagements for his first night in New York, he might do worse than pay a visit to the Four-Leafed Shamrock, where he was sure of a big welcome. The message ended with O'Shea regretting that he couldn't be there to greet Mick in person, citing pressing business in Boston as an excuse. Another note on the message board contained an invitation to the Irish Embassy, but by now that function would have been almost over.

Mick unpacked, showered and took a cab to the Four-Leafed Shamrock on Second Avenue. Outside the hostelry there was a long green canopy stretching from the kerb to the door, as portrayed in all the movies he had ever seen of New York. Instead of a liveried doorman sporting white gloves, top hat and a wide smile, however, there was what appeared to be a recent defector from the People's Liberation Army. In its early twenties, the creature affected a wisp of hair about its chin that just might have passed for a beard on a kid goat, and an unruly ponytail which forced its way out from under a black beret. One ear was pierced by a brass stud holding a large safety pin, the other supported two round ear-rings. Its clothes were of some black canvas material – possibly tarpaulin. They were several sizes too large, suggesting that they had been borrowed, or more probably stolen, from an obese undertaker. If the creature's deathly pallor was anything to go by, it could be putting some business the undertaker's way in the near future. Surprisingly, it also had the power of speech.

'Who're-you-an'-where-d'ya-think-yer-goin'?'

'Mick Flannery's the name – and I'm invited!'

The creature brightened considerably, flashing what it clearly imagined to be a welcoming smile.

'Great, c'mon in. We're holdin' a table for you. Dave was afraid you mightn't show. Over for the Parade, huh?'

Mick nodded perfunctorily. He wondered who the hell Dave was, until mention of the Parade reminded him that he should go easy on the drink tonight. He had taken on board an elegant sufficiency during the six-hour flight and this had already wrought havoc with his waterworks. The Doc would have described it as 'a frequency problem'. Much as devout Catholics could not pass a church without dropping in for a quick prayer, Mick now had the same problem with toilets – or 'Restrooms' as the sign to his left proclaimed. He took the narrow stairs two at a time. Squeezing himself inside the tiny cubicle, he noted that it doubled as a graffiti centre and message board. Phone numbers with subtitles of varying explicitness vied for space with slogans such as *Shamrocks suck* and *Ex-altar boy wishes to meet same* and crude depictions of genitalia. The most striking of these were a pair of three dimensional squares entitled '*Balls* by Salvador Dali'.

Back in the bar, he had more time to take stock of his surroundings. Of the pigtailed creature there was no sign. Presumably it had resumed its post at the door as final arbiter on who should be allowed to venture within. The front section of a very long room was an old-fashioned saloon dedicated solely to the consumption of drink. Behind a long wooden counter with a footrail sunk firmly in the red-tiled floor, a barman with a waistline even more impressive than Mick's headed a team of junior bartenders who were silhouetted against an illuminated backdrop of bottles from every corner of the globe. An uneven line of shamrock-shaped balloons proved a more recent addition to the *décor*. These would have given O'Shea – who had already pushed back the frontiers of bad taste well beyond acceptable limits when it came to shamroguery – serious pause for thought. They bore slogans that proclaimed *I'm an Irish virgin, make my day and have sex with somebody else*, or *I need more money and power and less shit from you people*, along with *I drink to make other people more interesting* and finally: *I'd slap you but shit splatters!*

Food was served in the rear of the saloon, where diners were packed like sardines around huge tables. Above the roar of conversation a band of some description invited Mick to *Come Back To Erin*. Nothing could have been further from his mind.

He had just spotted the proprietor, a fellow member of the legendary hurling team. They had last met on the field of battle after which the proprietor, one Dave Foley, had followed many of his countrymen to America. Foley was huddled in a corner, surrounded by burly men wearing startling green ties and matching caps that proclaimed *Irish and proud of it*! Mick had never seen such an outpouring of nationalist pride, and this was only the day *before* the big Parade. Back in Brulagh, the Parade lasted about ten minutes, with Father Jerry O'Sullivan in full priestly garb leading a motley procession of schoolchildren, and headed by the local brass and reed band, who had trouble keeping in step, not to mind in tune.

With a roar like a hippopotamus calling to its young, Dave Foley greeted Mick. 'Jaysus, if it isn't the man himself! Come over here to me and I'll introduce you to some of the lads!'

The lads, it transpired, were old drinking buddies of the proprietor and had been proving this over the past day or two, if one were to judge by the stubble on their chins and the aura of manic disarray that surrounds those far gone in drink. In contrast, Foley's face beamed pink and cleanshaven as that of a newborn babe. Clutching Mick by the shoulder lest he should try to make a run for the door, Foley banged on the counter with a heavy beer mug to attract the attention of his patrons. When the noise subsided to a gentle roar, he introduced Mick with another hippo-like bellow.

'Meet a legend in his own lifetime, boys — the only man in history to win four All-Ireland medals in a row. Mick Flannery, the greatest hurler ever!'

After that, everything seemed to go downhill rapidly. Drinks were pressed on Mick from every quarter, all with one thing in common. Regardless of their content, all had some element of green. Crème de menthe, green beer and Green Mexicans — a lethal mix of tequila and peppermint — coursed down his gullet until the ceiling began to take on a life of its own. Strangers vied with each other to be the first to shake his hand, and press yet another verdant vodka on him. It would have been boorish to refuse and Mick, whatever his faults, was not a boor.

The ceiling began to move more violently, like a turbulent green sea. Blearily Mick again looked at the steep stairs that led to something called a mezzanine wherein lay the 'Restrooms'. Why the hell they couldn't call them lavatories and be done with it still remained a mystery to him. From afar, a Brooklyn accent asked him if he would like a drink. Though normally such a question would have been purely rhetorical, this was one of those rare occasions when an internal debate was necessary to resolve the question.

'Here I am marooned in the Four-Leafed Shamrock Bar – of course I want a drink! What does the clown think I came in here for in the first place – a bloody haircut?' his confused mind blustered in response. But another, quieter voice – that of Sweet Reason – also tried to get a word in edgeways. 'That's all very well, but if you drink any more, you'll fall flat on your face.' With one ear cocked to the internal debate raging within his breast, the other heard a slurred voice that he had difficulty in recognising as his own, frame the reply: 'I'll have a large whiskey and a pint of stout, if you don't mind.'

His request echoed eerily across the crowded bar, causing the ceiling to heave again, this time not in synchronisation with the separate and quite distinct movements of both the floor and his stomach. Deciphering the sign by the stairs was difficult, despite an inner conviction that what it said was of some importance. The letters swam before his eyes like floating amoebae, coming together in great blobs only to drift apart just as they were about to make some sort of sense to his befuddled brain.

'What the hell,' he asked himself plaintively, 'are they advertising "beetroots this way" for? Whoever heard of bloody beetroots in a bar, for Jaysus sake?'

In a flash of lucidity that flickered just long enough to unscramble the anagram at the foot of the stairs, he realised that the amoebae spelt out the familiar word 'Restrooms'. If there was one thing in the whole wide world that he needed more urgently than anything else at the moment, this was it.

Once more he sought refuge inside a cramped cubicle. This time he went through a routine that had served him well in the past. Taking the large white handkerchief from the breast pocket of his suit, he flicked it open from its folds so carefully ironed by Maggie only two nights before. It felt more like two hundred years ago, he reflected woozily as he spread it out on the floor. He then hung the jacket of his suit on the hook provided by a thoughtful management for just that purpose. Meticulously he tucked the green silk tie inside his shirt with even greater care than he had shown in arranging the handkerchief on which he knelt as if worshipping the great white telephone into which he was about to speak.

It was in this supplicant position that he awoke the next morning. A loud banging on the door added to his discomfiture.

'Come on outa there for Chrissakes, or you're gonna miss the Parade.'

The owner of the Four-Leafed Shamrock sounded aggrieved that anyone should contemplate such an evasion, though Mick would have happily settled for a bed, any bed, rather than the cold canyon that was Fifth Avenue. Waiting with Dave Foley was a small agitated man with a goatee beard. He was introduced to Mick as his 'minder' from the Embassy.

The next thing Mick remembered was marching in a biting cold wind towards a large stone mausoleum that turned out to be St Patrick's Cathedral. From its steps, a figure that might have been Batman waved imperiously at those marching past in the Parade. This consisted of a myriad marching bands fronting a ragbag of Irish organisations drawn from every quarter of the United States.

Mick found himself leading the Ancient Order of Hibernians (Poughkeepsie Chapter). Behind them the Friendly Sons of St Patrick from some place he had never heard of sported an array of long-stemmed cheerleaders who kicked their legs high in the air and clasped giant tri-coloured pom-poms in what must have been their very cold hands. By way of contrast, those just ahead of him were a motley group, sashaying happily under an enormous banner that read *The Fighting 69th, Regiment of Maher of the Sword – gentle when stroked, dangerous when aroused.* Whether this slogan applied to the late Maher, those parading under his banner or to the regimental Mascots – a pair of giant Irish Wolfhounds – remained far from clear.

Mick watched enviously as one of the giant curs relieved itself against a fire hydrant. How he wished he could do likewise. His night in the Four-Leafed Shamrock now seemed light years ago. Watching the hairy brute reminded Mick that another visit to a restroom was long overdue. Just then a fellow marcher, an octogenarian in a green plastic bowler hat and sporting enough shamrock to feed a herd of buffalo, steered him towards Batman.

On closer inspection, the cloaked figure wearing the funny hat proved to be His Eminence, Cardinal O'Halloran bestowing his blessing on those marching in the Parade. The Prince of the Church extended his hand towards Mick as a black-clad assistant, possibly Robin, whispered Mick's name, together with a thumbnail *curriculum vitae*, into the episcopal ear.

Mick's first reaction from years of pressing the flesh was to shake the hand of the Cardinal. Just in time he remembered that he was expected to kiss the ring – an unhygienic exercise at the best of times. On this day of all days, hundreds must have already pledged their fealty that morning, many of them in a state of ill-health similar to his own. With this very much in mind, Mick clasped the Cardinal's hand to his face taking care to press his nose, rather than his lips, against the gemstone set in the heavy gold ring.

'Michael Flannery, is it not? I've heard all about your exploits both on and off the field of play!'

The voice twanged sharply as Mick looked up at the hawklike features to gauge whether the Sergeant's discovery of Josephine and himself *in flagrante* could have reached the Cardinal so quickly.

'Have you now, Your Eminence? Well, I only hope at least some of it was good.'

Rising from his knees for the second time that morning, he felt a rush of blood to his head that made him dizzy. The eagle-eyed cleric must have recognised the symptoms for he asked, 'Would you care to stand with me here for a while and review the Parade while you catch your breath? You seem tired and there's a long day to get through yet.'

No *Deus ex machina*, even if it did wear scarlet, had ever been more welcome.

'Nothing would please me more, Your Eminence. The jet lag was beginnin' to get to me there for a moment.'

The Cardinal's voice sounded perfectly innocent when he intoned, 'I know, I know. Quite a lot of politicians coming over from the Emerald Isle have the same problem. There's a lavatory round the back, in case you're interested. I often find jet lag takes its toll in that manner, don't you?'

Mick barely had time to nod his agreement before fleeing round the back of the enormous Cathedral.

The following day he located the radio station that O'Shea had told him about, in a sleazy part of town. Fifteen floors up in an elderly elevator did nothing to relieve the knot of tension inside Mick's stomach. This contrasted sharply with the dull throbbing inside his head that refused to go away, despite ingesting three Alka-Seltzers and a packet of Tums. Those green concoctions produced like rabbits out of a hat by Foley and his buddies were exacting a cruel revenge. However, Mick was never one to allow bodily ailments to stand in the way of self-promotion.

As both Mullarkey and Charley Halpin had stressed, his image of an international statesman debating matters of global import across the American airwaves would be vital in the forthcoming election campaign. Casual asides such as, 'Like I was saying only recently in a "coast to coast" interview . . .' would project the image of a major player on the global stage. A sense of *gravitas* — that word of Charley's that he could not remember for love or money back in Brulagh — was what he needed to acquire, if he were to garner the votes of an increasingly disillusioned electorate. That image, together with his plans to make Brulagh a major coal depot, might conceivably pull in enough votes to do the trick yet again. The Hall of Fame nonsense wouldn't harm his prospects either, especially if Charley wrote it up properly.

The lift doors opened on to a dingy hallway with black plastic rubbish bags, many burst or overflowing, stacked against peeling walls. Mick walked down a dimly-lit corridor, squinting owlishly at the names painted on the doors. *International Export & Import Consultants PLC* vied with *Mogul International Modelling Agencies Inc.* for his attention. So intent were the tenants of this corridor on debasing the word *International* that Mick decided there and then to delete it from all future Press Releases concerning the Coal Plan for Brulagh. In mulling over this, he almost missed his destination. A business card sellotaped to an unpainted plywood door, sporting a newly-replaced lock of impressive proportions, announced that within lurked *Station WBZC – FM/ NYC, a subsidiary of The International Goodwill Broadcasting Corporation.* From the outside, it seemed likely that the size of the corporate titles in this corridor might well be in inverse ratio to the floorspace they occupied.

A knock evoked no response, so he hammered, whereupon a slow drawl from within informed him: 'The fucking thing is open. Just push it in, for Chrissakes!'

The speaker was a fat man of indeterminate age. He was sprawled in a seat behind a table piled high with papers – mostly bills, Mick noted. He wore a black baseball cap turned back to front and a grimy tee shirt that read SAVE TIBET. His ample belly spilled out over faded jeans, the ends of which were tucked inside expensive-looking cowboy boots. These were resting on the table, their owner viewing Mick from between them like a gunner drawing a bead on the enemy.

'Yeah? Whaddya want?' Mick explained and Fatso softened a bit. 'Take a seat . . .'

He cocked a thumb towards a tubular steel chair with a plastic seat, currently occupied by the biggest cat Mick had ever seen. A notice just above it sternly warned: *Do not feed Rastus. The cat is on a strict diet for duodenal ulcers.*

Mick tipped the chair sideways, decanting the creature onto the floor, from where it glowered up at him, its back arched with hostility. Tiring of the floor, it sprang nimbly onto the table – an impressive feat when its size was taken into account. Mick decided to treat the animal with caution, lest its next leap might end in his lap. Taking a brief respite from whispering endearments into the cat's ear, Fatso picked up where he had left off.

'. . . Maria'll talk with you in a minute.'

This was the first indication of a female presence. For an uncomfortable millisecond, Mick feared this might have referred to the cat, still eyeing him with tiny, hate-filled eyes. Saner counsels prevailed, though, suggesting that Maria was a researcher who would go over with him the topics for discussion so that nothing untoward might disturb the great American people from its morning coffee. Mick clutched at this reassuring scenario much as a drowning sailor might cling to wreckage, however flimsy. Suspicious that O'Shea had dropped him in the shit, he was already entertaining strong reservations about the whole setup. It smacked far too much of Amateur Night for his liking. The poster on the wall above Fatso did little to allay his fears. It screamed at him in the vilest Dayglo purple: *The Yellow Ribbon is soaked in the blood of the Iraqi people!*

Taken with the SAVE TIBET tee shirt, the place might have been the secret headquarters of the People's Liberation Army (Lost Causes Battalion), one of whose recruits had greeted him outside the Four-Leafed Shamrock Bar yesterday. Further speculation along these lines was disturbed by the appearance of a tall girl with long black hair that reached almost to the micro-mini discreetly covering less than one per cent of her black fishnet tights.

Fatso jerked a thumb at Mick. 'The Irish guy.'

Almond eyes of the palest green swivelled towards him, locking like lasers on his own. She addressed him in a husky voice that he recognised as that which had been talking over the PA since he came in.

'Great to see you, Mick. Thought you mightn't show. That happens with politicians on my show sometimes, y'know . . .'

She smiled faintly at Fatso, who sniggered openly. Obviously a shared private joke. 'Now we've exactly twenty-five seconds before we go on air, so let's move!'

He followed behind her, hypnotised by the lithe movements under the stretched fabric of her miniskirt as she sashayed into the tiny studio and flopped down into a swivel chair. Adjusting the microphone some three inches from her lips, she indicated that Mike should do likewise. As the jingle plugging the virtues of someone's Deep Dish Pizza – made from only the finest organically-grown ingredients and completely free of red meat – faded out, Maria picked up a clipboard and scanned it briefly before purring into the mike: 'Welcome to the second half of *The Maria Marquesa Show*, the hour that brings the brothers and sisters up to date on the worldwide struggle for freedom. With us today we have Mick Flannery, a legend in his own lifetime. As the name suggests, Mick is an Irishman . . .'

A brief pause here while she shot him a smouldering glance and allowed her audience a moment to digest this nugget of information along with their prunes and Lite Kreem.

'. . . Visiting Noo York for the very first time. How d'ya like The Big Apple then, Mick?'

The question was phrased in such casual tones that he was unsure if an answer were expected of him. It was only when she arched her eyebrows inquiringly as she waited for him that he haltingly replied, 'Oh fine, Maria, fine . . .'

He would have developed on this at far greater length, had he not been pulled up short by: 'Great, great. Now, down to business. How's the war going?'

The question was lent greater impetus by eye contact of what Mick regarded as a highly erotic nature. Maria Marquesa was by far the most beautiful woman he had ever seen and he wanted her very badly indeed. This had the effect of making him forget whatever he was about to add to the sum of human knowledge on the current and future prospects of *Noo York*.

'Which war would that be, Maria?'

A joyous tinkle of laughter like a cut-glass chandelier caught in a sudden draught greeted this.

'Aw, c'mon Mick, stop playing games. Why, the War of Liberation in your own country, of course! I've already filled in the listeners on your family's record in the fight for Irish Freedom. Tell us like it was, Mick.'

In a changing world, one thing was certain: the true story of how Maggie's father and uncle conned future generations into believing that they had singlehandedly put the forces of The Crown to flight was not about to be revealed here – or anywhere else, for that matter. Flannery remembered as if it were only yesterday the shots fired over Tim's coffin as it lay by the graveside, draped in the national flag. It would not have surprised Mick had the old comrades who discharged the customary volley from rifles even more ancient than themselves, directed their fire into, rather than over, the coffin to make sure that the secret of the Brulagh ambush remained just that – secret. Now this gorgeous creature wanted Mick to spill the beans. Sorrowfully he decided it was about the one thing in the world he wouldn't do for her.

'Yerrah Maria, the only record I could talk to you about is the four All-Ireland medals I got, and that was nearly as long ago as the ambush.'

She remained tight-lipped, making it obvious that she and her listeners expected something better than this.

'As for Con and Tim, sure that was ages ago. The IRA they fought for were true freedom fighters, not like the lot that are going around today . . .'

'Oh yeah? How come?'

'Well, for one thing, the present lot just plant bombs and run away to somewhere safe. Then they set them off by remote control – and usually kill innocent civilians into the bargain. The likes of Con and Tim Murphy would turn in their graves if they were to be mentioned in the same breath as a gang of murderers like the present crowd.'

This approach evidently failed to meet with her approval.

'Are you trying to tell me that there isn't a War of Liberation going on in Ireland?'

'Too damn right I am. There is a bit of a civil war going on in the North, where Irishman is killing Irishman, but what it is they're trying to liberate each other from, I don't know. Unless, of course . . .' Mick paused here as the thought struck him for the first time '. . . it's from life itself. In which case, they seem to be doing it quite well!'

Mick would have been far happier trotting out his party piece – the one that he could recite robot-like in his sleep, about: '*The unbreakable links between the Auld Sod and the new generation of Irish-Americans who are about to inherit the riches of The New World.*' Never mind that all of those second-generation Irish to whom he had spoken declared that wild horses would not drag them back to the Land of their Fathers – not even for the briefest of holidays. Most of them had quit the island under poor circumstances and saw little point in reviving old ghosts and bad memories. He might have developed his 'Liberation from Life' theory further, were it not for an unexpected sensation in his groin.

Seconds earlier, as he was in full flight, he had noticed Maria stretching in her chair as though to ease a pain in her back. Now he discovered it was for the express purpose of placing her foot squarely on his most sensitive region. Her toes seemed to be searching frantically for something. Having found it, they beat a gentle tattoo on it. Mick found this such a distraction that he instantly abandoned the warring factions to their own devices to concentrate all the better on developments on the home front, as it were. It was not surprising, therefore, that he almost missed her next question completely.

It was: 'How soon should the Brits get out of Ireland?'

Had Mick been less preoccupied with things of the flesh, he would have evaded this loaded question by the simple expedient of ignoring it. Instead of risking an answer, he would have switched over to automatic pilot and delivered his 'unbreakable links' party piece. This denied even the most probing of interviewers a chance to get a word – or a question – in edgeways. It had served Mick well in the past and would do so again. But not today.

When the probing was done with the foot, Mick found himself at a distinct disadvantage. As he paused to gather his remaining wits, he heard: 'Address the mike, Mick,' which was accompanied by another piano concerto for toes. By now Mick was sufficiently aroused to declare war on the rest of the world if it would help get him out of the studio and into bed with the toe pianist across the table. To lend even greater urgency to the matter, Maria had now brought her other foot into play.

Mick heard a voice that he had difficulty in recognising as his own, reply: 'Yerrah the sooner the better, I suppose!'

Before he could retract or qualify this appalling *gaffe*, she dropped her feet from their target and signed off with: 'That's it for today, folks, from *The Maria Marquesa Show*. It's sure good to hear, brothers and sisters, from a power broker like Mick Flannery that it's high time those Brits got out of Ireland. I just wish you knew the trouble I had dragging it out of him . . .'

As she said this, she winked seductively at Mick and then continued, stifling at birth any thoughts he might have had of cutting in on her and amending the damning statement she had just attributed to him: 'Time to go now, so Adios to the brothers and sisters everywhere and keep up the good fight, one and all, from *The Maria Marquesa Show*.'

As they both removed their headphones, Mick was struggling with a series of conflicting emotions. The first was that he had landed himself in a hornets' nest of left-wing liberationists. Not just of the bra-burning sort, but of those who automatically sided with the rebels, regardless of who was right or wrong. He knew the type full well. The 'Do not confuse me with facts, my mind is made up!' school of thought. He had met quite a few second-generation Irish and most of them slotted into that category effortlessly. From a comfortable distance of 6,000 miles, they solved their island's problems without, however, bothering to go there and inspect them at first-hand for themselves.

Mick shifted uneasily in his chair as he tried desperately to damp down the fires of a growing passion. Racked as he was with regret at letting his heart – or points south – rule his head in the explosive issue of the British Occupation, all thoughts of what Mullarkey might have to say to him about it were driven from his mind by an overwhelming desire to jump on this sultry siren of the airwaves. As he looked on her through a red haze of lust, he quietened the distant voice that warned him that his 'sooner the better' remark would return to haunt him. How often had Mullarkey stated privately that the greatest single disaster that could possibly befall him would be for the Brits to quit Northern Ireland, leaving his administration to sort out the mess?

Now Mick, a Member of the European Parliament, had invited them to do just that! Ever the optimist, he tried to console himself as he watched Maria lean over the side of her chair to extract a comb from her bag, thereby exposing at least an acre of shapely buttock in the process, that no one except long-haired dopeheads and ageing flower children could possibly bother to tune in to such a load of leftie claptrap.

Then again, if he had misjudged the audience, and the Embassy minion who had rescued him from the Four-leafed Shamrock got wind of it, his future prospects would be gloomy indeed. The first thing a sceptical electorate looked for in their representatives was a sure pair of hands. If it were to be reported back home that Mick had uttered pro-IRA sentiments, his friends would assume that he was drunk. Non-friends, who made up the vast majority of the electorate, would not be so kind.

9

THE GAELIC PALACE was packed to the doors. Large and small, rich or slightly less so, professionals or blue-collar workers, the crowd appeared to have but one goal: the consumption of liquor to the value of, if not in excess of, the fifty dollars they each had paid for the doubtful privilege of seeing the legendary Michael J. Flannery in the flesh and witnessing his elevation to the New York GAA Hall of Fame.

By contrast, the stage was an oasis of emptiness where a solitary microphone stood rigidly to attention beside a table draped in green baize. On this rested a huge vase of Waterford crystal, a hurler in full flight skilfully etched on a frosted medallion cut into the chunky bowl of cut glass. Next to it in a heavy gilt frame was an illuminated address. Much of it was virtually illegible due to the flourishes and embellishments on the ornate Gaelic script. It had been commissioned for the occasion from the Little Sisters of the Poor, who – despite their title – had charged two thousand dollars for their labours. Their brief had been to incorporate every aspect of Mick's sporting career into the delicate filigree inscribed on the wafer-thin parchment.

To Mick's disappointment, it did not refer to his three decades of selfless public service. On the plus side, it failed to include certain less salubrious happenings that went to make up the rich fabric of his life, thereby leaving the scales of justice evenly balanced. Indeed, it may have been prudent to omit the undeniable contribution he had made to politics both at home and abroad because he had just been informed by a dampish whisper in his ear that some members of the Lower Manhattan branch of the Friendly Sons of St Patrick had originally refused point-blank to attend tonight's bunfight because of Mick's known lack of enthusiasm for the cause of Irish Freedom. His unexpected outburst in that now-famous radio interview had caused them to change their minds. They had gone so far as to bring their manifesto with them which, in due course, they would ask Mick to sign. It dealt with the early withdrawal of troops from Northern Ireland and a pious expression of hope for a United Ireland.

This – and much else – had been conveyed to him by the man from the Embassy whose task it was to make sure Mick stirred up no more hornets' nests. Life was difficult enough for Embassy minders such as he at the best of times, but it peaked a week either side of St Patrick's Day, when every redneck politician from the Old Country descended on them, expecting to be fed, found and fêted. Opportunities had to be laid on for them to bend the ear of a dozen different Irish organisations, ranging from the Hostile Sons of St Finian to thinly-disguised fronts for the Provisional IRA. And when it came to necks, he decided, they didn't come any redder – or thicker – than the one attached to his current charge.

Apart from the disastrous interview, and the protests outside Station WBZC that made prime-time TV, Mick had behaved outrageously ever since setting foot in the Land of the Free. Teaming up with his long-lost buddy, Dave Foley of the Four-Leafed Shamrock Saloon, Mick had laid waste to the bars of Manhattan until the Ambassador himself had called a halt to his frolics by sending the bearded Embassy minder to stay by his side night and day.

Mick did not appreciate this service, though it was doubtful whether he even remembered Foley rescuing him from the Restroom where he had passed the night. Foley had then passed Mick on to the bearded one, who had washed and shaved him before forcing him to swallow approximately a quart of black coffee. This was currently engaged in a life or death struggle with last night's alcohol.

The temptress of the airwaves had not been allowed near him, much to Mick's annoyance. If only Mick Flannery could be kept sober during this nonsensical Hall of Fame Award Ceremony, the Embassy man's promotion prospects would be greatly enhanced. He scratched his well-trimmed beard contentedly as he imagined how it would be when he broke the news to his wife. Imelda had always been critical of his slow climb up the diplomatic grease-pole. Of late, this had been expressed by her long-threatened retreat from the king-size bed with the satin sheets to the single bed in the spare room. As befitted a diplomat's wife, she implied rather than stated that her favours would be restored if and when his career prospects took a serious turn for the better.

Now all that stood in his way was the large figure in the natty mohair suit. The bearded one had grown to hate this political dinosaur from the backwoods. Goddamit, he thought, the slob might as well have come from another planet for all they had in common. The guy seemed to think the sophisticated city of New York was just one long bar counter. Part of the damage-limitation exercise had been to bring Mick on a sightseeing trip that included Central Park, the Museum of Modern Art, Wall Street and, as *grande finale*, a helicopter trip to Ellis Island and the Statue of Liberty. However, while the bearded one was standing in line for the chopper ride, Mick disappeared with a muttered excuse about 'taking a leak'.

He was run to ground eighteen hours later in the Four-Leafed Shamrock, draped across the bar and serenading the patrons, together with the bar-owner, a formerly solid citizen by the name of Foley, with choruses of *Galway Bay*. Unfortunately, before his charge could see the sun going down on Galway Bay through the window of Aer Lingus Flight 104 making its final approach into Shannon, it would first be necessary to despatch the fat bastard down to Louisville, for it was there that the idiot had, without as much as a 'by your leave' to the Embassy, embarked on some deal or other with coal-shippers from the Mississippi port. Part of the bearded one's brief had been to discover what Mick was up to in the Deep South. In this he had been unsuccessful to date. Any time he had brought up the matter, it was only to be politely fobbed off or given a look that might have suggested to someone better versed in the ways of the world than he that there was a bit more to Michael J. Flannery than the boozy exterior would at first suggest.

The good news, the Embassy minion reminded himself yet again as he watched his charge make his way through the crowd to the podium, stopping every so often to press the flesh or whisper something into a receptive ear, was that after this, his last task was to make sure Mick was on a morning flight out of Kennedy. Then, and only then, could he breathe easily and report to the fair Imelda that careerwise, things were looking up. There was also the vexed question of who had booked the idiot onto Radio WBZC – FM/NYC. Though claiming to be a subsidiary of the International Goodwill Broadcasting Corporation, this was widely regarded as a cover for a ninety-year-old Irish-American of immense wealth, who had been a lifelong supporter of creeping socialism and pale pink liberals of every race, creed and colour. The bearded one winced as he contemplated this conglomeration of everything he most despised.

The rumour wafting round the lower echelons of the Embassy chattering classes was that the nonagenarian had a brother some twenty years younger who had once owned a bar in Mick's home town somewhere way out in the asshole of nowhere. The O'Shea brothers had close connections with various illegal organisations and were suspected of channelling funds back to Ireland under such thinly disguised charities as the Republican Prisoners' Clothing Fund and God alone knew what else. Rumour also had it that Mick had once been the target of a subversive kidnap back home in Brulagh. It was a complicated saga that involved a moving statue of Mary, the Mother of God, and Mick's wife who, for a while, thought that she had been chosen to convert the People's Republic of China to the One Truth Faith. The younger, if indeed such a description could be applied to someone over seventy, O'Shea had to leave Brulagh hurriedly and under something of a cloud though his role in the strange sequence of events had never been properly explained. Alas, this rumour could not be confirmed or denied by the man at the centre of the storm. Mick, even when drunk, had sung dumb on that one.

In stark contrast to the emptiness at the front of the hall, the back was a seething mass of two-fisted drinkers, all speaking at the same time. Listeners were, as always, thin on the ground. Progress through this dense throng of drinkers was hampered further by strangers stopping Mick and engaging him in debate as to the merits of various teams of the past and battles long ago. It was therefore not all that surprising that the proceedings got under way before Mick reached the stage. A latterday leprechaun in a green velvet suit was rasping loudly into the microphone, un-deterred by the fact that no one was paying the slightest heed to what he was saying. It soon became apparent that he was reading out a list of those already honoured in this fashion.

Spotting Mick, the little man swiftly changed tack and said, 'I see the legendary Mick Flannery approaching the podium. As most of you here are only too well aware, Mick Flannery is one of the hurling legends of all time. No man has ever won four All-Ireland medals in succession; indeed, few enough have managed that number in a lifetime. Add to that over thirty years of unstinting service to the people of Ireland and you have really something to be proud of . . . Mick here is an example to all of us as to how an Irishman should behave himself at home or abroad . . .'

This was news to Mick; even more so to his minder. The Ambassador's instructions – delivered in what he mistakenly imagined to be the speech pattern of the native New Yorker – had been as clear as the impressive chunk of Waterford Crystal glittering on the table. *'Get the creep outa here as fast as his legs will carry him. If he really has to shag off to St Louis or Louisville or wherever the hell he's going, you just make damn sure that his ass is on that plane or your own ass will be in a sling, understand?'*

The Ambassador, a long-serving political hack who had himself failed on more than one occasion to find favour with a fickle electorate, had taken to New York like a duck to water. To date, his main task had been to bail out impoverished students who had either run out of money or run foul of the law – or both. He regarded Mick as an adult form of this annoyance and proposed to deal with him in a like manner: ship him back home before he could cause any more trouble.

Relations between the Embassy and the State Department were already strained over a ticklish matter of extraditing some unsavoury characters back to Ireland where they had a list of charges against them longer than a wet week in Westport. Meanwhile the velvet-suited leprechaun pressed on with his remarks, accompanied by the occasional electronic whine from the mike.

'. . . A devout Catholic, Mick has been an exemplary father . . .'

Further news for Mick. He wondered if he could get the text of the leprechaun's speech sent to Charley Halpin. It would provide hours of harmless amusement to friend and foe alike as they read this hymn of praise that crackled through the loudspeakers and crashed like foam-crested breakers over the heads of those gathered to pay him homage. He was now almost at the foot of the stage, having made his way through the crowd of wellwishers.

'. . . so without further ado, I would ask you all to give a big hand to our guest of honour who has come all the way from the dear old Emerald Isle to be with us here tonight. Ladies and gentlemen, I give you the one and only *Mick Flannery!*'

The drinkers at the back of the hall fell silent, awaiting whatever pearls of wisdom might drop from the legend's lips. If they were expecting a rousing denunciation of the old enemy, the perfidious Albion, they were in for a disappointment.

'My friends,' Mick began, 'I'm delighted to be with you tonight in the Gaelic Palace. I thank the last speaker for his kind remarks about me, but I must tell you that we're all here tonight for a far more important reason than the four medals I was lucky enough to win a few years back. The real reason we're gathered here tonight is to honour the GAA. Each and every one of us owe a debt of honour to the Association that nurtured us in our native sports and helped us to preserve our national identity both at home and abroad. I would be failing in my duty to its members back home in Brulagh if I didn't have a special word to say about St Fintan's, the club I played for all my life. I can promise you that some of those games I played for them were a damn sight harder than the toughest All Ireland . . .'

This evoked a spirited cheer that gave Mick a chance to recover his breath and take a sip from the glass of water on the table.

'Indeed,' he went on, 'I see some of my team-mates from the old days here tonight, especially Dave Foley who has been showing me the sights of New York . . .'

More cheering by those who knew the innkeeper by reputation.

'. . . Which is better for me than him showing me a clean pair of heels like he did on many occasions on the hurling pitch . . .'

This sally drew a ragged cheer but Mick sensed it was time to bring his remarks to a conclusion and quit while he was still ahead of the game. It was increasingly apparent that the drinkers were anxious to get on with the task in hand and having to applaud every now and then interfered with this process.

'Before I go, I'd like to invite the New York GAA to send a team to Brulagh next year to play on our fine new pitch. I dare say we could rustle up an All-Star team to take the field against them.

However, I would stress that the fixture would be more of a social than a competitive one. I would like those of you who might not have been back home for a few years to see the changes that have happened since you left. Some of these, like the new houses and factories are a bit more obvious than the ones that have taken place in the hearts and minds of those who remain at home. Most of the people I represent are heartily sick of the Troubles in the North. . .'

This was interrupted by cheering and a few raucous yells of 'Up the Republic!'

'. . . But they are even more sick of some well-intentioned but misguided Irish-Americans sending money home to people who actively support illegal organisations.'

The reception for this was mixed – with some clapping but catcalls and whistles of disapproval as well.

'The GAA that I am a member of wants no hand, act, or part of such organisations as NORAID and the National Caucus . . .'

He didn't get to finish. Those at the back of the crowd were arguing among themselves heatedly. A minority shouted, 'The man is right, let him finish!' but the majority were trying to drown out his words with hoots of derision and cries of 'Judas!' and 'Traitor!' As the mood of the crowd turned ugly, scuffles were breaking out in the tightly-packed hall. Then, without any warning whatsoever, the lights went out. In the darkness, someone plucked at his sleeve and whispered in his ear, 'Time to go, I think.' Mick picked up his glass bowl and followed the bearded one from the Embassy through a series of narrow corridors and doors, the last of which led out onto the street. From behind them came the sound of angry voices and running feet. They did not wait to find out if their pursuers wished Mick to return in order that he might conclude his remarks, or whether they had something less sociable in mind.

The bearded one hailed a passing cab from the kerb and manhandled Mick inside almost before it had come to a halt. He snarled, 'The Majestic on Forty-Second and Fifth!' before slumping back on his seat and going into a deep-breathing routine that was punctuated at regular intervals by the word 'Kee-rist'. This was accompanied by the wagging of his beard from side to side, meant to express utter disbelief that a kindly deity could visit such suffering on mankind.

Still out of breath and shocked by the reaction his words had evoked, Mick cradled the huge bowl in his lap, determined to salvage something of value from the evening. Staring at the rolls of flesh on the cab driver's neck he debated whether to overrule the bearded one and re-direct the cab to the Four-leafed Shamrock. There he would get a proper drink rather than one of those fancy concoctions with fruit growing out of them, so beloved of the native American. Suddenly remembering that he still had to pack and phone home before the early flight tomorrow, wiser counsels prevailed. The clincher was that he could no longer be assured of a warm reception among his fellow Irish-Americans now that he had put the record straight on the vexed question of Northern Ireland and those who would meddle in its affairs from afar. He would quit while he was ahead and go back to the hotel. To do otherwise would risk being thrown out of two establishments on the same night, a feat certain to attract comment in various quarters. In the foyer, the bearded one wished him a curt goodnight and requested that he be ready to leave for the airport at seven o'clock the next morning.

Mick poured himself a stiff drink from the Robobar in his suite before turning his attention to finding the exit code that would enable him to phone the Brulagh Inn. It buzzed twice before a sleepy voice answered.

'Hello, who's this?'

'Sean, your father here. How's tricks?'

'Ah Jaysus, Dad, do you know what time of the night 'tis?'

'Not the foggiest, but it's just after nine here. Anything strange at home?'

'Nothing much. Oh yeah – the *Clarion* had a big write-up about you.'

For a moment a clammy hand gripped Mick's heart as he wondered wildly how Charley could have heard about himself, Josephine and the Sergeant. He asked in as steady a voice as he could manage: 'Oh yeah, and what had Charley to say for himself?'

'Ah, just the usual. You know, the same old thing. *Mick Flannery in America on a vital mission. Full employment for Brulagh hangs in balance.* That kind of stuff.'

'I'm off to Louisville tomorrow,' Flannery told his son. 'They're flying me down there in a private jet, if you don't mind. That's about it then. Send my best to Jenny and your mother.' With that, he hung up and freshened his drink.

The next morning they were speeding towards the airport in a black limo, with the bearded one preserving an injured silence. This suited Mick perfectly. As he viewed the receding skyline of Manhattan with a series of appreciative grunts, his minder plied the driver with a stream of anxious queries regarding the traffic conditions between here and the airport. When these met with no response other than a helpless shrug, the bearded one became more agitated than ever. It seemed that the driver did not speak English – something Mick found hilarious. Not so his companion, whose aggravation was further enhanced by Mick offering him a drink from the well-stocked cabinet set in the back of the mute driver's seat. A curt shake of the beard indicated that it did not allow alcohol to pass through it at such an early hour. It was further implied by look rather than word that for Mick to have a drink would be a serious breach of etiquette.

The array of bottles was confusing. Because he didn't recognise any of them, he thought for a fleeting moment to make a virtue of necessity and close the cabinet again. At the last moment he recognised the familiar squat shape of a Courvoisier bottle. Pouring himself a generous measure, Mick sipped and he felt its delicious warmth spread to every extremity. The beard twitched ever so slightly to allow words to filter through the dense undergrowth.

'I must warn you that drink is expensive – about twice as much again as the exorbitant prices in the Robobar of your suite. The Embassy paid for them on that occasion, but their hospitality will hardly extend to paying for drinks while driving to the airport.'

Until now, Mick had done his best to remain civil to the little bollix, but the late nights, the Courvoisier struggling to silence the pneumatic drill behind his forehead and last night's ordeal in the Gaelic Palace all combined to make something snap.

'What the hell do you mean? I think it's about time you and I got a few things straight. I'm supposed to be the guest of your fucking boss. 'Twas he sent you along with me to make sure I got to the airport on time. I would have been quite happy to get a bus or a cab – that way I wouldn't have to put up with any more of the shit you've been giving me since I first laid eyes on you. Another smart remark from you and you'll be out of a job so fucking fast your feet won't touch the ground. As for this shaggin' drink, I intend having another one in a minute and if you don't like it, you know where you can shove it. What's more, you're goin' to pay for it, same as you are for this excuse for a shaggin' ambulance that we're travelling in. Now, for the last time, I'm askin' you to cut out the nonsense and have a drink for yourself, because that's exactly what I'm going to do!'

The minder huffily declined and they had maintained a decidedly frosty silence ever since. Soon afterwards they glided up to the Departures door. While a man dressed in the uniform of a Ruritanian Prince loaded the suitcases onto a luggage trolley, Mick caught sight of a placard being held aloft. It bore the name 'Mr Michael Flannery'. He turned to the bearded one who was reluctantly signing the chit for the limo plus extras.

'Hey, what're they doin' with my name on a piece of cardboard?'

'I suggest that you address that question to the gentleman with the placard. He may be able to enlighten you further. Good morning to you, Mr Flannery. Have a nice trip.'

From his expression, the minder would have been happy if Mick ended up crashing in the icy river that bordered the airport. They parted without a handshake and Mick approached the man who bore his name aloft for all to see.

'If you walk this way, Mistuh Flannery, I'll show you to the Executive Lounge. Here, let me take yoh bags.'

Avoiding the long check-in lines, Mick followed his luggage through a red door that led to a small room with a view of that section of the tarmac crowded with Executive jets.

'That's yoh aircraft just outside...' He gestured vaguely towards a gaggle of small jets, sleek as seals, basking in the watery sun. 'I'll load the bags and check with the pilot. There's a television, newspapers and telephone just over there beside the bar. Help yohself to anything you want.'

A few minutes later, a limo even longer than the one that had brought Mick here, pulled up at the stairway of an unmarked executive jet some fifty yards from where he was sitting. Two snappily dressed businessmen got out of the back and mounted the steps. A minute or so after they had disappeared inside, the phone rang, almost causing Mick to spill his drink. He wondered for a moment what he should do, then, as there was obviously no one else going to answer it, he picked up the receiver.

'Is that Mr Flannery? Good. I'm the pilot of the Gulfstream just outside your window. We have your luggage and the other passengers are already on board. We have just been given a take-off time so you should leave by the glass door leading onto the runway. We look forward to seeing you, Mr Flannery, in the next minute or two.'

There was a click and the line went dead. Mick was impressed.

As he walked the short distance from the lounge to the aircraft a blast of icy cold snapped at his cheeks. If it weren't for those brandies, he might never have made it. Climbing the steps, he noticed the name *Gulfsteam IV* painted on the side.

The pilot met him at the door and led him into a luxurious cabin where the two men he had seen boarding earlier were already seated. They had their jackets off, revealing power braces of red and blue respectively. The older of the two, a silver-haired man in his sixties, rose from the soft leather armchair and grasped Mick's hand in an iron grip.

'Good to see ya, Mick. I'm Max, the guy you talked to over the phone. This is Sammy, my associate.'

The younger man was in his mid-thirties, running to flesh with a bald, cleanshaven head set on the bull neck of a wrestler.

'Hello there. We've heard a lot about you, Mick. Even seen you on television a few nights back. You seem to have made quite an impression on the pinkos and lefties. Anyone who bugs that load of bastards can't be all bad. Glad to have you aboard.'

The bullneck turned to call over his shoulder: 'Break out the champagne, girls.'

Seconds later, two hostesses appeared from the galley of the aircraft bearing trays of canapés and dishes of caviar to go with the Dom Perignon. Max, the silver-haired one, smacked his lips. 'Mick,' he said 'I sure hope you like beluga. Sammy and I decided years ago that this was the only way to fly. We both got pissed off with delayed flights, losing baggage, seatmates who never shut up when you wanna work or sleep, panicky drives to the airport and the whole hassle of shitty airline food and over-booking, so we just agreed one day to get our own corporate plane.'

Mick broke off from the champagne and caviar long enough to

mutter something about the cost. He wasn't all that interested but thought it only polite to inquire. Somehow he got the impression that it was expected of him.

'Yeah, well, these birds don't come cheap, that's for sure . . .'

The younger tycoon nodded enthusiastically, his mouth even fuller than Mick's with the delicious tiny globules of beluga. 'This one cost Mineralco about twenty-five big ones with all the extras. If you look at the TV screen over there you'll see where we are the minute we get airborne. The satellite system projects an image of our plane against the terrain below. It's all computer-generated from maps – a bit like playing God as you watch yourself fly around the globe. We can charge the satellite system to expenses 'cos it also lets us phone or fax anywhere in the whole goddam world. The whole shebang costs about five big ones a year to run . . .'

Mick could restrain himself no longer. 'Do you mean five *million*?' he asked incredulously.

'Yeah, about that. The goddam fuel alone comes to nearly a grand an hour, for Chrissakes. But . . .'

The older man heaved a contented sigh as he pushed away the empty goblet of caviar and held out his glass for a refill while selecting a cigar from the humidor on the low table at his knees. When the cigar was drawing to his satisfaction, he picked up where he had left off.

'It's all deductible. The IRS are used to these babies by now 'cos there are nearly seven thousand of them flying around the world. Pepsico, Ford and Xerox have a couple each, for Chrissakes, but poor guys like us have to make do with just the one.' His face creased in a wolf-like smile while Sammy applauded this sentiment with a chuckle that came from somewhere deep down near his crocodile shoes.

The metallic voice of the pilot cut deep into the buzz of conversation: 'Please take your seats and strap yourselves in, folks. We are about to commence our take-off procedure.'

As the twin Rolls Royce fanjets revved up to sound like Maggie's vacuum cleaner at full stretch, Mick took another mouthful of Bubbly and tried very hard to relax.

10

THE PUBLIC ADDRESS SYSTEM squawked out his name. It emerged as *Flan-eerie*. Mick wondered who could know of his whereabouts and was relieved to learn it was only Max, calling from the Gulfstream on its way back to New York. They had dropped Mick off in Atlanta, from whence he would fly direct to Brussels for an important EC meeting on energy. Energy was, as it happened, something he was rapidly running out of. His flight had just been delayed indefinitely due to yet another go-slow of European Air Traffic Controllers. The pair on board the Gulfstream had somehow heard of his plight, and had arranged for him to avail himself of the American Airlines hospitality suite, where free food and drink would be available until his flight was called. Max did mention – a trifle *too* casually – that the suite was equipped with an excellent communications system. He just mentioned it in case Mick wished to call home and arrange for the advance payment of one million dollars to Mineralco Inc – or rather to their discreet offshore account. This would have to be completed before the rest of the plan could go ahead.

This blatant attempt to expedite arrangements was as transparent as it was understandable. Even though Mick had made it quite clear that he would first have to clear it at home and in Brussels, Mineralco were in a hurry to close the deal and get things, specifically the trans-Atlantic barges, moving. Apparently there were only a limited number of these monsters available at any one time and they had to be booked months, even years ahead. The one million deposit would be placed in a joint account in the Caymans and used only as 'show' money to the people who leased the barges as an earnest of everyone's good intentions. If Mick felt a niggling unease at being pressurised, he was too exhausted to reflect on it in any detail.

Halfway through his second frozen daiquiri, Mick had already concluded that next to Johnny Slattery's pure drop, this had to be the fastest way of getting alcohol into the bloodstream short of employing an intravenous drip, when a small, stocky figure tapped him on the shoulder. For a brief moment Mick struggled to put a name on the chubby face but it was the distinctive rasp of the New Yorker inquiring, 'How's it goin', Mick?' that triggered his memory.

'Abe – Abe Linovitz! Where did you spring from, for Jaysus sakes?'

Not as innocent a question as it sounded. Abe had left Brulagh hurriedly a while back when he was found to be ripping off Luke Divareli by selling phoney memberships in the Orchid Club*. It was only by waiving his share in the Club that Abe managed to escape in a fishing boat, just ahead of an agent from the US Attorney's Office armed with a warrant for his arrest.

'I might ask you the same question, ole buddy,' the voice rasped. 'I heard your name on the PA and wondered if it could be the same guy that parted me from my money but saved my skin. Then I saw you heading in here so I just followed you. You're a long way off base, ain't you? How are all my buddies back in Brulagh? The last I saw of it was you and that cop waving me goodbye from the pier. That bum Divareli still owes me seven points in his lousy Orchid Club.'

Mick decided that the reminiscences had gone far enough, so he cut in with a brief resumé of the coal deal. Abe's eyes narrowed as he asked what the two guys looked like. Mick described them as accurately as he could.

On hearing that one walked with a limp and the other had a wart on his forehead, Abe cut in, 'Just let me guess their first names. Samuel and Maximilian – am I right?'

Mick felt a cold sweat breaking out on his brow. 'Yeah, they called each other Sammy and Max,' he conceded reluctantly. 'How the fuck did you know?'

' 'Cos there's barely a dozen con artists left still pulling stunts like that.'

Mick's mind raced frantically. The office building which he had

* See *The Last Resort*.

been taken to had MINERALCO in letters twenty feet high on its roof. The bloody janitor obviously knew the two men, it was nothing but Mistuh Hartmann this and Mistuh Janecski that. Dammit for a story, they even had their names up on the doors in fancy gold paint! And what about the fucking jet? They couldn't have set up all those things just to con him. It was then he realised that the only genuine, one hundred per cent con man he had ever met was none other than Abe himself.

When he voiced these doubts, he was told; 'The name Mineralco is probably kosher – so is the office block, I guess. It's only the bodies *inside* it that were in on the scam. Did you say there was a janitor?'

'Yeah, an old black guy. Ran out of the building to open the door of the limo. Was bowing and scraping to Sammy and Max as if he knew 'em all their lives. Like I said, they had their shaggin' names on the doors up fourteen floors in the Executive Suite. One was President of Mineralco, the other was Chief Executive Officer – I can't remember which.'

'Doesn't matter. The names are probably okay too. The Sammy and Max I know are brothers. I won't tell you their real names in case you get trigger happy and go gunnin' for them. With a lawyer, I mean. But their real names sure as hell ain't either Hartmann or Janecski, so those guys are probably the real McCoy.'

Mick was getting angrier and more desperate by the second. 'Ah, come off it. I saw Max's photograph large as life on the wall behind a fucking enormous desk.' Even as he spoke, he realised that he must have been too hung-over to notice the absence of secretaries and receptionists in the outer office.

Abe stopped shaking his head sadly for just long enough to explain, as though to a backward child, that nowadays any damn fool could get his picture taken and enlarged in less than twenty-four hours.

'Stick it in a fancy frame and you can call yourself the goddam Pope if you want. That don't make you a real pope, though. Naw, it's my guess the offices and everything else were genuine. 'Cept, of course, they were closed for some reason or other. I'd bet my ass those two guys bribed the janitor to let 'em use the place for an hour or two while everyone legit was away doin' something' else. Did they make any call on the way in from the airport?'

'Yeah, they did. Called ahead from the limo for someone to expect us in ten minutes or so!'

'There you go – that was to warn the janitor guy to get the show on the road and make it look as though they were up and running. What happened when you pulled up outside the door?'

'Like I told you, the janitor was waiting on the steps, bowing and scraping. Then he led us to a bank of elevators and we went up to the President's Office and talked for half an hour or so. Max showed me the cranes loading the barges at the dock down below us. I signed a preliminary agreement and . . .'

'What does that commit you to?'

'Putting up a million dollars deposit as an earnest of our good faith. It's to be lodged in a joint account.'

'Offshore, I'll bet.'

'Yes, the Cayman Islands as a matter of fact. But so what? It's in the name of Mineralco Inc. Surely to God that makes it all right if the firm is genuine?'

'My ass it does.' The stocky little man was apoplectic at this suggestion. 'Have you any idea what it costs to set up a "Me Too" outfit in the Caymans? I mean, a company with the same name as a legit corporation?'

Mick shook his head. It was on the tip of his tongue to reply to the effect that Abe was the expert on that kind of thing but instead, he swallowed the unkind thought and waited to be further enlightened on the intricacies of offshore financing.

'About a grand, that's all. One lousy grand and you can call yourself Coca fucking Cola if you want. Ain't legal anywhere else but on the islands, of course. Better believe me, ole buddy, or else those two shysters are goin' to leave you hanging out to dry. Did you give 'em a cheque?'

'No, of course not. I'm not that big an eejit!' Mick could not avoid laughing aloud at the irony of it all after he had uttered those words. This time it was Abe's turn to let it pass.

'What'd you do after that?'

'We left the building and drove back to the airport. They dropped me off here and flew back to New York.' Mick could contain himself no longer. 'Now tell me this and tell me no more. How the hell do I know *you're* not in on this thing yourself, now that you seem to know so much about it?'

For a moment, he thought the little man was either going to hit him or get up and leave. After about a minute during which the tension became almost tangible, Abe began to laugh. At first softly, then louder and louder until it became a series of bellowing guffaws, so much so that the others in the hospitality suite were starting to look their way. A barman hovered anxiously nearby in case he might have the beginnings of a problem on his hands. At last Abe found the power of speech though his eyes were still streaming from the laughter.

'Naw Mick, I'm not in on it. Believe it or not, ole Abe is now strictly legit. I'm fronting for an outfit called AEF – the Alternative Energy Foundation. Set up by this African guy with more dough than he knows what to do with. He's Paramount Chief of Marabar with this crazy son . . .'

11

'YOU MUST BE out of your mind!'
    A blistering heat enveloped the dusty streets of Charles-
ville. It was just after midday, a time when even the dogs scurried
for shelter from the scorching sun. In the air-conditioned cool of
the Royal Palace, Freddie Okansu wished that he too could find
somewhere to hide. Not from the sun, however, but from the
searing blast of his father's temper.

The Paramount Chief was a small wizened man in his late sixties
without an ounce of spare flesh on his small frame. In sharp
contrast, Freddie had just reached thirty-five and had a comfortable layer of fat all over his body though it was most noticeable on
his face. This was usually creased in a smile but not on this
occasion.

The Paramount Chief was reading aloud a letter from the
management of Caesar's Palace in Las Vegas which requested
immediate settlement of a bill for Freddie's birthday party.
Attached to the document was an itemised account to the sum of
twenty-six thousand, four hundred and three dollars.

'How could anyone in his right senses spend that amount in one
evening?'

The Paramount Chief punctuated each syllable with a flick of
the ornate fly whisk that had become his seal of office. It was an
affectation that he had picked up from the late Jomo Kenyatta. It
had since become so closely associated with the ruler of Marabar
that it was incorporated into the national flag and appeared on
several denominations of postage stamps. On this occasion it was
waving at Freddie in such an intimidating manner that he decided
not to tell his father that spending that sort of money in any Las
Vegas hotel was very easy indeed. Especially when one bought
champagne for everyone at the blackjack table and invited most of

the hostesses back to the best suite in the house when the excitement of gambling began to flag. Nor did he think it timely to mention that it was a figure which paled into insignificance when compared with his gambling losses over the previous month. A new system for beating the blackjack dealer had unaccountably failed to work, leaving him owing various casinos a sum not far short of one million dollars.

In the ordinary way, this would have been a manageable amount. He would just have called Abe Linovitz and explained his problem. Then Abe would have used the vast resources of the Alternative Energy Foundation to settle the outstanding amounts with no one – least of all the Paramount Chief – being any the wiser. Now some idiot at the front desk of Caesar's Palace had sent the bill to his father. Whether this was a genuine mistake or a plot to embarrass him did not really matter at this stage in the proceedings. Abe's avenue to the Paramount Chief was through Freddie. Therefore, it was in his own interest to keep relations between father and son as cordial as possible. However, at this very moment the Paramount Chief was trembling with rage as he screamed at his son, Freddie.

'Just suppose, just suppose any of those cursed camel-dealers got their hands on this . . .'

He waved the letter with his free hand while continuing to flail the thin air with the fly whisk.

'. . . The bazaars would speak of little else for weeks to come. As for our neighbours, they would clap their hands in glee at our misfortune. The Number One Son of the Ruler of Marabar cavorting with floozies in Las Vegas, while his father's enemies are planning every hour that Allah sends to strip him of his lawful throne. They are telling the people lies enough to turn them against us without idiots like you playing into their hands.'

Freddie did not attempt a reply. Indeed, much of what his father said was true. There was mounting unrest and it was coming from outside their borders.

Before the Casino and the mud, things had been different. In those days Marabar was a sleepy place, no threat to its oil-rich neighbours. Its sole asset was an almost-unbroken stretch of beach along its coastline. Some of the wealthy families who had stayed on after Independence ran hotels in a desultory fashion. It was not until Abe Linovitz appeared with his plans for a resort complex that things really began to happen. In a surprisingly short time, the huge Town Hall of Charlesville, the capital, had been transformed into a luxury Casino where high rollers from all over came to play. Not Freddie, however. As a Director he was forbidden to play by the rules of the offshore company that controlled the Casino. A luxury hotel had sprung up across the square and all this was funded by Abe who described himself as an investment consultant.

Before the Paramount Chief approved Abe's plans, he had asked where the money was coming from. Abe explained that he had many backers who trusted his judgement in the matter of good resort locations. Generously rewarded at every stage of the construction, Freddie and his father were given a share in the profits in return for ensuring that everything within Marabar worked smoothly. Much of this money was transferred into the Alternative Energy Foundation, again set up by Abe, for the furtherance of research into fuels other than oil or coal. This was because their neighbours were rich in oil while Marabar had nothing to show for a succession of dry wells except a lot of strange-coloured mud.

Again it was Abe who came to the rescue. He took a sample of the mud to someone in Texas who declared it to be the finest drilling mud available. It was ideal for lubricating expensive bits and fetched a premium price from the exploration companies. Thus, the Paramount Chief and his Number One Son found themselves an asset more valuable than the oil for which they had been praying. Soon the coffers of the AEF were full to overflowing. This gave rise to something they had not had to contend with before – envy. The West African Republic of Marabar had become immensely wealthy overnight, at the expense of international oil companies. It was this envy, and the unease on both sides of the border that it created, that the Paramount Chief referred to as he continued his tirade. Freddie hung his head, as if in shame. He was waiting for the storm to pass. Then he would contact Abe. He would know how best to sort out what was, after all, a relatively minor problem – only a question of a mere million dollars or so.

Mick Flannery was stuck. Push as he might, the door of the toilet just would not open. From inside, the sound of the giant Rolls Royce engines suspended beneath the wings of the Irish Airlines Jumbo, was just a muffled roar. Fighting hard against the sudden panic welling up inside him, he sat down on the only seat available and buried his head in his hands. The cubicle seemed to have shrunk to the size of a matchbox as his temples pounded with the onset of claustrophobia. To calm himself, he ran the events of the past twenty-four hours past his mind's eye like a grainy, black and white newsreel.

Abe's voice was like a soothing balm: 'Look, Mick, it's gonna be easy enough to check out and I owe you one for keeping me outa jail that time back in Brulagh. I guess it's payback time right now so this is what I think we both should do . . .'

Back in Louisville for the second time in twenty-four hours, he had left Abe waiting in the cab as he ran up the steps of the Mineralco building. Inside, the same old janitor was perched behind his desk in the centre of the lobby, chewing gum and gazing intently at a tiny portable TV. Not the faintest flicker of recognition crossed his wrinkled face as Mick approached and asked to see Hartmann and Janecski. The old guy just rubbed his grizzled chin and eyed Mick suspiciously. When he did speak, he was courteous but firm.

'Ah'm afraid yuh need an appointment to see Mistuh Hartmann or Mistuh Janecski. They don't see no one without an appointment. Why don't Ah just take yoh name?'

'Flannery, Michael J. Flannery. You tell them it's urgent. I'm a Member of the European Parliament and I want to talk to them this minute!'

The old guy looked unimpressed. 'Okay, mistuh, I'll call Mistuh Hartmann's secretary.'

He dialled a number and a female voice squawked back at him testily. 'Yeah, what is it?'

'Gennelman heah wants to talk with yoh boss.'

'Does he have an appointment?'

'Nope!'

'Then tell him to make one. Mr Hartmann doesn't take callers in off the street. Tell him that.'

'Don't have to. He can hear every word yuh say.'

'Good!' The loud click signalled that she had slammed the phone down.

The janitor grinned at Mick and explained, 'They're all sick as dawgs this mornin'. Founder's Day picnic yesterday. Every year it's the same. Company hires a paddle-steamer and buys all the Moosehead they can drink. They bin comin' in here pale as ghosts and holdin' on to their heads like they was goin' to fall off on the ground.'

That solved the mystery of why there was no one around yesterday, but it still didn't get Mick up to the fourteenth floor. He leaned across the desk and spoke low and slow to the janitor.

'I can do one of two things. If you don't let me up to see Hartmann, I'm going to write a long letter to him on the official notepaper of the European Parliament, explaining how you were part of that circus yesterday. Hartmann and the other guy may not believe me, but then again maybe they will. In any case I'll tell them how this building was wide open on a day when it was supposed to be closed and how you welcomed two conmen and their mark like they were soul brothers and gave them free run of the place. On the other hand, I could walk over to that elevator and press the fourteenth-floor button. If I get to see my man, I'll just ask a few questions and leave you out of it. Now I've a cab waiting outside so make up your mind one way or the other!'

The janitor looked him squarely in the eye, thought about it for a second or two and then jerked his head in the direction of the bank of elevators.

The rest was easy. Flannery walked straight past a startled secretary and opened the heavy mahogany door that led into Max Hartmann's Presidential Suite. A silver-haired man in his seventies rose from behind the familiar desk and raised his eyebrows as he inquired sternly: 'I don't believe we've met. Do you have an appointment?'

Mick pulled his eyes away from the huge frame that held the portrait of the man now halfway out of his chair. The picture, as Abe predicted, had been changed since yesterday.

Mick spoke in a quiet, assured voice. 'Mr Hartmann, this'll take about two minutes of your time. While you were celebrating Founder's Day, I was sitting in this very office. Two men, one pretending to be you and another your partner Mr Janecski, almost conned me out of one million dollars.'

After that it was plain sailing. The two minutes of Max

Hartmann's time became a half-hour. At the end of their conversation, addresses had been exchanged, a letter typed up, signed by Hartmann and tucked into Mick's inside pocket and they parted with expressions of mutual esteem. It also appeared that the barges Mick had seen went *up* the Ohio River. Mineralco had yet to ship coal in barges across the Atlantic, and very much doubted if it could be done.

Back in the toilet serving the First-Class section of Flight EI 104, the newsreel was flickering again. The stocky figure of Abe crowded everything else off the screen of Mick's memory. He was taking leave of Abe at the airport when the last piece of the jigsaw fell into place.

'What about the Mineralco plane, Abe?' he had asked.

'What about it? Gulfstream have their headquarters just down the road from here in Savannah. Those guys not only sell planes, they lease and rent 'em as well. I'll lay you six to one there was no company logo on it.'

He was right – just *Gulfstream IV* painted on the door. Abe was again in full spate. He continued to shake with silent laughter as if the incident were the funniest thing he had heard of in ages.

'But don't worry. I know those guys from way back. They're genuine con-artists, not like the shysters you meet on every goddam street corner nowadays. Sammy and Max don't do drugs or blackmail. Setting up this scam has set them back mebbe ten grand at most. They're not going to come back at you for a small hit like that.'

There was another long silence before Abe unburdened himself of one final comment on the whole, sorry affair. 'I guess you're going to have to find something else to swing the election now . . .'

From outside, a loud knocking on the toilet door disturbed his reverie. The voice of a flight attendant called anxiously, 'You okay in there?'

When Mick explained his predicament, the answer was preceded by an audible sigh like a mother explaining something elementary to her slowest child. It was a *sliding* door. Furthermore, a notice to that effect was affixed to the top of the offending portal. Avoiding the stares of his fellow passengers who must have heard the commotion, Mick shuffled back to his seat and pretended to read the menu.

Despite whatever gloss Charley Halpin could manage to put on it, the plain truth was that Mick was coming back empty-handed. Doubtless the Farmers' Friend, Noel McBride, would be the first to point out that this was nothing new. Whatever way he looked at it, the coal fiasco was a serious setback. Fortunately, Charley Halpin hadn't mentioned the word 'coal' in print, preferring to focus on Mick's triumphal progress through New York. Nevertheless, too many had heard him voice his hopes of turning Brulagh into the coal capital of the south for the Farmers' Friend not to get wind of it sooner or later.

As Mick pondered on how to spike the little runt's guns, he read again the letter he had brought back with him from the real Max Hartmann – a Southern gentleman, if ever there was one, with a mop of silver hair and a drawl one could cut with a knife. Typed on Mineralco notepaper, the letter stated that nothing would please President Hartmann more than to supply all the coal in Kentucky to a fine man like Michael J. Flannery. However, after examining the project from every possible angle, both parties agreed that the complex infrastructure of roads and storage bunkers necessary to service a new loading jetty would impact too heavily on the environment of a small, tightly-knit community such as Brulagh.

The letter, at Mick's request, did not mention that the technology required to ship coal across the Atlantic by barge had yet to be developed. Max signed off by saying what an honour it was both for Mineralco and the city of Louisville to be graced by the presence of such an eminent European Parliamentarian as Michael J. Flannery, and expressing the hope that this would be the seed from which would spring a long and fruitful association between the citizens of Louisville and Brulagh.

It was much more than Mick had imagined could be salvaged from the wreck, but hardly enough with which to launch a campaign. Of course he would use the letter to prove that it was he who had aborted what could have been a profitable venture for Brulagh because of its impact on the environment. At least this should keep the bloody 'greens' off his back and allow him to emerge with his political skin intact, but it was not going to *win* him any extra votes.

Of course, there would be always be the Old Guard to rely on –

the hard core who would emerge from the mountains and remote farmsteads. Dressed in their best suits and Sunday caps, they would arrive at the polling stations, blinking and looking round them in amazement like insects that had crawled out into the sunlight from beneath a shady rock. Dutifully they would put a Number One opposite Flannery, Michael J., and then disappear from public view until the next election. Faithful followers like these would support him until the grave closed in over their heads. Sadly, that is precisely what had happened to many of them. As for the young, it would be foolish to expect them to share their parents' reverence for a sporting legend who last took the field almost forty years ago. To make matters even worse, the constituency for the European Parliament was much larger than his Dail one and extended far beyond Mick's sphere of influence.

In the four glorious years since he had filled the seat left vacant by the late James O'Rourke, he had acquired a taste for good food, expensive wines and first-class travel. Now all these might vanish in the twinkling of an eye unless he could conjure a new rabbit out of the hat. Furthermore, the voters would expect more from him than the usual pre-election castles in the air. As Charley Halpin had said, mixing his metaphors so effectively, this time Mick really would have to come up with the goods to bring home the bacon.

Already the Farmers' Friend was asking aloud what Mick had ever done for his fellow sons of the soil during his time in Europe – or during his three decades in the Dail, for that matter. Despite Mick's near-disastrous adventures in America, Charley had come up trumps yet again. If one were to believe the front pages of the *Clarion*, Mick had left behind him a great nation paralysed with grief at his departure. In particular the citizens of New York were portrayed as sobbing uncontrollably if not actually beating their breasts as Mick took wing.

Despite all the ballyhoo, even a seasoned campaigner like Charley would not be able to conceal his dismay were Mick blithely to announce that he was returning bereft of goodies. There was no need for the tubby reporter to remind Mick that being honoured by every Irish Association from Alaska to Acapulco wasn't worth a tinker's curse if he didn't have, at the very least, the *promise* of jobs. While jam today was preferable to jam tomorrow, anything was better than no jam at all. As for the coal depot, while it might have enraged the environmentalists, it *did* promise jobs – the precious motherlode of every hack seeing re-election since Adam was a boy.

As he speared the last of the French *haricots provençales* and poured another glass of champagne, Mick learned from the label that Champagne de Castellagne was made from grapes which come from the best vineyards in the Montagne de Reims, the Marne Valley and the Côte des Blancs. '*The cuvée is made in spring and the blending is the climax of the art of making champagne,*' it warbled. To take his mind off his plight, he tried rewriting this as a label for Johnny's poteen. When he could get no further than: '*A lethal blend of low-grade spuds and blackstrap molasses gives the apéritif its distinctive taste of a particularly delicate sulphuric acid*' he abandoned the exercise. Johnny Slattery's people, he reflected, had been in business every bit as long as the purveyors of the fizzy stuff. By the time old Dom Pérignon thought of tying down his corks with string and using stronger bottles at the end of the seventeenth century, the Slatterys and their colleagues in trade had been selling poteen for over one hundred years. Legally, too. It was not until later that Excise Taxes and the red-coated Revenue men had driven the moonshiners underground.

Swallowing the last of the champagne, he stretched back in the comfortable seat of the Boeing 747 and closed his eyes. Memories of Reims and Marne floated by, a grim reminder that unless he could conjure up something – and fast – the nearest he would get to such places in the future would be the travel agent's window.

Something Charley had said over a crackling telephone line to his hotel room in New York suddenly set Mick's mind racing again, even though his body craved sleep. A friend of the Colonel's called Derek Evans was conducting a survey of some sort or another on Brulagh Bog. When Mick asked what the hell anyone could want with a worked-out swamp like that for, he was told that it had to do with pelletised peat production. *Fireballs*, as Charley sneeringly referred to them before he dismissed the whole thing as the pipedream of some mad Welshman with a bee in his bonnet. Remembering what Abe had said about the Alternative Energy Foundation, suddenly Mick was not so sure.

12

THE BLACK MERCEDES slowed to a halt at the entrance to the American Embassy in Dublin, where a red-and-white-striped security barrier was manned by a pair of grim-faced Marines. One peered in the driver's window while the other scrutinised the two passengers in the back. The Private Secretary, a slim briefcase cradled in his lap, pressed the button that lowered the rear window and spoke curtly.

'Department of Foreign Affairs. We have an appointment.'

One of the Marines checked the floorpan of the car with a long-handled mirror while his colleague consulted a clipboard. Satisfied that everything was in order, he stepped back, saluted smartly and raised the red-and-white steel barrier. A steep ramp led down into the bowels of the circular fortress that was the American Embassy. Sinking back in the comfortable upholstery as the driver inched his way over the speed ramps, Kevin Mahony, the Minister for Foreign Affairs, grinned to himself as he contrasted this tight security with that of his own Ministry. His Department was located in an area woefully short of public toilets. It was not unusual for short-taken shoppers to persuade the security guard at the front door to let them use the toilets in an emergency. While this improved relations with the public, it did little for security.

Watching a crewcut hulk in a sharp suit that clearly profiled his shoulder holster, Mahony wondered idly if his own personal security should be tightened. The suggestion that the Department of Foreign Affairs was moonlighting as a public convenience would have thrown the inmates of this stockade into a state of deep shock. So what the hell? If the Yanks wanted to create a Fortress America in this quiet Dublin suburb, that was their business. Personally, Mahony believed that if someone was out to get you, they would succeed no matter what precautions were taken. Making an old building such as the DFA secure would be next to impossible so it might as well maintain its open-door policy.

Another crewcut, this one chewing the antenna of a walkie-talkie, waved them to an empty space in the basement car-park. As they got out he motioned for them to follow him across the tarmac towards the open door of an elevator. Leaving the driver in the car, they followed at a distance behind the crewcut. The Private Secretary could contain himself no longer.

'Do they think they're in bloody Beirut or what?'

The Minister just shrugged wordlessly. The only demonstration at the Embassy in recent times had been a good-natured affair. The crowd, mostly students, were protesting at the delay in processing their visas. That in itself was an indication of the state Pat Mullarkey had got the economy into, despite his public assurances that 'the fundamentals are sound'. True, inflation was pegged at two per cent and growth hovered around the same figure. Sadly there was another vital statistic that Mullarkey and his redneck supporters in the Country and Western wing of the party preferred to ignore. Unemployment was twenty per cent and rising. Hence the fuss about the delay in issuing American visas. It also explained Mullarkey's sudden drop in popularity – a point not lost on those who would be happier with a different leader.

In the bar of the Dail where the Government sat, the whisper was that Mahony at Foreign Affairs was the right man for the job. Mullarkey's power base had always been the rural vote, but now a new Messiah had appeared in his home constituency. The Farmers' Friend looked an odds-on favourite to beat Mick Flannery, the party candidate, for the last of three seats in the forthcoming European Elections. Should this come to pass, it could herald the beginning of the end for Mullarkey and his rednecks.

The crewcut inserted a card, waited for an answering bleep and then keyed in something on a numeric pad by the door. Inside the elevator they were alone. 'Wonder what the old fart wants? Did he give any indication at all?'

Kevin Mahony shook his head and wished that his Private Secretary would exercise a bit more discretion. It was quite on the cards that the paranoia of His Excellency, the Ambassador

Extraordinary and Plenipotentiary, extended to wiring the elevators for sound. At the best of times it was difficult to discover what was on the mind of the geriatric whose services to the American fast food industry and the Grand Old Party had been rewarded with an Ambassadorship. At a guess, it would be the extradition business, that threatened to develop into a major diplomatic row at any moment. Perhaps, the Minister thought, they're going to hand over the wanted man to us after all. Unlikely as this might be, experience had taught him never to be surprised at the u-turns and sudden policy switches of diplomacy.

The Ambassador was a grizzled hulk of a man with short grey hair and drooping jowls like an elderly bloodhound. His office was immense. A curved window of bullet-proof glass formed the outer wall. The vast expanse of polished maple floor was bare save for the skins of dead animals scattered at random. Two large Norman Rockwell originals gave a clue to the Ambassador's artistic preferences, confirming that he had once been a baker from Milwaukee. Next to them hung the Stars and Stripes and an enormous reproduction of the Great Seal of the President of the United States. From behind a battery of telephones and two computer screens the Ambassador struggled out of his deep leather chair to greet them.

'Good of you to come at such short notice.' The Ambassador tried to hide his pleasure at not having to deal with the Taoiseach. Mullarkey had been nothing but trouble since he burst on the political scene a few years ago. A backwoods man if ever there was one, the guy simply did not have the same respect for the United States or its Ambassador as his predecessor. His most recent demand – not a request but a goddam *demand* – was that some goon serving a sentence in Boston should be sent back to Ireland immediately. It had taken all the self-control the Ambassador could muster not to tell Mullarkey to find a lake and go jump in it. Thankfully, that nonsense appeared to have been shelved for the time being and today's problem was a far more cut-and-dried affair. The Ambassador cleared his throat noisily before continuing.

'I have a complaint here from the owners of the Gaelic Palace in New York. Seems they rent it out to various Irish organisations from time to time. Anyway, last St Patrick's Day, they decided to honour Mick Flannery by electing him to their Hall of Fame. In the course of his acceptance speech, he insulted his audience so much that they tried to break the place up. The owners now want an assurance from your Government that it will pick up the tab for the repairs.'

Mahony steepled his fingers. This was totally unexpected. Of course everyone in the Cabinet had heard rumours of Flannery's carry-on in New York. Only the Minister for Foreign Affairs, however, had the actual transcript of that disastrous radio interview in which Flannery had invited the British to leave Northern Ireland forthwith. In a clumsy effort to set the record straight, he had provoked the Hostile Sons of St Finian – or whatever they called themselves – to lay waste to the Gaelic Palace. What had been said on that occasion mirrored the official view of his Department, and if the lunatics in the Gaelic Palace didn't like it, too bad. What's more, those who caused the damage were American citizens and liable to due process in that country. He conveyed these views to the Ambassador.

'Of course Your Excellency will understand that while the Irish Government can in no way be held liable for the damage,' he concluded, 'it does very much regret that the remarks of one of its European Representatives could have been misrepresented. It is the view of the Irish Government that the question of withdrawal by the British from Northern Ireland is not a fit topic for debate in a public forum such as the Gaelic Palace. This is especially so when I believe that some of the audience represented organisations which have been sending funds, unwittingly or otherwise, to subversives in this country. I would urge Your Excellency to spare no effort in seeing that this unhappy situation is resolved as soon as possible. I would further suggest that a valuable first step in this process would be to return the man whose extradition we have already formally requested. This would clearly demonstrate that the United States of America does not offer sanctuary to those plotting the overthrow of the lawfully-constituted Government of this country . . .'

The Ambassador reached out of his chair to thump the desk. He had been struggling to find words with which to interrupt the flow but apoplexy got the better of him. With his free hand he pointed a stubby finger at them as though it were a loaded pistol. Suddenly realising that the cigar was still jammed in his mouth, he had to stop pounding the table to remove it so that he could splutter: 'Are you trying to tell me, Mahony, that your Government intends doing sweet damn-all about this . . . this . . .' again words failed him before he settled reluctantly on

'. . . goddam *riot*? It was started by this idiot Flannery using what was a perfectly ordinary social occasion to make an inflammatory speech—'

Now it was Mahony's turn to break in. 'Sorry, Your Excellency, but I have seen the transcript of Mr Flannery's speech, and what he said reflected my Government's views. While he was acting in an unofficial capacity, his words could in no way be construed as inflammatory – except of course by those hellbent on throwing democracy out of the window.'

The Ambassador had solved the problem of the cigar by smashing it out in the large ashtray with such violence that it set the telephones rocking in their cradles. His face was a dangerous shade of scarlet.

'Goddammit Mahony,' he expostulated, 'I've heard enough of this claptrap for one day. You have the almighty gall to sit there and tell me that you refuse to accept responsibility for the actions of a clown like Flannery who treats New York as one long bar counter. On the one hand you say that he was acting unofficially, while on the other you claim that what he said to spark off a goddam riot is official Government policy. Hell's teeth, you can't have it both ways!'

This time the Private Secretary went in to face the bowling. 'We take your point, Your Excellency . . .'

His voice was calm and oozing sweet reasonableness. He had heard rumours before now but this was the first time he had seen the Ambassador throw a temper tantrum. He feared that the message he had to impart would be no more welcome than his master's.

'It does, however, raise certain difficulties as the Foreign Minister has pointed out. One possible solution would be for you to take up such a delicate matter with Mr Flannery yourself.'

His minister nodded approvingly. He had been torturing his brain for some way of avoiding liability for the mayhem while, at the same time, availing himself of the welcome opportunity to lay the blame squarely at the feet of the Country and Western brigade of whom Flannery was a prominent member. The prospect of an official rebuke to Flannery from the American Embassy, preferably accompanied by a gigantic repair bill for the Gaelic Palace, was one to be relished. Of late, Mullarkey had seemed to be linking his fate with that of Mick Flannery for some reason. Now here was a perfect opportunity to sink Flannery, and with him Mullarkey, by holing him below the waterline. It would be easier, he mused, to launch a 'heave' against a sinking Taoiseach than one that was riding the crest of a wave. For that reason he would do everything possible to encourage His Excellency in his relentless pursuit of Mick Flannery. Sadly, the old buffoon was having none of it.

'How in tarnation can the pair of you have the goddam nerve to sit there and tell me you can do sweet damn-all about this guy Flannery? What do you want *me* to do? Get in my goddam car and drive down to wherever he lives with a goddam repair bill like some hick brush salesman with an overdue account?'

A silence descended like a black cloud as each of them examined his options. With rheumy eyes staring out into the middle distance, the Ambassador was in the throes of a massive sulk. Obviously Mahony's outright rejection of responsibility for the damage was something of a setback. Nonetheless it could be a useful bargaining counter when real pressure was exerted over this extradition business. The creep in a Boston jail had been caught trying to break into a military base. He had drawn five years but would probably get out in two if he behaved himself. However, he was on a murder rap in Ireland with further charges of being a member of an illegal organisation also pending against him. The Ambassador's instructions from the State Department on this issue were to stall for as long as possible. The last thing anyone wanted was for the affair to become a major issue in an election year. On the other hand, the suggestion that the Ambassador of the greatest power on earth should become a bill collector was more than flesh and blood could stand. As if he would stoop so low as to write personally to some pork-barrel politician asking him to pay up. It was a Mexican stand-off.

Summoning what dignity he had left, the American announced, 'Okay, boys, if that's the way you want to play it. But I gotta warn you that Uncle Sam can play hardball too!' With that the meeting was over.

The car glided past the security barrier and turned right into the heavy traffic. The Embassy of the United Kingdom and Northern Ireland was but a short distance away. Apart from the security barrier, the contrast between the two buildings could hardly have been greater. The British Embassy was a large house rather than a round fortress bristling with satellite dishes and antennae. If it felt itself to be a beleagured outpost, it concealed the fact remarkably well.

Once inside, over a dry sherry the Counsellor and Head of Chancery apologised for the absence of his Ambassador and explained politely what it was he wished to find out.

'A Mr Michael Flannery suggested on Station. . .' He paused here to sip his sherry and leaf through his notes until he found what he was looking for '. . . WBZC – FM/NYC of New York that the interests of both our nations would be best served by an early withdrawal of troops from Northern Ireland. What we at the Embassy wish to know, Minister, is whether these views reflect those of your Department?'

The question, though pointed, was put in such a polite fashion that even the most sensitive would have been hard put to take offence. Mahony wasted no time in setting the record straight.

'I am delighted to have the opportunity of explaining this unfortunate incident. The radio station in question is so small that we debated long and hard whether to formally apologise on behalf of Flannery to Her Majesty's Government, or just to let it pass in the hope that no one of any importance was listening at the time. The station describes itself as a subsidiary of the international Goodwill Broadcasting Corporation. Our investigations tell us that it is an umbrella group for mainly leftist organisations, and how Flannery ever came to be there is one of the great mysteries of all time. He was on a private visit to New York and was representing no one but himself. It is hardly necessary to assure Her Majesty's Ambassador that such views in no way represent those of the Government to which I belong . . .'

At this point Mahony shot a quick glance at the Counsellor. His eyes were half-closed but the gentle nodding of the head indicated that Mahony should continue.

'In fact, it may have escaped your notice but at a function some time later, Flannery went to considerable pains to redeem himself. So much so, in fact, that the affair broke up in disorder. As for the radio interview, I have a transcript of it back in the Ministry. You are welcome to a copy of it if you wish.'

He was cut short by the languid drawl of the Counsellor. 'That won't be necessary, as I have one here. To be quite fair to your Mr Flannery, it would appear that he had already evaded several loaded questions from a Miss Marquesa and indeed had tried, albeit unsuccessfully, to set her right on the Northern Situation. It was only at the very end of the programme that she sprang the question on him . . .' Again he paused to find the relevant sheet of the transcript before adding '. . . "*How soon should the Brits get out of Ireland?*" to which your Mr Flannery replied – unwisely, I think we all agree – "*Yerrah the sooner the better, I suppose!*" The programme ended on that rather unsatisfactory note.'

They finished the sherry in silence. The Counsellor then summed up. 'We at the Embassy were anxious to be reassured that your Mr Flannery was speaking for himself and not for the party to which he belongs. We are perfectly happy to accept your assurances on that score and I would thank you for taking the trouble to brief us. Thank you, gentlemen.'

On the drive back to the Department of Foreign Affairs, the Minister regaled his Private Secretary with the various tortures he would happily inflict on the corpulent person of Michael J. Flannery. On a more private level he was composing a memo regretting the damage caused by untutored country bumpkins to the reputation of his country abroad. This would accidentally fall into the hands of a favoured political correspondent and provide the basis for a series of articles savaging Mullarkey and his rural rednecks. It would be the first small nudge in what Mahony confidently expected to result in a major 'heave'.

The man in the eye of the storm was also indulging in a spot of fence-mending. Since he got back, Mick's telephone had scarcely stopped ringing. The organisers of the Hall of Fame Award had a repair bill for the Gaelic Palace running well into five figures, and were wondering aloud as to who was going to pick up the tab. Having shredded several drafts of what he considered to be an appropriate retort, he eventually handed the missive to Patsy, his secretary. She embarked on a holding operation. Her reply, on behalf of Mick, managed to disclaim all responsibility for the incident and the subsequent damage to fixtures and fittings while thanking the organisers profusely for the signal honour that they had bestowed on him, along with the large glass bowl, and wishing them well for the future.

Opening a second front, Mick scribbled a hurried note to Dave Foley of the Four-Leafed Shamrock Bar, confirming that a Brulagh All-Stars team would be delighted to take the field against a New York Selection in the Flannery Stadium. Originally the proceeds had been earmarked for the local St Fintan's GAA Club. However, in view of the difficult attitude being adopted by the owners of the Gaelic Palace, Mick wondered if part of the gate receipts could not be set off against the repair bill. He ended with more confidence than he felt by saying that he had no doubt that Foley would sort the whole thing out.

This was a mere pinprick compared to the other slings and arrows that rained down on him. Job, he reflected darkly, had had it easy compared to him. The bearded one from the Embassy had sent back a full report of his activities. There ensued angry if one-sided telephone conversations with Taoiseach Mullarkey, in which it was pointed out that Mick had done the two things he had been specifically warned against. In case they had been forgotten, Mullarkey repeated that these were to 'Turn up sober and don't mention The North.'

In words that brooked no argument, Mick was told that far from projecting the image of a Statesman with a safe pair of hands, he was nothing but a loose cannon on the Ship of State. From now on he would have to sink or swim without the backing, financial or otherwise, of the ruling party. As a parting shot, Mullarkey told him that the Department of the Environment would not contemplate the transforming of Brulagh Harbour into a dump for Kentucky Coal Barons. Having plunged this last spear into the still-twitching corpse, Mullarkey hung up. Mick did not bother to tell him that the coal thing had already fallen through anyway, lest Mullarkey should seek a new stick with which to beat him. Far better to let the miserable little bastard believe he had delivered the *coup de grâce* to Mick's electoral prospects.

Even without Mullarkey's intervention, these were far from rosy. Over the phone, Charley Halpin had reported glumly that the Farmers' Friend had got hold of the transcript of the radio interview in which Mick invited the forces of The Crown to quit the North. He was now quoting this at every Church Gate meeting the length and breadth of the constituency. Charley had done his best to counter it by printing the relevant bits of the Gaelic Palace speech in which Mick castigated those 'well-intentioned but misguided Irish-Americans sending money home to subversive organisations'. The effectiveness of this had yet to be measured, but at least it got the attention of the media. Unfortunately, so did the shenanigans in the Gaelic Palace. The New York tabloids had a field day, the *Daily News* describing it as a 'Paddy's Day Donnybrook'. Nearer home, the *Irish Times* was less amused. In an editorial penned more in sorrow than in anger it moaned, 'We have disgraced ourselves again!'

Sitting in the snug of the Brulagh Inn, Mick was struggling with the problem of how to break the news to Charley that the coal thing had fallen through. Reluctant to admit that he had been conned in Louisville, he was racked by indecision. In the meantime Charley had been filling him in on developments of a more local nature.

'The new Sergeant has Johnny Slattery's heart broke from patrolling the mountain. Johnny can't make up his mind whether it's the widow or his *poitín*-still the hoor is more interested in, but it's causing a hell of a shortage, I can promise you. Oh yes, and Tom Donnelly's back on his feet again . . .'

'Out of dry dock, you mean,' Mick growled as Charley pressed on with the local news round-up.

'Did Maggie get on to you about the rock concert?'

'Yeah, we had a stand-up row about it. Now we're not talking because of it!'

Charley was unmoved by this news item, though it did prompt him to add: 'Herself and Julia May are supposed to be organising protests against it, if you don't mind!'

Mick would have expected no less from either his wife or the priest's housekeeper. Both of them were religious maniacs as far as he was concerned, and could be relied on to oppose anything that remotely smacked of enjoyment. Their idea of a night's fun was five laps of the rosary beads while dressed up in the blue and white regalia of the Legion of Mary. Still, they could make things awkward if they had a mind to.

'What kind of protests?' he asked wearily.

'Yerrah who knows?' Placards and that sort of thing, I suppose. I hear they mean to take it farther if they don't get their way.'

Mick was perplexed. 'Farther? How do you mean, *farther*?'

'Oh, the Bishop, no less. If you'd only bothered to listen to his Pastoral Letter you'd know he's dead set against things like rock concerts.'

Mick shrugged helplessly. For the concert *and* the coal-jetty to disappear down the tubes at the same time was just unthinkable. Then he remembered what it was he wanted to ask the tubby little reporter.

'What were you saying over the phone about this friend of the Colonel's? The Fireballs thing?'

Charley drained the last of his pint and wiped the froth from his lips before explaining. 'Oh, the Welshman's called Derek something or other? He's some relation of the Colonel's. The Editor sent me to interview him but his idea was so crazy we never got around to publishing it.'

This did not put Mick off the scent. Ordering two more pints, he got Charley to tell him everything he knew about Derek and his Fireballs plan. Long after the little man had left, Mick stared thoughtfully out to space. Then his face split into a wide grin. He went through the bar, into the kitchen of Sean's home and picked up the phone, then dialled a number from a rather crumpled business card Abe Linovitz had given him before they parted.

After much difficulty, Abe was located in the West African Republic of Marabar, where he was closeted with the Paramount Chief and his son, Freddie Okansu. Both of them were listening intently to the stocky American and with good reason. Was it not Abraham Linovitz who had turned the golden beaches of Marabar into a playground for the rich, and an oddly-coloured mud into something far more valuable than the oil-wells it helped to drill? Now that money was drying up and the natives were becoming restless, who else would the pair turn to but Abe, whose financial wizardry had served them so well in the past?

When Mick's call came through, Freddie Okansu was trying to explain away an unfortunate quote he had recently given to a British Sunday newspaper. 'Dammit, even old Jean-Jacques Rousseau confessed that democracy was fit more for angels than for men! And let me tell you, our people are no angels. It's not so long since we ate missionaries for breakfast!'

This unfortunate remark was widely reported and came back to haunt him time and time again. Indeed, one of the reasons for the crisis meeting with Abe was to devise some way of spiriting out even more funds from Marabar in case the balloon should go up unexpectedly. It was, therefore, not the best time to interrupt Abe with a phone call.

'Whaddya want, Mick? This'd better be good. You're interrupting an important meeting!'

Abe listened as the outlines of the peat project, code-named 'Fireballs', were explained to him. He, too, was underwhelmed. It was all too vague at this stage. Nevertheless he asked Mick to put a presentation together and fax the details to his New York office. Then he hung up without even saying goodbye.

Not the most encouraging start, Mick reflected, yet a drowning man had to cling to whatever flotsam drifted within his reach. He would have to arrange a meeting with this Derek person to discover the precise details of what he had in mind for the Brulagh Bog. Mick prayed silently that, whatever it might be, it would meet with the aims of the AEF, in which case all might not yet be lost . . .

13

'WHAT WE HAVE here, Mr Flannery, is a giant compost heap . . .'

Derek had not yet become accustomed to addressing Mick by his first name, despite frequent requests to do so. The two men were standing close to the outflow from the Colonel's lake. From this vantage point, the vast palette of muddy browns and moss-greens were spread below them like a giant, rumpled blanket, the stagnant pools and bulging peat outcrops gashed here and there by eruptions of piercing yellow gorse. The whitewashed walls of a lone cottage, crowned by its roof of golden thatch, was the only trace of human habitation. It was the home of Johnny's uncle, the fiddle-player and the last man in Brulagh still cutting turf from the bog. This was confirmed by small black mounds drying in the watery sun well to the west of the tiny cottage.

'Not a very efficient one, mind you,' Derek continued, 'because of all the water flooding down into it from the Colonel's lake just above us. Luckily, the danger zones are far away from where we will be milling the turf.'

He waved a hand towards the far side of the bog. 'I would build the processing plant over there and tuck it in behind that stand of trees for appearances' sake. Not that it's going to be especially big or ugly – quite small, as a matter of fact. The drying plant is fuelled by the peat pellets so the thing literally feeds off itself. Electricity consumption is low so we won't need bloody great power pylons buggering up the landscape either. As for the road, if we widen it a bit and slap on some more tarmac, that should do the trick. The only heavy traffic will be during the actual construction. After that, just the workers' cars mostly.'

Mick looked at him sceptically before demanding: 'How the hell do you get the end product out of here so, if not by road?'

'Pipelines,' came the tranquil reply. 'The pellets will be pumped by compressed air along the same sort of pipelines used for gas or oil. That goes for the waste product, too – a brown liquid which happens to be a superb fertiliser. We can either dry it on site and package it, or pump it along another pipeline . . .'

'To where?' Mick interrupted.

'Well, I was just coming to that.' Derek swallowed hard before continuing. 'For this project to be viable, the Power Station eight miles to the north of here must be converted to burn pellitised peat.'

He held up a hand to forestall Mick's yelp of protest. 'That is not a major problem, by the way. All it needs is re-tuning of the burners, which would cost very little. You may remember that it was originally designed as a turf-burning station until the Turf Board people decided that Brulagh Bog was worked out. Then they switched to oil. Did I read somewhere that it was slated for closure?'

'You did. The cost of oil makes it uneconomical.' Mick knew the grim details only too well: seventy good jobs about to go down the drain in the very heart of his constituency. He had already met a delegation from the workers but the Electricity Supply Board were adamant that the costs were way out of line. It suddenly dawned on him that these cost figures might no longer apply if Derek and his peat pellets came to the rescue. Suddenly Mick formed a picture in his mind's eye of the *Clarion* banner headline;

FLANNERY SAVES SEVENTY JOBS!

'Anyway,' Derek promised, 'the saving on fuel costs at the Power Station would pay for conversion inside a week!'

Mick paused for a moment to digest this welcome item of news before raising a different issue. 'Would the Power Station use enough of these pellets to keep the plant here working at full stretch?'

'No, nothing like enough. That's where the existing pipelines from the Power Station to the oil-jetty further up the coast come into play. Instead of pumping oil *in*, we pump the peat pellets and the liquid fertiliser *out*. Our only major expense, apart from erecting the plant out here beside the bog, will be running the pipelines the eight miles or so to the Power Station. Much cheaper than roads, of course. Less damaging to the environment as well. No bloody great lorries thundering to and fro with all the disruption and pollution that entails. There will be no waste and the vapour from the driers is quite harmless to the environment.'

'Substituting exports for imports . . .' Mick thought aloud. It would make a shaggin' great slogan across a big picture of himself looking suitably Messianic.

'Absolutely.' Derek's Welsh accent was piping with excitement. 'A whole new industry that could cut the country's oil-bill in half, not to mention the jobs it would create . . .'

'How many?' Mick had been waiting for the chance to ask that right from the moment they had looked out across the bog for the very first time. At the end of the day, jobs were what really counted. The Farmers' Friend could rant and rave till he was blue in the face, but the first candidate to come up with a credible jobs package would bring home the bacon. Saving the jobs at the Power Station was one thing, but *creating* new jobs was even better. The snag was that there was a world of difference between a vague promise, and a package that was signed, sealed and delivered before the punters cast their votes. Derek was being coy on the actual job numbers.

'Difficult to say, really. Two hundred or so at the construction stage. Then eighty permanent staff to run the plant. Spin-offs like catering, security, maintenance and that sort of thing might raise the total to near one hundred.'

Good, but not good enough. Those figures would have to be confirmed by Derek's parent firm and then cleared with Abe and Mullarkey before being made public. Nonetheless they were heartening. Mick cocked an ear as the Welshman warmed to his theme.

'I'm telling you, man, this will revitalise the whole bloody neighbourhood without doing the slightest harm to the environment. That's a damn sight more than you can say for oil-wells or bloody coalmines, even if you had any round here!'

Mick nodded, but just like those job projections, he was going to need a lot more than Derek's word for all this. That Wildlife crowd would raise blue murder should there be the slightest threat to their precious environment. Old Daphne, despite being as deaf as a stone and daft as well, was Trouble with a capital T. A stout old Dowager in her seventies, she had taken to painting the flora and fauna of Brulagh Bog and was making a very good thing out of it. Long before that, she had espoused the cause of wildlife preservation to the extent that she had almost prevented the building of Divareli's golf course among the sand-dunes because it might have endangered something called the Bee Orchid. It was only when her niece, the Lady Aphra, married Divareli that she relented. Her concern for wildlife preservation, moreover, had not prevented her from hunting foxes with the Gallerick pack of foxhounds for well over half a century.

Bitter experience had taught Mick Flannery that any protests from that quarter could cost him votes. With that miserable little bollix Mullarkey suddenly going all 'green' and knocking the coal depot on the head, this peat-pellet plant would have to be cleaner than the driven snow. That said, everything else about it was almost too good to be true. As luck would have it, the Department of Finance had recently published a report on the dire effect imported oil was having on the balance of payments. With those Doomsday figures still fresh in the public mind, even Mullarkey would find it hard to turn the project down. If he did, it would spell curtains for him – and for Mick Flannery. But that was for later, Mick reminded himself. What was needed now was an absolute guarantee from this Welsh genius that the wildlife issue would not be a problem.

'How can you stand there and tell me that building a shaggin' factory out here isn't going to wreck the wildlife?' he probed anxiously. 'Any eejit in his right mind will tell you that the noise alone will scare the shit out of every bloody bird for miles around. What's more, are you honestly trying to tell me that the fumes and the harvesting machines won't wipe out those shaggin' flowers that old Daphne gets all that money for painting? Get on the wrong side of her, me boy, and you can kiss the Fireballs Project goodbye. She'd have a mob of protesters on the site before you could scratch yourself!'

Derek explained as patiently as he could that it was the wetlands on this side of the bog that supported the rare White-fronted Goose and the Bog Cotton. Part of his plan was to fence off this area and turn it into a wildlife preserve where no hunting or shooting would be permitted. In this way the geese could increase and multiply, undisturbed in their breeding by hunters or naturalists trampling all over their breeding grounds. The same went for Bog Cotton. This, in time, would turn the whole area into a mecca for wildlife enthusiasts who could view the endangered species to their heart's content – but from a safe distance. It would, Derek added, also give a useful fillip to the off-peak tourist trade.

He went on to explain that the conditions which made the wet part of the bog ideal for wildlife also rendered it quite useless for peat-harvesting. It was far too wet for the milling machines to operate and the surface crust, for the most part, was too fragile to walk on. However, the vast flatlands – until now considered worthless – would yield an endless supply of raw material for the pelletisation process. When Mick wanted to know how one part of the bog could be too wet while the rest of it was ripe for processing, Derek walked him round the edge of the bog to show how the water from the Colonel's lake saturated one area to a dangerous extent while leaving the far side untouched because of the drains put in by the Turf Board before they abandoned the site.

'What do you mean by "dangerous extent"? Apart from falling into a boghole, how can a bloody bog be *dangerous*?'

'Bogbursts.' The voice was matter-of-fact. 'Much the same as a mudslide down a mountain. They usually happen after a lot of rain. In Finland there were springs under their bogs which caused the pressure to build up under the bogcrust like a balloon about to burst. Anything standing in its way is swallowed up in a foul-smelling mixture of turf débris and bogwater. You can trace the path of a bogburst for years afterwards by the black trail it leaves behind – quite like lava from a volcano and almost as deadly. The water from the lake would have much the same effect, I expect.'

Seeing the worried look on Mick's face, he sought to reassure him. 'Don't worry. It usually only happens where a bank of turf has been cut, like that one over there . . .' He pointed to a ridge of peat cut from the raised bog by hand, and Mick recognised it as the stretch harvested by Johnny Slattery and his uncle. A tall bank of ebony mud formed a steep cliff crowned with green moss and patches of Bog Cotton.

'It would just spew out all over that flat stretch of land, well away from where we would be working.'

Now that Derek had shown him what to look for, Mick could see the enormous build-up behind the bank from which the turf had been cut. Large pools had formed at its base, caused by the brackish water forcing its way through the face of the cutting, making it glisten like polished black marble in the sunshine. Nearby, carefully-built clamps of turf that looked like black henhouses bore mute testimony to back-breaking hours spent prising the turf from the bog with narrow spades. Behind them lay the entrance to a saucer-shaped valley, the amphitheatre in which Aphra planned to stage the rock concert.

At that moment, almost a mile away and hidden from their view, Aphra and the Colonel were straining to catch a faint sound on the wind. It resembled two pieces of dry timber being scraped together, and it came from somewhere between them and the dark menacing mass of the bog in the distance. The sharp grating noise became clearer. Now it seemed to be coming from two places at the same time, one quite near and the other much further away.

'What's that?' Aphra thought the sound seemed vaguely familiar.

'That, young lady, is the cry of the corncrake. The female of the species is telling her mate to get a move on or his dinner will get cold. My late wife, God rest her soul, did much the same thing by beating the dinner gong.'

This was followed by a throaty chuckle that quickly turned into a racking cough as he tried for the umpteenth time to light his pipe in the stiff breeze. The Colonel's wife, Derek Evans' only sister, had died some time ago. Shortly afterwards he came to live in Ballyglen. For a while, a succession of elegantly-coiffeured ladies well past the first blush of youth had called regularly to his lonely house by the lake. Whether they were merely ships that passed in the night or had plans of a more permanent nature remained a mystery. All anyone knew for certain was that they stopped coming when the Colonel started calling on Deaf Daphne. He would join her at the Orchid Club where she had a studio. Standing beside her as she painted, he bellowed happily into her hearing aid. Aphra was convinced that her aunt had the gadget switched off most of the time.

This sudden burgeoning of not-so-young love did not sit well with the Eleventh Earl of Gallerick. Until Luke Divareli married

Aphra, bringing a much-needed injection of funds into the Gallerick household, Daphne had kept an iron grip on the purse-strings. As the only Gallerick with any serious money, Gally had cultivated her for years in the expectation of an inheritance. Now the Colonel posed a serious threat to funds Gally had long since regarded as his own. Indeed, he had borrowed extensively from the dried-out Tom Donnelly on this expectation.

Of late, the banker had taken to wondering aloud when Gally's overdraft might be reduced – or at least, brought within its agreed limits. It was pressure of this nature that had driven the Eleventh Earl into the vintage port business with Harmon. Like other ventures he had undertaken before this, it had not been blessed with success. Now it looked as if his only chance of assuaging Donnelly was to rent the back field for the proposed rock concert. So far, he had steadfastly refused every request for it in the hope of getting a decent sum in the end. That this had infuriated his daughter Aphra was to be regretted.

'So it is,' Aphra said now, tilting her regal head to catch the bird's creaking call. 'I haven't heard one in ages. Why, I wonder?'

The Colonel finally abandoned all efforts at lighting his pipe and thought for while before muttering darkly, 'I expect that Pat Mullarkey, our great and good leader, is one bally reason.'

Aphra tossed her head scornfully. 'I know politicians are blamed for everything, but how can you possibly pin the absence of corncrakes on that horrid little man?'

'Quite simple, really. Before he decided to lead the country out of the Dark Ages and into the blinding glare of the twentieth century, our hero was an Agricultural Adviser hereabouts. He turned the local farmers against the gentle art of hay-making and pointed them towards those dreadful plastic-covered silage pits. Not only do they look bloody awful but the effluent from them kills fish like nobody's business.'

'That may well be, but how does the corncrake fit in?'

'Well, until Mullarkey converted the farmers to silage-making, the meadows were cut once a year by a noisy mowing machine that gave the corncrake plenty of time to scamper out of its path. Now those damned forage harvesters swoop through the meadows two or three times a year, hoovering up the grass and anything else that gets in their way. Your corncrake likes nothing better than lurking in the meadows and tucking into a nice feed of spiders, worms and seeds. These are also disappearing, of course, since Mullarkey's modern farming methods caught on. At the best of times, the poor old corncrake isn't a good flier. How he can expect to make the long flight to Africa on an empty stomach is quite beyond me. In the autumn, he heads for the sun like the sensible chap that he is. Now,' he cleared his throat noisily and looked sternly at Aphra, 'I daresay you didn't bring me all the way out here just to hear about the corncrake.'

'No, actually I need your advice. This is where we plan to hold the rock concert — assuming that Gally gives his permission, that is. Just at the minute he is being stubborn as a mule but I expect we'll talk him round to it in the end. Anyway, leaving that aside for the minute, I have the Manager of The Howling Dogs . . .'

The Colonel interrupted to inquire what dogs had got to do with the subject under discussion.

'Oh, that's the name of the rock group. Their Manager, Mr Jagger, is coming here to inspect the site before he'll confirm the booking. I need you to tell me how to turn this place into a giant theatre in the round. Actually that isn't the problem because, as you can see, Nature has taken care of that already.'

Which it undoubtedly had. The site was a huge natural amphitheatre, almost completely surrounded by grassy knolls that rolled gently down to the centre where the sound-stage would be erected. A rough track meandered from the edge of the bog through a valley between the rolling hills that would seat the thousands of fans Aphra confidently expected to greet The Howling Dogs in concert.

She pressed on quickly before the Colonel drifted into another woolgathering exercise like that of the corncrake: 'What I must be able to show this Manager person is how he is going to get the generator trucks and all the gear for the sound-stage from Brulagh out to here. I was hoping that a man of your military experience . . .' Deliberately she let her voice trail off, playing the helpless female card to perfection.

The Colonel tapped out the ash from his pipe on the sole of his boot and stroked his chin thoughtfully. 'Well, I must confess it *is* a rather out-of-the-way spot, but I can see the advantages from your point of view. That excuse for a road down there is the only access for the trucks and, of course, the fans. You will have to set up a checkpoint at the narrowest part of the road between here and Brulagh to collect the tickets. I presume it *is* a ticket-only affair?' Aphra nodded without interrupting the flow. 'Good, so you can control the crowd in Brulagh by leading a steady stream of people onto the access road. Of course that will require policing but I expect you've already thought about that.'

Again Aphra nodded confidently. In fact she hadn't thought of it at all, but was reluctant to reveal the fact. Instead, she made a mental note to speak to Sergeant Johnson about it in the near future.

'Now let's take a proper look at the road. It should be all right. Derek, my brother-in-law you know, has already surveyed the stretch from Brulagh to the bog. According to him, even though it doesn't look much, the foundations are excellent. If the damn road is good enough for construction trucks, it has to be all right for your job.'

They scrambled down the slope to the centre of the amphitheatre and listened to their voices echo eerily round them. As the Colonel observed aloud, the natural accoustics were good enough for the London Philharmonic, not to mind a pack of Howling Dogs. Having walked the road along the floor of the valley to where it skirted the edge of the bog, he pronounced it adequate in dry weather. However, he delivered this warning.

'If you get a lot of rain, you can forget about the whole business. Not only will the trucks get bogged down, but the crowds will turn the whole damn place into a sea of mud. That is, of course, assuming that the silly buggers are daft enough to turn up in the rain in the first place!'

Aphra dismissed such a doomladen prospect with a curt, 'That's taken care of! The weather insurance is going to cost us an arm and a leg, but what else can we do? No wonder every glass box monstrosity in every damn city is owned by some focking Insurance Company or other. It's absolutely infuriating. Only for Luke, the darling, twisting a few arms, the swine wouldn't have insured us at any price!'

They lapsed into silence, contemplating the enormity of the undertaking. When Aphra had calmed down, she introduced the next item on her agenda. 'What about the loos? How many do you think we'll need, and where should we put them?'

The Colonel scarcely heard the question. His mind was racing down another path. Having found the ideal spot to practice the bagpipes without his brother-in-law complaining, the Colonel wondered how best he might broach the topic of his giving a recital at the Orchid Club. The delicate feelers he had put out to join the Brulagh Céili Band had been strangled at birth by the Doc, of all people. His verdict was handed down in such a charming manner that the Colonel didn't grasp its full import until much later. His exact words had been, 'We've always kept a soft spot for the bagpipes round here, Colonel . . .' The sting was in the tail of the sentence: '. . . the bog!'

Mick Flannery was lost in thought. In his private Valhalla, there were no worries about elections or opinion polls. It was a gentle Paradise where sporting legends ruled supreme, their lustre undimmed by the passing of the years. Reluctantly quitting this land of fantasy he allowed his senses to come to grips with the real world. The first thing to register was that the snug of the Brulagh Inn reeked of a particularly foul-smelling tobacco. Derek had remarked, only half in jest, that it was all too obvious what his brother-in-law smoked in his blasted pipe. The mystery lay in how the hell he dried it. What was the Welshman's surname again? Derek *Evans*, that was it! Mick had called after him, 'You'll be round here for a while more, won't you? There's someone I badly want you to meet.'

The reply was reassuring. 'Of course I will. Unless the Colonel . . .' at this point he gave an exaggerated wink followed immediately by a stage whisper from behind his hand as he pointed to the Colonel's retreating back '. . . drives me out of Ballyglen with those damn bagpipes of his!'

Before he had got up to leave, the Colonel had emptied his pipe into the ashtray. There the tobacco lay, smouldering away like a damp sod of the turf – a commodity to which Mick had suddenly become very much attached. Indeed, it would not be too much to say that his future, and that of the Fireball Project, were now inextricably linked.

Standing like mourners round a funeral pyre, an array of empty glasses surrounded the ashtray. The last hour had been spent closeted in the privacy of the snug, with the Colonel and Derek

Evans. Mick would have much preferred it if the old warhorse had left them alone to discuss the Fireball Project but it was not to be. Despite his presence, Mick had got more than enough data to alert the three people who would progress the idea further. They were Abe Linovitz, Pat Mullarkey and Sir Geoffrey Farmingdale. The last-named was Assistant EEC Commissioner for Fuel and Energy, and Chairman of its sibling offshoot, the Fossil Fuel Conservation Committee.

This Fireball Project should be right up Farmingdale's alley. The crafty old blueblood had managed the seemingly impossible feat of boosting output from Britain's North Sea oil-rigs while discouraging oil exploration anywhere else. ELF, the French oil conglomerate had christened him 'le nouvel Albion perfide', a label he wore with as much pride as if they had decorated him with the *Légion d'honneur*.

Sir Geoffrey's FFCC got away with it on the pretext of preserving a rapidly-dwindling resource while safeguarding the environment. It was widely believed that his elevation to the peerage had more to do with the effect his policies had on the British Exchequer than on the European environment. Mick, who also sat on the FFCC whenever he could find the time, hoped that the wildlife preservation element in Derek's plan, together with the utilising of natural resources, should be sufficient to prise worthwhile funds loose from Sir Geoffrey and his committee. Already he was composing a begging letter to the FFCC as an opening shot in his campaign.

To be fair, the Colonel hadn't been quite such a bloody nuisance as Mick had expected. In fact, the old warhorse had some useful observations to make on the site for the rock concert. He had just been there with Aphra, who had dropped him off at the door of the Brulagh Inn but declined his invitation to come in for 'just the one'. Before the Colonel arrived, it had become clear that Derek's scheme, so rudely dismissed by Charley Halpin and his Editor, was a proven, hi-tech method of revitalising Brulagh Bog. The prototype plant outside Helsinki proved that beyond any reasonable doubt. That the Finns declined to pursue it further had more to do with politics than any inherent flaw in the revolutionary process. They could get all the oil and gas they wanted from the Russians in exchange for their engineering and chemical products. A neat arrangement, as Derek pointed out, that did not apply here.

Quite the opposite, in fact. The cost of shipping oil and coal to a rock some distance off the European mainland was hurting the Irish economy. Anything that could change that for the better was like money in the bank where votes were concerned. Derek was satisfied that there were sufficient reserves in Brulagh Bog to fire the Power Station for the next forty years. Furthermore, there would be enough surplus to fuel another six stations of the same size for a similar period. By using the existing pipelines, the possibilities were endless.

Last, but not least, the waste from the manufacturing process was a brown liquid. When spraydried, it made an excellent fertiliser. In liquid form, it could be pumped as ballast into giant oil-tankers returning empty to the Gulf. With the oil-jetty already linked by pipeline to the Power Station, imports would be suddenly transformed into exports. It was just a matter of pumping out the peat-juice into the empty tankers. The only investment needed, Derek assured him, was a second pipeline beside the one that would pump the peat pellets from Brulagh Bog to the Power Station. Dammit, he told himself as he banged the counter to attract his son Sean's attention, it was just the break for which he had been waiting.

To crown it all, ecologically speaking, the Fireball Project was clean as a whistle. As Sean came back with a fresh pint and a whiskey chaser, his father roared at him, 'How's this for a slogan?

IMPORT JOBS — NOT OIL!
VOTE MICHAEL J. FLANNERY
FOR YOUR NO. 1 IN EUROPE
THE MAN WITH THE PLAN!'

14

APHRA DROVE FAST along the narrow road, hemmed in on both sides by blackthorn bushes and wild woodbine. It was the same road that eventually petered out behind the amphitheatre. Here and there, gaunt trees sprouted up out of the undergrowth, their bare branches stark against the fresh spring sky. She had long been on nodding acquaintance with the Colonel, but had only got to know him well when he became close to Deaf Daphne. On the way back from their reconnaissance of the concert site, he had invited her to an evening's fishing on his lake. He had also asked a favour: would she please drive him to Johnny Slattery's lair high up on Mount Brulagh as he had something to collect from the bootlegger and his own car wasn't big enough. Also, he didn't know the way – or so he claimed.

Aphra wondered what the Colonel could possibly want with the likes of the bootlegger as she steered the Land Rover between the stone pillars that led to Ballyglen House. The short avenue snaked downhill until the house came into view from behind a giant copper beech. A small period residence, it remained in poor repair while the Colonel tried to make up his mind whether to stay in Brulagh or sell the place and return to England. The paint was flaking from the wooden window sashes, and where the ivy failed to grow, the plasterwork was pitted and cracked. A broken upstairs window covered with plywood did little to dispel the air of decay.

Crunching across the gravel, Aphra picked her way through a vigorous crop of weeds. These complemented the wider selection that grew in even greater profusion on the lawn. The doorbell had an 'Out of Order' sign sellotaped above it, and no alternative means of alerting those within presented itself. However, the big hall door – with a splendid half-moon fanlight above it – stood ajar. A sheepdog lay curled on the front step. It blithely ignored Aphra by feigning sleep, barely cocking an eye at her as she stepped over it to go inside.

A narrow hallway stretched far into the distance. Just inside the doorway stood a large marble-topped table. This incorporated a stand that held three fishing rods and an assortment of elderly golf clubs, their leather grips flapping loosely. The pegs of the hat-stand were empty save for a floppy tweed hat with trout flies impaled in it. The marble slab was strewn with envelopes, most of them bills of one sort of another. The largest of these was a rectangular brown packet with the legend *Allied Banks of Ireland, Brulagh Branch* printed on the top corner. Like the others, it remained unopened.

A chandelier, draped with cobwebs, hung by a slender chain from the high ceiling. Next to the hall-stand and catching the light from the open door hung the portrait of an elderly ruffian. Affecting mutton-chop side whiskers, he glared balefully into the middle distance as though furious at being imprisoned forever by the heavy gilt frame. A moth-eaten tiger skin lay on the parquet floor; one of its glass eyes was missing, which gave the beast a lopsided, piratical look. As Aphra made her way down the hall, she passed an array of dangerous-looking spears, any one of which might have reduced the tiger to its present state. Above the weaponry hung an oar of impressive proportions. The gold-leaf lettering on its blade had faded but the word *Cambridge* was just discernible.

As this was Aphra's first visit to Ballyglen, she ventured down the hall with some trepidation. The hurried arrangements made as she dropped the Colonel off outside the Brulagh Inn were that she would drive him up the mountain immediately after lunch. That would get them back to the lake in time for the evening rise. Sounds were coming from behind a door at the end of the hall. Opening it, she found the Colonel and a stranger sitting round the kitchen table, drinking from coffee mugs.

'Ah, there you are, my dear. This is Derek Evans, my brother-in-law.'

A thin man wearing faded jeans and a denim workshirt open at the neck stood up and extended his hand. He exuded the healthy glow of one who has spent much of his life out of doors.

Wandering around the Finnish wetlands, not far from the Arctic Circle, had given his face a colour quite like that of the Colonel's, even if its origin was very different.

'Pleased to make your acquaintance, Lady Aphra,' he said cordially. 'I've heard a lot about you.'

The accent was that of the Welsh valleys. It reminded her of threatening slag-heaps stark against the horizon, and mining towns covered in a film of black dust – pretty much what Mick Flannery planned for Brulagh, the focking idiot. How anyone could even think of turning a village like theirs into a focking coal depot was beyond belief. If Mick was serious about going ahead with the idea, he would soon find that he had bitten off more than he could chew, jobs or no focking jobs. She hoped it wouldn't come to a showdown between them because she liked the old reprobate despite his all-too obvious failings. He made her laugh –and she could forgive a lot of anyone who could do that on a regular basis. What is more, if she *had* to oppose him on this coal madness, Mick might change sides on the rock concert issue, leaving her very much out on a limb. Further speculation along these lines, however, was cut short by the Colonel, who refused to be pushed backstage for long by Derek's social niceties.

'Thought you had got lost, m'dear . . .' he broke off to explain briefly to Derek '. . . Aphra hasn't been here before, y'see. The plan is for us to scale the mountain, with Aphra as our trusty guide. We collect the stuff from Johnny, check with the blighter that everything is in order for you to start digging holes in the bog, Derek old man, then we dash back here and go out on the lake. By then, the trout should be leaping out of the water. What d'you both say to that?'

As the question was plainly rhetorical, the two just nodded. They climbed into Aphra's Land Rover and left Ballyglen in a spray of gravel. She noticed in her rear mirror that the front door was still ajar and the dog still had not moved an inch.

When the Colonel explained the purpose of their mission she nearly drove off the road with the shock.

'Do you mean to tell me that you've the focking nerve to ask me to drive through Brulagh and back here with a load of Johnny's gut-rot in the back? What happens if Sergeant Johnson stops me?

There's a focking great fine for even being in possession of the stuff, in case you didn't know.'

The Colonel was somewhat taken aback. The last time he had heard such language was in the Barrack Square. Yet he would not be deterred from introducing Derek to the mysteries of the 'pure drop'.

'I *didn't* know about the fine, now that you mention it, but don't worry, dear girl. Should anything go wrong, I will assume full responsibility. You have the word of an officer and a gentleman. Anyway, your dear Aunt Daphne would never forgive me if I got you clapped in irons.' He turned a deeper purple than normal at the thought of his beloved, and conversation lapsed as Aphra turned off the tarmac road up what at first glance appeared to be the dried-out bed of a river.

Two drystone walls ran about ten feet apart and roughly parallel to each other. The line was broken now and again by a gap leading into a field. Sometimes this was guarded by an elderly gate secured with rusted barbed wire. Those gaps in more frequent use – to judge by the trampled earth and fresh cattle droppings – relied on a large thornbush to act as a gate. This was pulled aside when the cattle were being moved. The stone walls that bordered the road were only to be seen now and again; for the most part, they were overgrown with heather, brambles, weeds and ferns of every description.

A light skin of tarmacadam had once covered the road surface but this had long since worn through. It was now a rough track with a centre aisle of grass and weeds that brushed noisily against the exhaust pipe. The wheel-tracks were of bare earth, compacted by the passage of an assortment of vehicles. Here and there, large stones had worked their way to the surface. Taken in conjunction with the crater-like potholes, it all made for a rough ride. Aphra concentrated on avoiding the more obvious pitfalls as her passengers commented on the vista that unfolded behind them as they climbed ever higher.

Derek, who must have been used to the rolling Welsh hills and valleys, declared himself astounded by the piercing beauty of what he saw. As for the Colonel, for a recent arrival he seemed to be remarkably well informed. He knew all about Mick being kidnapped in Rose Cottage where he had been having it off with

Josephine Donnelly*. This had happened when an attempt to rob her husband's bank had gone awry. The Colonel was also familiar with the saga of Maggie Flannery and the moving statue at the grotto. So much so in fact, that he might well have been a witness to these events himself. Indeed, far below them the neon halo of the Madonna could be seen glinting in the pale spring sunshine.

At a spot where the view was particularly fine, the Colonel called a halt. The two men struggled to the top of a low stone wall from where they examined the lie of the land. Aphra chose to remain at the wheel and smoke a cigarette rather than brave the chill wind blowing in from the sea. An opaque curtain was slowly blotting out the horizon where the sky met the sea. It was a rain shower, the first for several weeks. They were just a short distance from Johnny's farmyard and not far from the barren summit of Mount Brulagh. Above her the terrain was a moonscape of grey rock, worn smooth by the elements save for where it was deeply scarred by the passing of primeval glaciers. Out of these cracks, furze bushes grew despite overwhelming odds.

How man or beast could wrench a living from such a barren, even hostile environment was a mystery. It was understandable, Aphra reflected as she watched the two men silhouetted against the darkening sky, that Johnny and his aunt should seek other ways to augment their meagre incomes. Bootlegging had been a tradition of the Slattery family for as long as anyone could remember − but witchcraft was a more recent addition to their lifeskills. The apple-cheeked old lady who played the squeezebox so expertly in the Céili Band was reputed to have magical powers. Her 'bottle' was rumoured to bestow the gift of eternal youth on whoever drank from it. Josephine Donnelly was a customer of hers, as was Deaf Daphne . . .

Could that, Aphra chuckled to herself, explain the Colonel's infatuation? Before she found the two men sitting in the kitchen of Ballyglen House, her quest had led her into an empty room leading off the hall. The walls were covered with Daphne's most recent paintings − a substantial investment for even the most dedicated art collector. This was even more so since Daphne had been per-suaded to add a nought to her prices, which now averaged out at

* See *The Neon Madonna*.

£500 apiece. With at least a dozen or so hanging on the wall, the mystery of who was snapping up the paintings almost before the paint was dry had been solved. Except that Aphra didn't have the nerve to tell the Colonel of her discovery. It would have looked as if she were snooping.

As she watched the two men drinking in the scenery, she pondered how such a large investment in art fitted in with the unopened bills and bank statements on the hall table. Just at that moment, the Colonel was pointing, like Stout Cortez, towards the enormous saucer of dark yellowish-brown that was Brulagh Bog, backed up by the silver sheen of the lake beside Ballyglen.

The vast stretches of bog, long since abandoned by the Turf Board, lay dark and flat. It was from these, Derek explained, that the peat for the driers would be harvested. A much smaller area, full of stagnant pools and green hillocks of bogcrust, would form the Wildlife Preserve. To the left of this, and right on the edge of the bog, was the black scar where turf was still being cut by hand. It was quite near the natural amphitheatre where Aphra and the Colonel had spent most of yesterday afternoon.

Hardly anyone except Johnny and his uncle bothered to cut turf any more. It was far easier to buy it in neat bales of briquettes rather than to hack it out of the bog with long spades. Even then it had to be stacked neatly to dry in the sun before drawing it from the bog in baskets – called creels – slung across a donkey's back. The reason the Slatterys were still willing to engage in this form of slavery was that the aforementioned creels were also ideal for smuggling *poitin* down the mountain, where it would be stored in the uncle's cottage which was beside the bog. From there Charley Halpin, in his own time, would distribute the 'pure drop' to favoured clients. Until recently, that is.

Since Kevin Johnson, the new Sergeant, had started courting Nora O'Brien, things had become difficult for the bootlegger. The bottles made a jangling noise that would have alerted even the dumbest of policemen, and whatever they might say about Sergeant Johnson, no one had ever suggested that he was dumb. In fact, the general consensus was that, if anything, he was a bit too clever for his own good. His increasingly frequent visits to the widow enabled him to keep Johnny under close surveillance, which was far more pleasant for him than crashing blindly through the heather at all hours of the day and night in relentless but futile pursuit of the will o' the wisp bootlegger and his still.

The tall Welshman could scarcely contain his excitement as he climbed into the back of the Land Rover to resume the climb upwards. 'Absolutely perfect, bloody perfect!'

He pronounced it *purrrrrfecked* and his voice became even more sing-song with the excitement. Aphra, concentrating on keeping the Land Rover from sliding off the narrow track, didn't bother to inquire what it was exactly that aroused his enthusiasm. It had now started to rain, making her task even more difficult.

Soon, the outhouses around Johnny Slattery's thatched cottage loomed up out of the drizzle. They were built with the same cut stone as the walls by the road – flat, jagged slabs laid on top of one another and held together only by their own weight. But these stones were closer-fitting and roofed with what had once been red-painted sheets of corrugated iron. Some of the latter had rusted right through, leaving them to flap disconsolately like sails in the wind.

An untidy heap of wooden pallets and garish plastic bags bore witness to the fact that Johnny Slattery believed in giving Nature a helping hand with artificial fertiliser. Its effect was apparent on the pastures close to the farmhouse. These were lush with grass, in stark contrast to the yellowing, weed-strewn squares surrounding them – islands of greenery in an ocean of weeds and yellow sedge-grasses. All the fields, good or bad, shared the same characteristic – eruptions of rocky outcrops, which put any mechanisation of the daily grind out of the question. Further proof, if such were needed, that the precious topsoil was a barely tolerated intruder. Already, several fields had been overwhelmed with thickets of brambles, furze-bushes and nettles – witness to the unequal struggle between man and Nature. Impenetrable to all but the most foolhardy sheep and goats, it was the sort of terrain through which Sergeant Johnson had been led a merry dance.

As Aphra manoeuvred carefully through the farmyard gate, the land fell away behind them, a panorama that swept the eye irresistibly from the barren slopes of Mount Brulagh down to the tiny harbour far below, its pier jutting bravely out into the sparkling sea. The landscape changed gradually from blazing furze-bushes that erupted in an explosion of golden yellow, to purple clumps of heather set against a backdrop of brambles and scrawny weeds. This, in turn, gave way to rock-strewn stretches of hungry grass from which a sheep could scratch out a meagre existence. Further down, the patchwork of squares stitched together by the grey stone walls turned a deeper emerald, many of them dotted with ant-sized black and white cattle.

The fertile plain that nestled at the foot of the mountain was greener still. It was here that whitewashed cottages, far grander than the bootlegger's, snuggled comfortably into the folds of the rolling foothills. Many of them were further protected by groves of tall trees so that only the golden thatch of the roof was visible to the naked eye. Overhead, gulls washed white by the scattered rainsqualls wheeled and screamed against a sky still defiantly duck-egg blue. But not for much longer, as a treacherous-looking black cloud heaved itself above the horizon.

The sound of the engine echoing off the walls of the yard had alerted Johnny to the fact that he had company. He poked his head cautiously round the door of the farmhouse. Relieved to see that it wasn't the law, he forced a welcoming smile. Pausing only to wipe the drop off the end of his nose with the back of his hand, he strode towards them, the same hand outstretched in greeting. It was Derek who reluctantly shook it, taking care to furtively examine his own palm the moment the exercise had been completed.

'*Céad míle fáilte*, Colonel. A hundred thousand welcomes to the lot of ye. By God, Miss Aphra, 'tis ages since the last time we laid eyes on you up the mountain. I think 'twas the aunt you were visiting at the time, about some relation of your husband's, unless I'm mishtaken.'

Aphra just nodded. The wretch was quite right. 'The aunt' as he referred to the old lady who combined a fine talent for music with reputed healing powers, was also possessed of a phenomenal memory. This she had put to good use in helping Aphra trace an important link between her family and that of Luke Divareli. Being a delicate matter, she had no desire to air it further. As the Colonel and Derek made their way inside the cottage, Johnny turned back to the Land Rover in which Aphra was sitting.

'Would you mind, Miss Aphra, if I asked you to drop off a bit of a message at my uncle's place?'

Thinking it to be a verbal one, or at most a small parcel, she nodded without enthusiasm. Johnny's uncle lived alone in a tiny cottage right on the edge of the bog, a mile further up the same road that ran past Ballyglen and meandered past the amphitheatre. The message, whatever it might be, could not be delivered until after the fishing expedition, by which time darkness would have fallen. There were better things to be doing, she reflected, than traipsing around unfamiliar backroads in the dark.

It was, therefore, something of a surprise when quite a long time afterwards she saw the three men emerging from the cottage, staggering under the weight of brown cardboard boxes that clanked ominously. Hardly believing her eyes, she screamed at Johnny, 'You don't think I'm going to drive down the mountain with a full load of your focking paintstripper, do you? I expected a few bottles at most. What happens if we meet Sergeant Johnson?'

She drew a sharp breath and swallowed to control her tongue. It was one thing to oblige the purple-faced old warhorse because Deaf Daphne had asked her to as a special favour, but this was quite different. Aphra hadn't expected to have to carry half Johnny's annual production down what passed for a road and which was frequented by the new Sergeant.

'I hear that he's spending quite a lot of his time around here these days,' she added pointedly.

The bootlegger ignored this jibe, preferring to go straight to the heart of the matter.

'Yerrah Miss, what would he suspect you for?'

Moments later they were careering down the mountainside, the Land Rover so laden with contraband that every so often its rubber mudflaps scraped noisily along the uneven surface of the track. The bottles rattled noisily and her passengers seemed highly amused by the racket, especially Derek, whose accent had become even more sing-song than usual. To confirm her worst suspicions, she took a second glance at him in the rear mirror. Any lingering doubts she might have had were dispelled when she examined the Colonel out of the corner of her eye. He was pissed as a newt. Under cross-examination, the two men confessed to drinking 'one for the road'. Several, in fact. On the strength of the tasting session, they had each purchased a case of the 'pure drop'. The rest of the cargo was destined for Johnny's uncle. Well, Aphra sighed to herself, that's all I need. Two drunks and load of poteen aboard when I meet the focking Sergeant!

Her passengers nodded off contentedly as Aphra set about negotiating a particularly treacherous stretch of the track. Half-way round a sharp bend, with the brambles growing in such profusion that they snatched greedily at the wing mirrors, she almost ran straight into a familiar blue car with the word GARDA picked out in black on a white roofsign. Sergeant Johnson was at the wheel, with Nora in the front seat beside him. Her children were bouncing up and down excitedly in the back.

Unnerved by the unexpected fulfilment of her prophecy, Aphra reversed madly back down the road to a gateway, where she hoped the Guardian of the Peace would have room to pass without stopping. She had almost reached its sanctuary when one of the rear wheels skidded off the track. The Land Rover slid backwards down into a narrow but deep gully, completely hidden by the long grass. There was dull thud as the tailgate struck the stone wall, which jerked the two merrymakers into startled wakefulness. Trying to accelerate with the four-wheel drive engaged only made matters worse, causing them to slide even further into the gully. They were well and truly stuck.

The lake was a flat mirror of gold, unscarred by the rippling rings of a rising fish. It hadn't rained for ten minutes but they were still uncomfortably damp after the last downpour. The boat lay still in the water. The Colonel had emphasised the need for as little movement as possible. In hushed tones he had stressed that stability was of the essence. Any rocking back and forth of their craft would alert the canny trout to their presence. It was the first time Aphra had fished from a boat on a lake and already its restrictions were beginning to irk. Casting a fly into a fast-flowing river – the sort of fishing she was used to – was simplicity itself compared to the iron disciplines of the Colonel.

The fact that both Aphra and Derek had managed to break most of his commandments did nothing to improve the Colonel's humour. This continued to deteriorate rapidly as the fish declined to put in their hoped-for appearance as evening approached.

To make matters worse, the after-effects of the 'pure drop' were starting to take their toll on the Colonel's digestion. A sudden attack of heartburn that felt like a flamethrower operating at full throttle somewhere about his navel scattered the remaining shreds of his usual heartiness to the four winds. Their slack lines he attributed to any number of factors. These ranged from the splashing of Derek's oar, Aphra cursing too loudly as her line snagged on some floating weed, too much movement in the boat or, as now, the shadow cast by the boat itself on the pellucid waters of the lake.

Even before they had left the shore, there were signs that the Colonel might undergo a sea change the moment they pushed off from the jetty.

'I never allow more than two to fish out of my boat at any one time,' he announced. 'Otherwise lines get tangled or, worse still, someone gets hooked. When casting, a hook can become an offensive weapon, y'know. Oh yes, one last thing. If you do catch something, *I'll* land it with the net, if you don't mind. That way, I won't have to pull you and the blasted trout out of the water at the same time!'

He needn't have worried. After more than an hour of flogging the lake with their lines, they hadn't got as much as a nibble. As they dipped their oars in the still water that had changed from gold to a flaming orange, the sun slipped down behind Mount Brulagh. A light breeze brushed the lake, shattering the still surface into millions of glittering diamonds that trapped the last rays of the dying sun.

It wasn't until they had tied up at the jetty close to Ballyglen that the Colonel gave full vent to his feelings.

'I'm most frightfully sorry for such a damnable waste of time. All I can say in my defence is that this time last year, the little buggers were practically flinging themselves into the blasted boat.'

Derek sought to calm him. 'Probably shy, that's their trouble.'

The Colonel's face turned puce with rage. He spluttered as he tried to get the words out without choking on them. 'Shy my . . .' he cast around frantically for a word that could be used in the presence of a young lady. Having found it, he put lots of spin on it before continuing. ' . . .*Foot*! They've all been poached – that's if they haven't been netted or dynamited, of course.'

Aphra chipped in: 'Or stroke-hauled. Don't forget that your friend Johnny Slattery is the crown prince of stroke-haulers.'

This was news to the Colonel. Stroke-hauling was the foul-hooking a fish on purpose and, as such, beneath contempt.

'Surely not!' He sounded absolutely aghast. 'I could scarcely credit that. Are you saying that the man who rented us the bog, entertained us at his fireside and supplied us with *poitin* when none was to be had for love or money, is one and the same chappie that's poaching my fish? Surely not, m'dear!'

' 'Fraid so, Colonel. At least, that's what Harmon says. If he's to be believed, Johnny is a stroke-hauler *par excellence*. He can see a fish in the water a mile away and have him landed on the bank before the poor thing can flick its tail. Hardly a day goes by without Johnny trying to sell fish to the kitchens at the Orchid Club. Harmon swears there isn't a fish born that's safe from our Johnny. Now to be fair I don't honestly believe that he would stoop to nets or dynamite, but night-lines . . .'

The Colonel was speechless. Night-lines, as their name suggested, were long, baited lines left in the water overnight and stripped of fish as the sun was rising. Used in a small lake like this one, they could decimate the fish stock inside a month. In the hands of an expert, they were almost impossible to detect.

Aphra had let her voice drop until it was hardly more than a whisper. There was little to be gained from pointing the finger at the bootlegger. It was quite on the cards that the Colonel would go straight back to Johnny's lair at the top of the mountain and confront the wretch with what she had just said. The bootlegger wouldn't thank her for that. Instead, she took her leave. If Johnny's hoard of poteen was to be stashed safely out of sight of the prying eyes of the Sergeant before nightfall, then she had better get moving right away.

'I really must be off,' she said breezily. 'Thanks for the fishing. It was fun even if we didn't get a bite. Where exactly is this blasted cottage?'

The Colonel gave her precise directions and both men watched the Land Rover bump away down the narrow track that led to the edge of Brulagh Bog. 'Beautiful girl, that,' Derek said almost to himself.

The Colonel just harrumphed and muttered something into his moustache about the filly being a little too highly strung for his taste. He was far too preoccupied with his fish – or the lack of them

– to be bothered by what Derek thought of Aphra. In his opinion Harmon accusing Johnny of poaching was akin to the pot calling the kettle black. Every dog in the street knew that old Gally and his faithful manservant flogged the antlers of his wild deer for wall trophies to the guests of the Orchid Club. What was less well known was that the pair were up to their necks in an even more lucrative trade. The private parts of the male deer, when dried and cured, were much in demand as an aphrodisiac by the Japanese. Referred to as Deer Pizzles, they fetched a handsome price on the Tokyo Commodity Market.

Not a subject for discussion with the fairer sex, of course, even if she *were* Gally's own flesh and blood. It did, however, call into question the trustworthiness of what she had just said, especially when quoting Harmon as her source. No, the jury was still out on the matter of Johnny Slattery, the Colonel decided. Trying to get to the bottom of anything in Brulagh was akin to trapping a blob of mercury with a fork. Nevertheless, something niggled incessantly at the back of his mind, and it came to him just before they sat down to dinner.

Derek had been prattling on again about his daft scheme to make peat-balls. To hear the chap talk, one would think the bog was going to turn into a gold mine overnight. 'Fool's gold,' the Colonel muttered, but kept his counsel to himself. Derek was a decent enough chap, even if he knew bugger-all about how to behave himself afloat. The poor sod needed something to occupy his mind since the Finns pulled the rug out from under him. If he wanted to believe that the bloody swamp was ready for some newfangled process, then let him. It was a damn sight better therapy than drinking Johnny's firewater for breakfast, anyway. Everyone in their right minds knew damn well that all the peat had been worked out by the Turf Board – who rejoiced in the name of *Bord na Mona* – before they packed it in years ago. He had told Derek this a hundred times over but the blighter just laughed and nattered on about pipelines, access roads and the like.

It was the thought of roads that jogged the Colonel's memory. Those damn tyre-marks, that was it! He had spotted them close to the jetty. At the time he had been so upset that they didn't register properly. Tyre-marks of any description had no business being there unless . . . Immediately after dinner he phoned the Sergeant.

'Ye-e-es dammit, *tractor* tyres. Absolutely plain as a pikestaff. Some blasted poacher has been bringing his bloody *tractor* to the water's edge to haul away my fish, that's what! Yes, of course I'll show them to you. Tomorrow morning will suit admirably, Sergeant. Ten o'clock on the dot.'

15

'ANY FOCKING IDIOT could see that the damn thing was full to the gills with bloody bottles rattling around in cardboard boxes. Coming from Johnny's place, that could only mean one thing . . .'

The Doc nodded encouragingly while Mick Flannery stared silently into the bottom of an empty glass. Aphra was becoming more animated as her story unfolded, slicing the air with a well-manicured hand for emphasis.

'. . . I had visions of spending the rest of my life in a filthy cell, sewing focking mailbags when, to my amazement, he just tipped his cap and bade me good day. Everyone knows he has his heart set on catching Johnny redhanded. Why the hell's blazes didn't he take the best chance the focking idiot is ever going to get? I need hardly tell you I didn't wait around to find out. I pushed my two passengers back into the Land Rover and was gone from there faster than shit through a goose.'

This soliloquy, delivered in a machine-gun like staccato, raised so many questions that Mick scarcely knew where to start.

'Who was with you?'

When she told him and explained why, as well as the purpose of her mission with the load of bootleg liquor, a corner of the veil lifted on the mystery. He asked her if Derek had mentioned the Fireballs Project.

'The what?'

Obviously not. Mick thought to dismiss the matter and speak of something else, but suddenly changed his mind. He would have to tell both Aphra and the Doc some time, so why not now? It would serve as a practice run for the inevitable Press Conference he would stage to launch it on an unsuspecting world – but not until all the pieces of the jigsaw were in place.

'The Fireball Project, that's what. Derek's firm has developed the technology to manufacture peat pellets – we call 'em fireballs – from the Brulagh Bog. It'll employ two hundred while it's being built, then there'll be about a hundred permanent jobs after that . . .'

Aphra could contain herself no longer. 'What about the focking coal thing? Are you still going ahead with that crazy idea?'

Mick shook his head and told his first lie of the day. 'No, I had to tell the Yanks that it failed to measure up to our environmental standards. They were disappointed, of course. In fact they practically went down on their bended knees to get me to change my mind, but you know how it is. Let there be the slightest hint of a threat to the environment and Mick Flannery will fight it tooth and nail . . .'

This last remark was addressed to Charley Halpin who had just joined them in the Doc's front room. As if on cue he chimed in with an appalled, 'Jaysus, Mick, if that coal thing of yours is banjaxed, how're you going to pull the election out of the fire?'

Despite the mixed metaphors, the question was relevant. Mick shot him a pitying look before answering. 'You know me, Charley. Principle before profit at all times. Now,' he continued hurriedly, lest his audience felt he was overplaying his hand, 'don't be worrying about the election for the moment. I was just telling them about the Fireball Project—'

Again Charley burst in with, 'D'ya mean that mad idea of the Welshman, What's-his-name?'

Mick fought hard to keep the annoyance out of his voice and answered as calmly as he could, reminding himself that this would be just the sort of hardship he would have to endure during a real Press Conference.

'It's *not* a mad idea, Charley. Nothing of the sort,' he smiled insincerely. 'It's a *proven* system, already tried and tested in Finland. I'll tell you something else, too. It's going to be the making of Brulagh, that's what. Jobs galore and no more young people bailing out of here, looking for work across the water. Better still, the whole process is clean as a whistle – so much so that I'm going to get the EC to put up a Wildlife Park right next to it. If that doesn't show how clean the Fireball Project is, then I'd like one of you to tell me what does. The peat pellets will be burned in the Power Station and the waste turned into fertiliser so it's a moneyspinner any way you look at it. Now I don't want to say any more about it until all the financing is in place, so I'd be much obliged if you all kept your mouths shut about it for the time being. Anyway, this meeting is supposed to be about the rock concert. On that score, I believe Aphra has some news for us.' He flapped a hand at Aphra and lapsed into silence.

She began hesitantly. 'The Manager of The Howling Dogs, a chap called Julian Jagger, wrote to me. He wants to see where we intend staging the concert before he'll agree to a booking. If he's pleased with all the arrangements, then he'll be looking for a deposit in advance. A big one.'

'How big?' It was the Doc's first contribution to the feast of reason and flow of the soul. He sounded anything but enthusiastic.

Aphra pressed on, albeit a trifle lamely, 'I don't know, but someone in New York told Luke that they were getting a hundred thousand dollars up front for each gig of their world tour. They open in Europe, then go on to America. After that, they come back to England and they end their tour in Brulagh . . .' she added with a sigh '. . . hopefully.' She reported that the Colonel thought the amphitheatre was fine just so long as it didn't rain. This did not go down well in view of the fact that it had been raining for the past week and showed no signs whatsoever of letting up.

'What do you know about this Julian character?' The Doc was pursuing the matter with the determination of a dog worrying a bone. He sensed that there was an air of uncertainty still hanging over the whole concert thing, even if no one was prepared to come right out and admit as much.

'Not a lot,' Aphra replied. 'He hopes to get here late July or early August. We'll put him up at the Orchid Club – for free, of course,' she added, lest the Doc should balk at any further expense attached to something he so obviously loathed. 'It's the least we can do. Now the next problem is that Daddy still hasn't given us the back field. I'm sure I'll win him round in the end but it may take a lot more time than I thought.'

When Charley Halpin was quite sure that she had finished, he chirped: 'There's another problem, too, in case ye don't know. Mick's wife and Julia May are organising a protest committee.

They've already had a preliminary meeting. What's more, they've issued a Press Statement. I just got hold of it on my way here. That's what had me late, as a matter of fact!'

A silence descended on the group as they reacted to this in different ways. Aphra was appalled, as was Mick. He was relying on his association with the rock concert to win over the younger voters. Or those of them, he thought grimly, who haven't already shagged off outa here to find work abroad. The Doc was delighted. Admittedly, he would have preferred someone other than the two aforementioned ladies to organise a protest but, as he reminded himself gloomily, necessity oft made strange bedfellows.

Mick was the first to break the silence. 'Well – are you going to read out the shagging thing?'

Charley tried to refuse, citing the confidentiality of the document entrusted to him. Mick would have none of it.

'For Jaysus sake, won't it be all over your shaggin' paper next week? The very least you can do is to let us know what is in the shaggin' thing before anyone else.'

The logic of this seemed irrefutable. Charley produced a handwritten sheet of paper from his inside pocket. 'Will I read it out so?' In answer to a series of nods from the others he began in his piping voice.

'*We, the undersigned, wish to register our protest as concerned citizens at the proposed rock concert. We understand that it is to be staged in a field outside the village and will be attended by thousands of young people. We ask what supervision will be in place to guarantee that drinking, drug-taking and fornication will not be freely practised by these strangers whose visit to our village can only result in one thing – disaster! Despite what some greedy people – who stand to gain commercially and in other ways by this abomination – would have you believe, the vast majority of concerned citizens totally reject the very idea of a rock concert. Apart from the mess and general disruption, such an event will pose a grave threat to faith and morals. His Grace the Bishop has already pointed this out in his last Pastoral Letter . . .*'

There was a lot more of the same. It made Mick feel even more sorry for himself than ever. First the coal thing falling through and now the shaggin' rock concert looking to be headed the same way. Even without the intervention of the Legion of Mary in the person of his wife and Father Jerry's housekeeper, the bloody thing was already at risk from the weather. He expected this Julian person to be a long-haired creature clad in faded denim who, between puffing marijuana and popping pills, would immediately give the thumbs down to staging a concert in what he would regard as the arsehole of nowhere. The meeting broke up momentarily as they helped themselves to drinks from the large sideboard.

Mick took Aphra aside and whispered in her ear, 'Do you think your husband would mind if Abe Linovitz came over here for a few days?'

Her reply was sharp to the point of rudeness. She too was exasperated at the way the rock concert was heading for trouble and subconsciously, she blamed Mick for not keeping his crazy wife on a tighter rein.

'For crying out loud, how the hell would I know? Why don't you ask him yourself? You hardly think I'm going to stick my neck out for you in something like that. Luke, the baa lamb, doesn't like to talk about the old days before he met me, y'know. I *do* know that he refused to testify against the little shit when those dreadful people he calls the Feds wanted him to. Personally I would have clapped Abe Linovitz in irons and then cut his balls off with a rusty razor and boiled them in oil – but there you are . . .' Her tone changed from shrill anger to a note of quiet resignation. 'No two people are the same, I suppose.'

They both stopped to reflect on this nugget of wisdom until Aphra moved over to the Doc, who was pouring himself what looked to be a large vase of whiskey. It was her turn to whisper anxiously. 'Did those tests come back?'

The Doc nodded grimly and shook his head as he murmured, 'Negative again, I'm afraid.'

It was time for them to take their places once more round the big dining table. As the meeting droned on, the rain lashed ever harder against the window panes.

Everything was hotter and dustier than ever. As he walked along the seafront, Abe examined the dirty stain at the water's edge. Bunker oil from passing tankers emptying their ballast tanks stained the white sand a revolting oily black. Swimmers would have to walk through this gunge to reach the sea, still that elusive shade of turquoise that once lured tourists from far and wide. Not any more. The empty beaches that he had walked for the past two hours testified to that. Tourism was dead. Already suffering from rumours of political unrest, the goddam oil would put the tin hat on it.

As he left the seafront and walked up the street, Abe could sense the tension in the air. Before now the people of Charlesville had always been a friendly lot, waving and smiling at him as he passed by. This, too, had changed. Now they gathered in small knots at the street corners, staring sullenly as he strode past them clad only in shorts and sneakers with the sweat pouring off his ample figure.

The letters MLF with a circle round them were everywhere to be seen. They had even appeared on the doors of the Casino, where traces of the red aerosol paint still lingered. Like the oil, it defied the most strenuous efforts to remove it. Built by the French as a monument to their Empire, it had been transformed at Abe's behest into a lavish gambling den that until now, had yielded vast profits. Of late the powerful camel-owning families had banded into the illegal Marabar Liberation Front – little more than a collection of malcontents united only in their lust for power, if Freddie Okansu were to be believed. Whatever the truth of that, it was clear that the MLF and the dirty beaches had brought the West African Republic of Marabar grinding to a standstill.

Inside the Royal Palace, the air-conditioning threatened to turn Abe's sweat to ice. His only gesture to formality was to don a short-sleeved shirt that depicted Hawaiian flowers. From a distance it looked to be on fire. Up close it merely caused the eye to blink involuntarily. Freddie and the Paramount Chief were listening intently as Abe informed them that the unpleasantness over the birthday party at Caesar's Palace had finally been cleared up by a cheque drawn on the AEF account in New York. There was also bad news from the New World. The Internal Revenue Service were pressing hard for evidence that the AEF was a genuine foundation. They now required proof that it had indeed funded projects, as its name implied, to encourage alternative sources of energy to the regular fossil fuels. It had not escaped their notice that AEF disbursements to date had more to do with entertainment expenses than Research and Development.

As his listeners' brows furrowed, Abe tried to cheer them up with the news that he had found a likely prospect for investment. Mick Flannery had sent him the details of the Fireballs Project and invited him to meet with one Derek Evans at the earliest possible opportunity. Until the IRS suddenly put the squeeze on, Abe had been in no particular hurry to oblige. What he had seen in his walk through Charlesville today removed the last lingering doubts he might have about the advice he was about to dispense.

'Folks, in my opinion the time has come for you to cash in your chips and move on. Marabar is finished as far as we're concerned. The locals want you both outa here and tourism is a dead duck once word of those filthy beaches gets out. You can see for yourself that the Casino is almost empty 'cos the high rollers want somewhere safe to lose their money. The slightest hint of political hassle and they're gone. With this MLF bunch paintin' the walls, you can forget about the Casino.'

The Paramount Chief just listened while Freddie reacted predictably. 'Easy to say, Abe, but harder to do. Where would we go and how do we get the money out? We can't just head for the airport with suitcases of cash. Anyway, most of it is abroad, isn't it?'

Abe nodded. Over the years, much of the proceeds from the Casino and the drilling-mud operation had been deposited in Geneva and New York. To get the money out of Switzerland should be simple enough, but the IRS boys could make New York something of a problem.

'The way I see it, America is the place for you. The trouble is that if you just run out of here, the guys who take over are going to holler foul! That way Uncle Sam might just freeze your assets which would be embarrassing to say the very least. So what you've got to do is arrange a State Visit somewhere so that both of you leaving the country at the same time won't look funny.'

Freddie exploded with anger. 'Are you telling us to run away from a rabble like the MLF? Why, they're nothing more than a gang of camel-thieves! Even if we were to leave – *with* the money, of course,' he added hastily, 'that crowd would be at each other's throats inside a week!'

'All the better,' Abe chuckled. 'Then they might even ask you guys back again to run the goddam country. Either way, you get out alive before the shit hits the fan – *with* the money.'

The Paramount Chief spoke for the first time. He had been listening intently to every word that was said, and now he nodded solemnly at Abe's last remark.

'There is much good sense in what Abe says. He has been our friend for so long that his motives are not in doubt. However, certain problems arise from his suggestion that we leave our beloved Marabar. For one thing, who is going to invite us on an official State Visit? Equally important, how do we collect all our money in a safe place *before* we leave?'

Freddie was about to say something but Abe cut in first.

'I think I can sort both those things out. A State Visit requires an official plane, right?'

They both nodded, mystified by where this was leading.

'Okay, so I get us an executive jet in the States. I know just where I can pick up a Gulfstream on wet lease – that's with a pilot and cabin staff included. Then I draw out the New York money, all of it, on the strength of this Fireball thing. I stop off in Geneva to pick up the rest and fly back here with the money on board. Then we leave immediately on this State Visit. Except, of course, that we don't come back!'

There was a brief lull while they examined this. Then Freddie put his finger on the obvious weakness to Abe's plan.

'We still haven't a State Visit laid on. Without that, your idea won't work.'

Abe agreed and suggested that they leave it at that. It would take three months or so to draw up a development plan for the Fireball Project that would convince the IRS. In the meantime, he would need to meet with the people involved. As for the State Visit, he would organise that too. At this early stage, however, he would rather not reveal the location he had in mind. For the moment he would just require their agreement for the Fireball thing, which he now proceeded to explain. He ended with: 'There should be tax breaks in it for us. The guys I'm talking about are screaming out for jobs and the price of oil is killing them. What I've got to do is get the politicians to row in with us. If I can swing that, we're home and dry.'

He was on his way to the airport before Freddie and his father realised that they still didn't know which country the Fireball Project was to be based in. Walking across the tarmac to the plane, Abe winced as the temperature read 103 degrees F.

The tyre-marks the Colonel had shown him beside the jetty had been those of a tractor. He had often noticed those big arrow-shaped imprints himself, on the way up to Nora's cottage. Of course there were plenty of other tractors around apart from Johnny Slattery's ancient Ferguson, but the tracks had stopped outside the old uncle's cottage. Furthermore, they had then turned round to go back towards Brulagh. When the road improved as it neared the village, the tyre-marks had been washed off the smooth tarmac by the rain. Under cover of darkness, the bootlegger was probably smuggling a larger than usual consignment of *poitin* to his uncle for safekeeping. Then, deciding to kill two birds with one stone, he had stopped off at the jetty to inspect his nightlines. 'Well, Johnny,' the Sergeant muttered to himself, 'that's where you made your big mistake.'

It was odd, though, that Johnny should be building up such large stocks at this time of year. It was still a long time till Christmas, the busy period for bootleggers. In the ordinary way, that load in the back of Lady Aphra's Land Rover should have kept Johnny's customers happy for the forseeable future. Oh no, he hadn't missed that, despite what her Ladyship might think, with her posh accent and snooty ways. It was just Kevin's unbelievably bad luck that he had Nora and the kids in the squad car with him at the time, otherwise he might have had the pleasure of charging her Ladyship with possession of an illegal substance.

However, with unauthorised persons in the squad car, it might have come out in court that he had been using Government property for a purpose other than the designated one. Something like that would not have escaped the notice of his Superintendent, to whom he had already applied for a transfer. Nothing urgent, of course, but he needed a posting to a much bigger place if he were to further his career. Brulagh was his first posting as Sergeant and there was nothing wrong with the place except for its size. He needed more scope to cast his net wider if he were to come to the notice of those charged with promotion within the ranks of the *Garda Síochana*. The only fly in the ointment was Nora. Since crashing in on her unexpectedly the night he was chasing Johnny across the mountain, he had grown ever closer to her and the children. They had even taken to calling him Uncle Kevin. He brought them shopping in the village twice a week and often dropped in out of the blue for a cup of tea and a chat. He would justify this, were he asked, by saying that in pursuance of his duty he was keeping a suspected bootlegger under close surveillance. However, it was harder to justify it to himself. He still could not make up his mind whether he was spending more and more time with Nora because he loved her, or merely to put the bootlegger's nose out of joint. Any further reflection along these lines was halted by the arrival of an unexpected visitor. Mick Flannery's bulky figure filled the doorway of the dayroom of Brulagh Garda Barracks.

'Hello, Sergeant. Hope I'm not disturbing the good work!'

This was a civil-enough comment in view of the circumstances of their last meeting. The Sergeant still had not fully recovered from the shock of seeing two heaving, naked bodies slowly disentangle themselves, trapped like moths in the glare of his torch. Since then no reference, however veiled, had been made to the incident by any of the parties concerned. Kevin hoped Mick was not about to bring it up now.

Politicians like this one played an important role in a Sergeant's career prospects. Nowadays Mick's sphere of influence was Europe. Despite that, he had been a member of the Dail for nearly thirty years and would still have friends in all the right places. Because of the embarrassing incident in the Bank, it was most unlikely that Mick would help in getting him a worthwhile transfer. The opposite, however, was much more likely. Should Mick be so inclined, he could see to it that the Sergeant got a transfer all right – but to a place like Achill Island where he would spend the rest of his days giving parking tickets to seagulls.

In view of this, the Sergeant forced a welcoming smile on his face before replying, 'Not at all, Mr Flannery. Always a pleasure to see you . . .' his voice trailed off as he wished he hadn't used that phrase. It seemed to shriek the unspoken word *naked*.

In fact, Mick was delighted at the reception and equally relieved that the subject of their last encounter had not come up. Rather than engage in idle chitchat, though, he came straight to the purpose of his visit.

'Would you mind, Sergeant, checking a file for me? Gus

Moriarty, your predecessor, told me that it's here somewhere. The name is Linovitz – Abraham Linovitz.'

'Certainly, Mr Flannery, that's no problem. Could you tell me . . .' the Sergeant hesitated for a moment as he searched desperately for a diplomatic way of asking the question '. . . ah, what precisely it is in connection with?'

Mick had his answer ready. 'Mr Linovitz wants to make quite sure there are no charges pending against him before he comes here. That's all there is to it. If it's too much trouble I can always—'

He didn't have to finish. The Sergeant was out of his chair and rifling through the files in the cabinet as he assured Mick, 'No trouble at all, Mr Flannery. I just have to know what you're looking for.' He found the right file after a minute or so of frantic rummaging. Blowing the dust off the cover, he brought it over to the desk and sat down. It didn't take long to read through. He looked up at Mick and reported, 'No charges were preferred against this Abraham Linovitz. Sounds an interesting person.'

Mick confined himself to a curt, 'He is! Now, I need a note from you to that effect, saying there are no charges outstanding against him,' he added helpfully, as though to a small child.

Trying to hide his surprise at this unusual request, the Sergeant plucked a sheet of official Garda notepaper from a drawer and inserted it with some difficulty in the sit-up-and-beg typewriter before him.

When Mick had left with the signed note, the Sergeant phoned his Superintendent. His request for a search warrant made out in the name of Johnny's uncle was greeted with some reluctance, until he promised the Superintendent that this time, Johnny Slattery was as good as behind bars. Nevertheless, the extra men he asked for were reduced from six to two. Rubbing his hands together, the Sergeant took this minor setback in his stride and began to lay his plans for the raid.

16

JUST AS THE meeting in the Doc's front room was ending, Father Jerry was gazing down wide-eyed at the Alps bathed in moonlight. The sharp finger of the Matterhorn pointed accusingly upwards at the Alitalia Boeing 747 as it sped towards Rome. This was his first return visit since he had left there a sick man. His boss in the Vatican Diplomatic Corps had been Luigi Marco Castelli, one time Archbishop of Milan and later Cardinal Dean of the *Corps Diplomatique*. His was the last name to be eliminated before the Pole streaked home a surprise winner in the race for the Papacy. Castelli was still weaving webs of intrigue within the Vatican, but Father Jerry did not plan to see him. It wasn't that there was bad blood between them. Rather it was that despite having worked together for such a long time, they no longer had anything worthwhile to say to each other.

It had not always been thus. There was a time when Father Jerry had scurried around the globe at the behest of Castelli. That was just after the war, when the Vatican was a discreet link between warring nations as yet reluctant to establish diplomatic relations with former enemies. When they eventually did so, the Vatican's role in international affairs shrank overnight. Father Jerry had been a victim of this. Eventually, when his health deteriorated, Castelli took it as a heaven-sent opportunity to reduce his staff. With an almost indecent haste, Father Jerry was shipped back to Brulagh. There he would either recover or die peacefully — depending on the will of God.

He inherited his predecessor's housekeeper, Julia May, who announced to one and all her intention of putting some 'meat on the poor craythur!' As a cure for ulcerative colitis, overeating was not to be found in any medical textbook. Yet it worked. He swallowed every morsel set before him and soon began to put on weight. Doc Buckley could not confirm that the illness had been fully routed, but he conceded that it appeared to have retreated in some disorder from Julia May's cooking. The likelihood was that the colitis was hiding out somewhere, biding its time before launching another attack. Father Jerry was quite happy to settle for that. Life in Brulagh had taken on a rhythmic pattern that he had failed to find anywhere else. It came with the realisation that his true vocation was not to save the world, as he had earlier believed. Rather it was to save his own soul, a difficult enough mission in itself. His routine of walking, praying, eating and dispensing advice only to those who sought it had brought him an inner tranquillity that only his dear friend Agostini could match. The rest of his colleagues in the Church seemed to be chasing their tails and losing their heads in the process.

The roads out of Rome were gridlocked. He applauded his decision to book into a Holiday Inn on the northern outskirts as he manoeuvred the tiny Fiat into a space in the car park. Getting used to the language was far easier than remembering to drive on the right. In the short trip from the airport to the hotel, he had had two brushes with death; one with a Lambretta scooter, the other with a truck laden down to the axles with vegetables.

Resisting the temptation to take a taxi into the city, perhaps even to drop in unexpectedly on Castelli, he settled instead for a delicious veal *piccata* in the dining room and then retired to his room. Sipping a nightcap of Glenmorangie malt whisky, he browsed through a complimentary copy of *La Repubblica*. Things hadn't changed much. Political scandals still shared the front page with pictures of scantily-clad starlets displaying their wares on the Lido.

Il Venerdi, its Friday supplement, listed forthcoming events throughout Italy. *Aïda* was playing in Verona, as usual. Perhaps he could persuade Agostini to accompany him there, even though his friend had never been an opera buff. It was a long way to travel, but the open-air Arena was a sight worth seeing in itself. In flicking through the rest of the paper, Father Jerry almost missed the half-page advertisement on the back page. The Howling Dogs were opening their world tour in Siena three nights hence. Before sleep came, he wondered if he could peruade Giuseppe Manolo Agostini, shepherd of the tiny parish of Boggola, to go with him to

The Howling Dogs instead. Since they had both left Rome, they had corresponded at irregular intervals. It was Agostini, for example, who had told him all about the Divareli family bank when Luke first came to Brulagh.

The next morning, he set off early, leaving the *autostrada* to climb in tight loops high into the Apennines. He had forgotten what a hard, impoverished land much of Tuscany was, like the upper slopes of Mount Brulagh. As he climbed, the Fiat engine whining in protest, a vista of rock-stewn sandy slopes unfolded. These were hard put to support the occasional cypress or scattered clumps of pine and scrub. The light up here was clear and sharp, throwing everything into a strong, three-dimensional relief. Unlike the Alps, there were no sharp peaks or deep gorges, rather the rolling hills and valleys that reminded him of home.

As he turned off onto the rutted road that led downhill to Boggola, the hillsides became more satisfying to the eye. Squat silvery olive bushes and slender dark cypresses crowded the skyline, while the slopes were squared-off into neat vineyards, some of which were shrouded in a bluish heat haze. This was the very heart of the Chianti region.

Every Christmas, Agostini sent him a case of Chianti Riserva and some *extra virgine* oil from the olive press at the back of his tiny church. There was also a minuscule vineyard sloping down to the mist-laden valley. An ornamental pond full of fat carp and a colony of strutting peacocks completed the land-locked Ark. As a Vatican trouble-shooter, Agostini was known behind his back as the Grand Inquisitor. Any cleric misbehaving had to answer to him. Many preferred to resign on the spot rather than submit to his tongue-lashing. How such a fearsome interrogator could become shepherd of a tiny flock miles from anywhere had mystified those who stayed on in the Vatican. Banished by Castelli, some said for delving too deeply into Vatican finances, Agostini had fetched up in the closest thing to Paradise that Father Jerry had yet seen. In Boggola, the one-time terror of errant priests pottered happily round his vines, wearing a threadbare cassock and dispensing advice to those parishioners who bothered to seek him out.

On his previous visit, *en route* to an early retirement, Father Jerry had fallen in love with Boggola. Now, like Agostini, he too had found peace far from the Vatican. An excellent reason, he reflected, to spend as little time as possible in the Eternal City. As for the good wishes that Julia May had insisted he deliver, in person, to the Pole, he would just have to dream up some excuse. In view of the Pontiff's incessant trips abroad, a white lie to the effect that he was not at home might just fit the bill. Father Jerry might have been more concerned about this were he aware that just then, Julia May was preparing to call on the Bishop . . .

At a meeting of the Legion of Mary that very evening, Julia May had asked for volunteers to accompany herself and Maggie Flannery on a protest delegation. It came as something of a shock to discover that none of her fellow members could make the trip to the Bishop's Palace. In the end, Maggie took her own car and collected Julia May from the Parochial House.

As she turned the key in the hall-door, the housekeeper complained, 'I hate leaving the place empty like this, but what can I do with himself off gallivanting in Italy? When I asked him if he would give my best wishes to Our Holy Father the Pope, do you know what he said?'

Maggie shook her head as she concentrated on moving off smoothly. Driving was not her *forte*, and she avoided it as much as possible.

Julia May paused briefly to catch her breath before continuing in an aggrieved voice: 'He said he had no plans to visit Our Holy Father. Seems he's going to stay as far away from the Holy See as he can, if you can credit it! Just imagine a priest visiting Italy and not going to see the Pope! Honest to God, there are times when I ask myself what Our Holy Mother the Church is coming to!'

Maggie barely noticed what her passenger was saying for she was lost in her own worries. When she had told Mick about going to see the Bishop, he almost hit the roof.

'In the name and honour of Jaysus, what's got into you? Can't you see how important that shaggin' concert is to me? How else am I to get the young ones to vote for me if I don't throw something like a concert their way? They don't give a tinker's curse if I won four *hundred* shaggin' medals. That was back when Adam was a boy as far as they're concerned. All that worries them is finding a job and having a good time. Now, just when I think the jobs might be sorted out, you have the neck to stand there and tell me that you want the concert to be stopped! Are you going out of your mind or what?'

She hadn't bothered to answer him. Mick had long since gone his own way. He had been promising pre-election jobs for as long as she could remember – not that anyone in their right minds would believe him any more. However, his latest stunt of buying votes by corrupting the young with rock concerts had struck a new low. She wondered aloud if it would be too much to hope that the Grace of God would enter his soul – even at this late stage – to make him see the error of his ways?

Julia May just grunted, then sighed, 'Men, is it?' Answering her own query, she intoned gravely, 'Even the best of them aren't good!'

They lapsed into silence as Maggie drove nervously over the mountains. Every crossroads brought back a different memory of the night Mick had returned in triumph with his last All-Ireland medal. Bonfires blazed in celebration, lighting up the excited faces that were flushed with drink as they waited for the return of their hero. It had been a long journey from the railway station to the outskirts of Brulagh. The convoy of cars and coaches stopped at every village for more drink and handshakes from delirious supporters unable to make the trip to distant Dublin. The impetus from that last game had been enough to give her husband three decades of political free-wheeling. The snag was, Maggie concluded bitterly, that free-wheeling could only be done when going downhill.

She remembered that night, too, for another reason. Climbing down from the team coach, almost speechless with excitement, Mick had sought her out in the huge crowd, and taking her in his powerful arms, had proposed to her there and then. How could any young girl in her right mind refuse someone who was a legend in his own lifetime? Their marriage, like his political career, had freewheeled downhill almost from the start. Well, maybe not right from the start, she conceded, but certainly from the time the children were born. After that, Doc Buckley had warned her not to risk further pregnancies. It was how this was to be achieved that caused the final rift between them. She opted for abstinence while Mick had suggested other means – all of them pagan practices condemned outright by her Church. It was then that she moved to the spare bedroom.

It was no secret that he had sought solace elsewhere, but what could she do about that? If it came to a choice between saving her immortal soul and a rapidly disintegrating marriage, then she had no doubt as to where her duty lay. Still, the memory of that night of the bonfires would live forever in her memory. Her father's crystal set, crackling with static and whining atmospherics, announced that with only seconds left in the game, Mick's team were losing by two points. Then the commentator, hoarse with excitement, shrieked across the airwaves: '*Mick Flannery . . . the ball on his hurley stick ten yards out from the net . . . lifts and strikes . . . A GOAL!!! And there goes the final whistle . . . It's all over!*'

She hadn't thought about those days in a long time. Soon after they were married, her father died and Mick won his seat in the Dail. The rockier their marriage became, the closer she felt to God. In the Bishop she had found a true friend. She was not blind to the fact that His Grace sometimes used her to get at Mick, but she no longer worried about things like that. In fact, she rather enjoyed playing the part of God's chosen messenger, though she wouldn't admit it – not even to Julia May.

The opening of the new school was a case in point. Complete with Mitre and Crozier, the Bishop declared that while it was the duty of the State and its representatives to build the school – and pay for it – the responsibility for *educating* the young must always remain firmly in the hands of Our Holy Mother, the Church.

When Mick rose to reply, he prattled on as usual about the service rendered to education by generations of nuns and Christian Brothers. However, he could not resist suggesting that the twentieth century demanded more of its young than just a solid grounding in the one, true faith. At this the episcopal brow darkened. When Mick went on to hint that perhaps he who pays the piper should call the tune, the Bishop's '*Harrumph!*' of disgust reached to the outer fringes of the large gathering. It was a public duel cleanly fought and relished by both parties. Then with the honours about even, the two stars of the opening ceremony adjourned to the Parochial House for bacon and eggs followed by hot whiskies. Thus was the balance between Church and State maintained.

The Palace was nothing like its name implied, being merely a handsome house set in its own grounds deep in the leafy suburbs of a large provincial town. His Grace opened the door himself and ushered Maggie and Julia May into a small sitting room. The walls were lined with books. Rain spattered against a French window leading out to a patio. Beyond that lay a trim lawn, bordered by neat flowerbeds. It looked much the sort of place that might have belonged to a wealthy merchant or professional man. The same applied to the interior of the house – or what they could see of it. Apart from a crucifix in every room and rather more holy pictures than one might have expected, there was little to indicate that this was the home of an anointed successor, however far removed, of the Twelve Apostles.

Over the telephone, Maggie had alerted the Bishop to the Legion of Mary's alarm at the prospect of a rock concert. He now intended transforming this alarm into something more tangible by coming straight to the point.

'I believe you ladies wish to ask my advice on the matter of the concert?' It was more of a statement than a question. Without waiting for confirmation, he pressed on: 'By coincidence, I had alluded to precisely this sort of thing in my most recent Pastoral Letter. It is almost as if the organisers – whoever they may be – deliberately set out to flout the wishes of Our Holy Father.'

Noting the look of surprise on the faces of his listeners at the mention of the Pope, he dropped his voice as though to take them into his confidence. 'Oh dear me, yes. Our Holy Father often directs his Bishops as to the contents of such letters. I need hardly tell you that his abhorrence of drug-taking, alcohol abuse and promiscuity is shared by all of us. So when you . . .'

He looked straight at Maggie for the first time. Until then, his head had been lowered as though he were addressing the highly polished coffee table.

'. . . alerted me to this dreadful business, my first reaction was that the Forces of Darkness had selected Brulagh as their next battleground in their eternal struggle against Our Holy Mother the Church.'

He then went on to tell them that after further reflection on the matter, he had phoned Father Jerry, only for Julia May – here he paused to beam winningly in her direction – to inform him that the good man was already winging his way to Italy. Having brought them up to date, he now set about his task in earnest. They would not be surprised to hear that it had come as a very great shock indeed to hear that the village of Brulagh, known throughout the land for its piety and moral probity, was about to take its first, faltering step down the slippery slope that led to perdition. Rock concerts, he felt it hardly necessary to remind them, represented all that was most evil in our modern society. Past experience had shown that drugs, alcohol and contraceptives would not only be freely available to those attending such an event, but in all probability would be forced on the young and innocent.

Anyone claiming that such an event had any cultural – or indeed *musical* – significance clearly had not listened to the words of what passed for songs nowadays. Blasting from powerful amplifiers, the lyrics would bring a blush of shame to the cheek of the most foul-tongued sailor. In these circumstances, even those God-fearing Christians who would not dream of attending such an occasion of sin could not close their ears to the vile corruption.

Looking Maggie straight in the eye, he begged her to exert whatever influence she could to defeat this pagan ritual. A ritual, he added darkly, that must inevitably corrupt the young and dismay the not-so-young as surely as night follows day. Of course, as a mere Bishop without any power over the civil authority, there was little he himself could do to change the hearts and minds of those misguided people hellbent on foisting this outrage on the good people of Brulagh. Once more he looked deep into Maggie's soul as he expressed the hope that surely to God – and His Blessed Mother – there had to be *someone* who could use their influence to see to it that the whole thing was stopped in its tracks before it got completely out of hand.

Suddenly, Maggie knew as clearly as if the Lord had spoken to her Himself, that it was her bounden duty to get Mick to cancel the concert, even if it cost him the election. Saving her immortal soul was far more important than a few miserable votes. Any lingering doubts she might have had on this score were dispelled when the Bishop pointed out that the so-called musicians would be perform-ing their antics on a stage not far from where some good people – here he paused dramatically to again look searchingly at Maggie – believed that Our Lady had appeared with a message of hope for humanity. He ended by assuring the two women of his support in any action they might take in opposing the aforesaid Forces of Darkness.

When she got home, Maggie left a handwritten message in Mick's bedroom. On reading it later that night, he cursed quietly and fluently as he crumpled it in his fist. That cute hoor of a Bishop was up to his old tricks again. Just like the old days when there was no money available for building new schools. His Grace would announce off the pulpit that it was a crying disgrace that more schools could not be built for a young population thirsting for knowledge. He made it abundantly clear that the only barrier to their thirst being slaked was the appalling foot-dragging of certain public representatives. As Mick was then the only one answering to that description for miles around, there could be little doubt as to whom His Grace referred.

This would be followed by a pincer movement, in which he would promote Maggie to an exalted position in one of the many prayer groups catering for the devout and those who wished to appear so. A whisper in Maggie's ear decrying the fact that boys and girls could not get a decent Christian education in the Land of Saint and Scholars was enough to set her snapping at Mick's ankles. Even when the bloody school *was* built, Mick reflected just before sleep came, the shaggin' Bishop never gave him an ounce of credit for it.

17

MICK FLANNERY GOT up early next morning. He needed time alone to think things out. Try as he might, he just could not shake off the feeling that events were beginning to control him rather than the other way round. He smoothed Maggie's note out and read it again to memorise it for future reference before popping it into the kitchen stove. This was referred to as Sellafield because of the noxious fumes it gave off when the wind blew from a certain point.

Before he even thought about how to counter the Bishop's move to sabotage the rock concert, Mick decided to take another look at where the Fireball Project would be set up. Every detail of it would have to be crystal clear in his own mind before he could even think of selling the idea to others. He closed the back door quietly so as not to wake Maggie, and set off down the avenue at a brisk pace.

After a long trek across soft ground, he made it to the vantage point beside the outflow from the Colonel's lake. Though he was puffing hard and out of breath, he lit a cigarette and gazed down at the huge expanse of bog laid out before him. It had stopped raining for the moment, but what had previously been a trickle from the lake when he and Derek Evans had been here before was now a gushing torrent that disappeared into the wetlands below him. Despite this, Evans had been right about the drainage left behind by the Turf Board. The flatlands from which the peat would be harvested remained dry as a bone despite the almost constant downpour.

Between the lower slopes of Mount Brulagh and the sea lay a fertile plain, much of which was drained by the streams feeding into the lake. He recalled the teacher in the old school telling his class how, long before the bog was formed, such streams wormed their way through the soft limestone. In time they were sealed over by deposits of clay and lime to form a maze of underground tunnels. The glaciers of the Ice Age further helped this process by forcing the streams ever deeper under the bog crust, leaving in their wake the deep crevices that scarred the rockface of Mount Brulagh.

In the stiller, stagnant shallows the peat had already started to form. Dead plants of every description piled up on top of each other as the generations passed, raising the level of the lake bed and allowing fresh stands of bulrushes and reeds to bloom erect and further impede the already sluggish waters. When these waters became a trickle, too shallow to support the water-loving bulrush and reed, they were replaced by smaller sedges and mosses. In a flood, these became floating islands of soggy turf. As the base of the bog filled up with silt and decaying vegetation, the floating islands grew bigger as more plants took hold, binding the mass together even more tightly. About now, the Bog Cotton that Daphne painted with such effect first became apparent.

This process took about ten thousand years. Even now, channels of brackish water encircled the humps of 'raised bog'. It was here − where no drainage or grazing existed and dark sphagnum moss prospered − that Derek would put the Wildlife Preserve. In such a place, Bog Cotton and the Greenland White-fronted Goose could increase and multiply to their hearts' content.

Mick took one last look at the peaceful scene before walking back towards the cottage in which Johnny's uncle lived. As he drew nearer he was surprised to see two vehicles parked outside. On closer inspection, they proved to be police cars. Mick gave them a wide berth as he hurried back home so as not to be late for Aphra.

When he got back to the house Maggie was at Mass so the inevitable argument about her note would have to be postponed for the time being. Looking at his watch, he saw that Aphra was late. He silently cursed womankind in general and the only daughter of the Eleventh Earl of Gallerick in particular. If she didn't arrive soon they would never make it to the airport in time.

The sound of a dog barking preceded the crunching of gravel as Aphra turned the big car with some difficulty on the small crescent in front of the Flannery farmhouse. A horn hooted impatiently. Seconds later, a well-bred voice called out, 'Hurry up or we'll be late!'

The sheer injustice of this cut Mick to the quick. He had been cooling his heels for the past twenty minutes, waiting for her to arrive, and now she was telling him to hurry up! The Bentley was one of the few extravagances Luke and Aphra allowed themselves. Even then, it was only wheeled out for special occasions.

Anticipating an injured riposte, Aphra spiked his guns by grinning apologetically and murmuring, 'Keep your hair on, I was only joking. Actually I got delayed talking to the Doc – about the concert,' she added hurriedly, in case Mick thought her to be sick or, worse still, pregnant. It wouldn't have surprised her to learn that the Legion of Mary were running a sweepstake on whether the stork would call at the Orchid Club this year. She could just imagine what that old cow Julia May was saying about her. All the more infuriating when she and Luke longed to start a family.

Mick pricked up his ears at the news that the Doc had been talking about the concert. He had always understood that the Doc was dead against it. That he should even discuss it with Aphra could well be a breakthrough. As they nosed out of the narrow gate and onto the main road, he pursued the matter further. 'Still as stubborn as ever, I suppose? The Doc, I mean.'

Aphra nodded absently. Her more immediate problem was her father. Gally still refused to be pinned down on whether or not he would loan the back field for the concert. To make matters worse, Deaf Daphne was now up in arms because the noise from the amplifiers would frighten her latest craze, the White-fronted Goose. This was a handsome grey bird with a white forehead and a black-striped waistcoat. The twenty thousand or so still to the good spent some of the year in Greenland and the rest in Scotland or Ireland. Quite a large colony of the endangered species made their home in Brulagh Bog. But Mick already knew all about them, as he explained – much to Aphra's surprise.

She was not to know that Derek Evans had filled him in on the life and times of the species when explaining how the Fireball Project would enhance, rather than endanger, its natural habitat. If Mick's dream came true, the whole village – not just some shagging goose – would benefit from the Fireball Project injecting new life into a rundown bog. For a mad moment, he even flirted with the idea of fighting the election on the slogan 'What's good for the goose, is good for you!' before common sense prevailed. In the meantime, Aphra had been talking nineteen to the dozen. He tried without success to get the drift of what she had been saying.

'. . . So when we saw him on TV, we almost jumped out of our skin with the shock. There he was, looking just like the Pope, gazing down on the crowd from a balcony above the square. Talk about *posh*!' She paused for breath, waiting for his reaction.

Not having the faintest idea of what she was talking about, Mick launched a speculative, 'Is that so?' That started her off again.

'Absolutely! The cameras were doing a long pan of the gorgeous old buildings around the square, contrasting the old with the new sort of thing before they focused back on The Howling Dogs. Anyway, they zoomed in on this balcony and, all of a sudden, there he was – Father Jerry, large as life and beaming down on the crowd as he waited for the concert to start.'

Still mystified, Mick fired another sighting shot. 'Are you saying he was on television? When?'

She took a hand off the wheel to wave in exasperation. 'You haven't been listening to one word I said, have you? Miles away in some focking daydream or other.'

Her voice took on a new note, that of a kindly teacher explaining something to a backward pupil. 'Luke and I were watching TV last night. It showed a clip from the opening concert of the Howling Dogs' world tour. With me, so far?'

Her voice was sweet as treacle yet the sarcasm was unmistakable. Mick quickly assured her that he was.

'Good! Suddenly, out of the blue, there was our friend the priest, caught by the cameras, smiling and cheering with the best of them.'

Mick was still confused. Father Jerry appeared to have the gift of astral travel. 'I thought he was gone to Italy.'

Aphra gave a long sigh of utter despair before declaring with exaggerated slowness, 'That's the whole *point*. The focking concert was in Siena. Honestly, there are times when I'd like to take you by the scruff of the neck and shake you!'

Suddenly, the jigsaw fell into place. They were on their way to collect the manager of The Howling Dogs. Aphra had indeed mentioned earlier that Jagger would be flying from Pisa, via London, but it hadn't registered with Mick to any extent. Now it all made sense. Except, of course, what Father Jerry was doing out there. Still, that was his own affair – unless his housekeeper got wind of it.

'Did Julia May see it, I wonder?' he inquired.

'Probably not. I doubt if the mad old bag watches anything except the God Slots. But never fear, she'll have heard about it by the time Father Jerry gets back. Rumour has it that Maggie and herself are organising some sort of protest campaign – do you know anything about that?'

Mick shrugged. Aphra was well aware that he had no control over what Maggie said or did. If his wife was determined to make a complete eejit out of herself, she would go right ahead and do so, come hell or high water. As she said in the note, if it cost him the election then that was *his* bad luck.

He explained this to Aphra and conversation drifted into other things as they approached the airport. It was one of the smaller regional ones, serving the UK and internal flights. The only aircraft in sight was already disgorging its passengers.

Aphra and Mick scrutinised each arrival closely. Their task in identifying Julian Jagger was not helped by the fact that they had never met him.

Even now, as the reluctant Jagger claimed his bag from the luggage carousel, he could not quite explain how he had allowed himself to be talked into coming to some backwoods called Brulagh. The fact that it did not appear on any tourist brochure did not augur well for its chances of making it as a suitable rock concert venue. However, the lady with the posh accent who called herself Aphra, point-blank refused to take no for an answer. When the air tickets arrived on his desk with a brief note to the effect that he would be met at the airport and conveyed to somewhere called the Orchid Club where he would occupy the penthouse suite as a guest of the organising committee, he had little option but to go along with the arrangement.

The concourse was crowded as he walked through the Arrivals area, looking around expectantly for someone to claim him. After a while the metallic voice of the PA invited Mr Julian Jagger to make himself known to the lady behind the Information Desk.

Waiting for him there was a large florid man in a blue mohair suit that struggled vainly to contain a lifetime of over-indulgence.

Beside him stood a tall, raven-haired beauty in her twenties, dressed in a silk trouser suit that combined a casual elegance with good breeding. She seemed somewhat taken aback at his appearance – which, he supposed, was understandable. Their only communication thus far had been over the phone. Probably she had been expecting a long-haired, demin-clad refugee from the Sixties rather than the middle-aged executive type standing before her, wearing a smart Italian suit and carrying an overnight bag.

Her voice did not disappoint him. It cut through the buzz of conversation around her like a hot knife through butter. 'Huh . . . huh . . . how nice to meet you. Quite frankly we had been expecting something a little different.'

Giving her the benefit of a dazzling array of expensively capped teeth, he said smoothly, 'Not to worry, happens all the time. People expect me to dress like the band on stage. Quite understandable,' he explained, 'but the sad truth is that I used to be a stockbroker. Still dress like one, or so my wife tells me. Old habits die hard, I expect. Now you must be Lady Aphra. Aren't you going to introduce me to your friend?'

On the way back to Brulagh, Jagger told them how he had come to manage The Howling Dogs. The lead guitarist lived quite close to him in Exeter. When the Dogs hit the big time, they had turned to him for advice. 'The rest . . .' he chuckled happily as he gazed out at the hedgerows flashing by '. . . is history.'

There was quite a crowd gathered in front of the entrance gates to the Orchid Club. When the Bentley purred into view, figures in flowing robes of blue and white held placards above their heads. The Legion of Mary were staging their first protest. Sergeant Johnson, his face red with embarrassment, was shouting at them to get back onto the footpath. At the very last moment, as if by magic, the sea of blue and white parted, leaving just enough room for the car to pass. One demonstrator, her face contorted with rage, banged a placard on the side of the car. Jagger looked straight ahead and didn't comment until they were on private property where the protesters dared not follow. He was inwardly delighted at this unexpected development. Since accepting the invitation to come here – in the belief that his phone wouldn't stop ringing until he complied with the Lady Aphra's wishes – he had nursed a growing conviction that a gig in Brulagh was out of the question. This demonstration, though mild by Italian standards, should bolster his argument when the time came to put his cards on the table. He worked hard to inject a hint of reproach in his voice.

'You never told me there would be protests against the concert.'

Mick tried to explain it away as something that had sprung up overnight and would disappear just as quickly as it had erupted. Jagger sounded unconvinced. 'I wouldn't care to bet on that. We had much the same thing in Siena two nights ago. The *carabinieri* had to move a few dozen demonstrators out of the Piazza just hours before the gig was due to start. Most unpleasant. Just what we didn't need for the opening night of the tour! The Italian Press made a meal of it, of course. I hope we're not going to have a repeat performance here. The old biddy with the placard back there looked to me as if she meant business.'

There was a pregnant silence in the car until Aphra explained: 'That old biddy, as you called her, happens to be Mick's wife!'

The arrangement was that they would all meet for a drink before dinner. When Jagger went downstairs later, the bar was empty save for a raffish-looking character reading *Country Life*. He was wearing startling tweeds and sipping a gin and tonic. Jagger guessed correctly that this was Aphra's father, the Eleventh Earl of Gallerick. He introduced himself, whereupon Gally bought him a drink and then immediately launched into a tirade against something he had just read about hunt saboteurs.

'Bloody criminals, that's what I call 'em. Should be horse-whipped, then flung into jail and left there to rot, the whole damn lot of 'em. Can you imagine anyone sinking so low as to spray bloody mace at a defenceless hound?'

Gally was almost speechless with anger. His face had turned a dangerous shade of purple, so much so that Jagger felt obliged to take over the conversational reins lest the Earl had a seizure.

'Your daughter tells me you keep a kennel of hounds,' he said quickly. 'I'd like very much to see them, if that could be arranged. I breed them myself – only in a small way, of course.'

'Really?' Gally was fascinated. He, too, had been expecting the worst when he heard that the manager of a rock group was coming to look things over. Arrangements still hadn't been finalised about the back field but, he groaned inwardly, Aphra would probably get her own way in the end, as usual. Now things were looking up. This chap seemed a decent sort – well-dressed, and one could actually understand what he was saying. Now to cap it all, he was a foxhound breeder.

'Do you hunt them at all?'

'No, I haven't the time. I'd certainly like to, though. Maybe at some stage in the future when life gets more orderly. Actually, my wife does most of the work. We supply a lot of the hunts in the South of England with breeding stock. Some of the older packs have become so slow and cross-bred that they can hardly keep up with the field . . .'

Gally almost knocked over his glass with excitement. 'Just what my son-in-law has been saying – you'll meet him in a minute. He's been plaguing me to import American stock. I wouldn't hear of it, of course. Y'see, I run my own hunt here and strictly between you and me, some of the hounds *are* rather slow. Wouldn't admit that to anyone, least of all Luke, but still it's the truth. Now, if your hounds are as good as you say, and they are *English* stock after all, then there's nothing I'd like better than to hunt a couple next season to see how they go.'

Jagger readily agreed to bring over two stallions the next time he was in Ireland, which would be the time of the rock concert. Gally's mood changed at the mention of the concert. He was perplexed.

'Tell me, old chap. How can a respectable bloke like you get mixed up with a shower like those Howling Dogs?'

Julian shrugged and tried to explain. 'They're not half as bad as they're painted. Quite civilised fellows, actually. Did you see them on television? They started a world tour in Siena the night before last.'

Gally was flabbergasted. 'D'you mean to say they let them play there?'

'Oh yes. The Dogs, despite their reputation, are really very decent. Some of them hunt quite a bit, actually. As for the kind of stuff they play, the fact is that they are highly regarded as musicians. Two of them compose most of the songs – write symphonies and operettas in their spare time, that sort of thing. All highly respectable. It's the fans are the problem sometimes. Tend to give the group rather a bad name. Still . . .' he sighed happily. 'It keeps us in the headlines. Like they say, there's no such thing as bad publicity.'

His tightly closed eyes and furrowed brow indicated that Gally was thinking. After a while he looked straight at Jagger and said: 'Look here, what you've said just now about the Mongrel Curs, or whatever they call themselves, is a bit of an eye-opener. To be quite frank, I had them down for a gang of drug-crazed thugs, musical saboteurs kind of a thing. In fact, I had refused Aphra a perfect site for the concert. Now I'm having second thoughts.'

Further discussion was interrupted by the arrival of the others. The dinner was taken up with reassuring Jagger that the demonstration outside the entrance to the Orchid Club was a storm in a teacup, Mick outlining the Fireball Project, and some speculation as to the likely effect of Father Jerry's TV appearance on his housekeeper's blood pressure. Just before the port arrived, Gally announced – much to Jagger's alarm – that he would be delighted to make the back field available for the concert.

As it was nearly midnight, the others drifted off, leaving Jagger and Gally alone at the table. They lit fresh cigars before launching a final onslaught on what was left of the port. Wallowing in the warm feeling of someone who has dined well, Jagger suddenly realised that if he didn't get up out of his chair this instant, he would fall asleep over the table. With an effort he shook himself fully awake and suggested to Gally that they view the Gallerick pack before retiring to bed.

'You're absolutely right. I'll be interested to hear what you think of them,' Gally said as he tinkled a small handbell on the table beside him.

Harmon materialised out of nowhere and drifted silently towards them, an inquiring look on his wrinkled face. 'You rang, milord?'

'Bring us another bottle of port, like a good chap. Make damn sure it's the real thing. And get us a flashlamp, as well. Mr Jagger and I are going to view the hounds.'

They walked somewhat unsteadily through a large courtyard at the back of the kitchens. Jagger carried the port while Gally brought along the glasses. Sounds of muffled whinnying and large bodies moving uneasily in confined spaces came from the stables.

The kennels were some distance from the house so that the barking would not disturb the guests. At the sight of Gally the dogs yelped excitedly, thinking he was bringing them a midnight snack. Instead, putting the port glasses carefully to one side, he leaned over the wooden barrier and waited until the largest dog in the pack shuffled over to lick his hand. Then with a deft scoop he lifted it up and placed it reverently at Jagger's feet.

'He's the boss, the lead hound, aren't you, old boy?' He patted its head affectionately before elaborating on its virtues. 'This chap's bloodlines go right back to Cromwell, y'know. He gives excellent tongue, practically tells me where the fox is, but all his progeny are slow as snails. No turn of foot whatsoever. Even in full cry, the hunt almost trample the hounds into the ground. What they need is some extra pace . . .'

Jagger was prodding the hound with his finger as though he knew what he was doing. After a while, he stood back to get a better look at the conformation.

Gally continued in an exasperated voice, '. . . Luke has his heart set on bringing in some dreadful American breeding stock. My God, can't you just imagine it! Bloody hounds giving tongue in a Yankee accent! Not on your life, I told him. Actually he's still quite upset, come to think of it.'

Further reflection on his son-in-law's humour was disturbed by the lead hound making a dash for freedom. In a flash he had darted between Jagger's legs and was heading for open country at a rate of knots that belied the alleged slowness of his family strain. In the process, Jagger almost lost his balance and had to make a grab for the wooden barrier with one hand while clasping the bottle of port in the other. Such an impressive feat of gymnastics did not pass unnoticed by Gally, but it was what Jagger did next that won his undying admiration. Without a moment's hesitation, off he sprinted, bottle in hand, in hot pursuit of the errant hound. The Eleventh Earl of Gallerick brought up the rear, trotting at a more sedate pace, a glass in either hand and giving a fair imitation of the huntsman's *'Halloo'* by blowing through pursed lips.

The hound might well have been recaptured then, were it not for the fact that Jagger was so poorly shod. Gucci slip-ons were quite unsuited to the going. The heavy rains of the past month had reduced the ground to a squelching, quivering mass of mud.

Despite this, he looked to be closing on the fugitive and might well have caught him at the brow of the hill were it not for a further development. Suddenly all three participants in the chase were rooted to the spot by a high-pitched wail. It was as though a platoon of tomcats were being doctored simultaneously. Then, as suddenly as it had begun, the terrifying noise trailed off into a strangled burble. During rehearsals with The Howling Dogs, Jagger had been exposed to some weird sounds but never anything remotely like that which was coming from the far side of the grassy hummock just ahead of them. Quivering with fright and whimpering like a frightened child, the lead hound had stopped dead, its tail tucked firmly between its legs.

When the sound abruptly stopped, Gally was first to move. With trembling hands he held out the glasses and indicated wordlessly that it was high time for a drink to steady the nerves. The cork had already been drawn and then replaced by a considerate Harmon, so it was but the work of a moment for Jagger to whip out the cork with his teeth and pour out the best port the Gallerick cellars could produce. To their relief, Harmon had somehow found the time to decant it before putting the cork back in. They did not wait to savour the rich bouquet conferred on it by age, but swallowed it by the glassful until their nerves had ceased jangling. Gally strove manfully to regain the priceless gift of speech. When it eventually did come, it poured out of him in a torrent.

'The *banshee*, that's what it is. The bloody Gallerick banshee! Harmon was right, after all – said he'd heard it a few times himself this past week. It's a harbinger of death, y'know. Dammit, this is the first time I've actually heard the bloody thing. Like I say, legend has it that *"A banshee cries before a Gallerick dies"*. Always thought it was just more of the Nabob nonsense. I never believed a word of it until—'

Another mournful wail cut him short. This time it was much louder as it rose and fell on the night wind. It drowned out the machine-gun chatter of a jacksnipe and the lonely cry of a curlew calling to its mate somewhere far out in the bog. As the hound fled in panic back towards the house, the two men struggled to the top of the hill and paused there to catch their breath. Just then the moon came out from behind a dark cloud to bathe the vast amphitheatre in its pale, eerie glow.

Jagger gasped in amazement. 'Perfect, absolutely perfect for a concert!' Then he felt damp cold mud seeping into his fashionable shoes and had second thoughts.

Suddenly Gally poked him in the ribs and pointed speechlessly at a lone figure marching out of the mist. Their first reaction was to follow the example set minutes earlier by the lead hound and run for their lives. Then curiosity overcame their initial shock. In tacit agreement, they sat down unsteadily on a rocky outcrop and watched with a mixture of terror and amazement as a ghost-like figure in a kilt marched slowly across the bottom of the natural amphitheatre. As it drew ever nearer, the source of the banshee's wail revealed itself.

Colonel Thompson had found somewhere to practise the bagpipes.

The two spectators had barely recovered their composure when yet another surprise manifested itself. From somewhere in the distance came a muffled roar, like that of a river breaking its banks, but suddenly increasing in crescendo. Then a wall of liquid mud appeared, roaring into the amphitheatre like a black tidal wave and threatening to engulf the Colonel, who was struggling ineffectually against it.

The bog-burst predicted by Derek Evans had come to pass.

Without a thought for their own safety and fortified by the port, the two men floundered through the evil-smelling morass, managing to pull the Colonel free in the nick of time. The old warrior clung to his bagpipes like a mother suckling her baby.

Strange objects began bobbing to the surface of the flood that had by now completely filled the floor of the amphitheatre. On closer inspection, the mysterious floating objects proved to be bottles. Gally retrieved one, removed the cork and sniffed its contents. All of a sudden his aristocratic features lit up with a smile even brighter than the moon.

'I believe we've hit the jackpot this time. This is some of Johnny Slattery's best!'

Sensing that Jagger had failed to get the drift, he explained: 'Johnny's the local bootlegger. He sent a load of *poitin* to his uncle who lives beside the bog. Tricked Aphra into carrying it for him . . .' He eyed the Colonel bleakly before contining the *resumé*. 'Anyway, the old uncle is nobody's fool. He must have hidden it in the clamps of turf so that when the Sergeant raided his cottage, there was nothing to be found. The sad part is that the flood swept all the bottles away, as well . . .' he nodded hastily lest the Colonel might feel his brush with death was not meriting the attention it deserved '. . . as nearly drowning our friend here. Dammit, I nearly forgot, you two haven't met before, have you? Colonel Thompson, this is Julian Jagger.'

The Colonel adjusted his *pince nez* which had miraculously survived the deluge and examined his new acquaintance.

'Ah yes, the chap with The Barking Bloodhounds or whatever they call themselves. Aphra was discussing the lie of the land with me just a few days ago. That was when I realised what an excellent spot it was for practising the pipes.'

Gally chipped in happily with, '*Was* is the very word, Colonel. After this the damn site will be a swamp for the rest of our lives, that's a racing certainty if ever there was one. No more bagpipes and definitely no concert, don't you agree, Julian?'

Jagger nodded. Inwardly he was delighted. The idea of staging a concert in Brulagh was a non-runner right from the start: he had seen that from the first moment he set foot in the place and had been racking his brains ever since trying to think of a tactful way of breaking the bad news to Aphra and Mick Flannery. Now that Nature had come to his rescue, he tried hard to keep the note of glee out of his voice.

''Fraid so,' he replied. 'Definitely out of the question now with all this muck floating about. Even if it could be removed, the place is going to smell like an open sewer for years. Do you think we might drink a toast to the Colonel's lucky escape before we go back to the house?'

As they had lost the glasses, they passed the bottle from hand to hand. When it was empty, Jagger volunteered to salvage another.

Harmon discovered them snoring loudly shortly before dawn. He reported back to Aphra that he would require her services and those of the Land Rover to bring back the revellers.

As they loaded the inert bodies into the back, Aphra looked out over the amphitheatre, now a heaving mass of black, and thought of what might have been. Then she remembered how nauseous she had been feeling all morning and that cheered her up a little.

18

DAWN CAME QUICKLY, high up in the Apennines. Looking out of his window, it was if a white gauze sheet shrouded the view as the dull glow of the sun crept over a sharp mountain ridge. Soon it started to burn through the opaque curtain. At first the terraced vineyards and tiled roofs of the nearby farmhouses and villas swam into view. Birds began to flap lazily in the cool morning air as if to disperse the last streaks of haze that clung stubbornly to the floor of the deep valley. Swallows cut through a morning silence so profound that Father Jerry thought he could hear their wings slicing through the still cool air.

Out of the mist loomed a village old as time. Perched on a distant hill, its red-tiled roofs formed a random pattern like a crazy pavement after an earthquake. The rolling hillsides were lined by neat rows of dark green vines and fatter olive trees. Files of slender cypresses formed boundaries, some dating back to the mysterious Etruscans. This was Sangiovese, where the finest wine and olive oil in Tuscany was to be found. Then again, if Agostini were to be believed, the beef from the lumbering white oxen was the best in the world, too.

The last few days had confirmed what Father Jerry had long suspected – that Boggola was as close to Paradise as he was likely to get. He and Agostini sauntered along mountain paths for days on end, delighting in the bright sunshine yet cooled by the mountain breeze that blew steadily from the northwest. The men and women who worked the hillsides were a hardy people. To plough a straight furrow on the steep, terraced hills and then harvest the fruits of their labours in the hot sun bred a hardy race. These were mountainy men, like Johnny Slattery and his elderly relations; the sort who ploughed the slopes of Brulagh with the aid of two donkeys, pausing only to lever rocks from the path of the furrow with an iron crowbar.

Indeed, the Tuscan system of sharecropping was not unlike the landlord-tenant arrangement that spawned a rural gentry like the Gallericks. The *mezzadria* system allowed the peasant to work the land with materials supplied by the landowner, with the produce to be divided equally between them. It was only recently that this tradition had broken down, leaving empty farmhouses to be snapped up by British holidaymakers. The peasants had sought a better life in the towns, while the expats were fleeing the rigours of modern Britain, turning the area into what was sneeringly referred to as 'Chiantishire'. The parallels between Boggola and Brulagh were not lost on Father Jerry, but he kept them to himself.

All thoughts of Verona and the opera were soon abandoned. The journey was too far and the tickets too expensive. Anyway, if they could make the effort to go that distance to an opera, Cardinal Castelli would surely wonder aloud why they could not make the far shorter trip to visit him in the Vatican. So instead the two men talked and walked for days on end. Agostini's parochial duties appeared to be even less demanding than Father Jerry's. Fewer than thirty souls bothered to turn up for Sunday Mass in the tiny chapel beside the fishpond.

The priests' only outing had been to Siena. Surprisingly, Agostini was all in favour of going to The Howling Dogs' Concert. It was staged in the Piazza del Campo, where the horse race known as the *palio* was run twice a year. Agostini always watched it from the window of an apartment owned by a friend. They did likewise for the concert. In fact, they spent two nights there after the concert as the family who lived there were away on vacation. Strolling through dark, steep streets lined with towering Gothic mansions of rust-coloured brick, they talked of times past when they ran to do Castelli's bidding. Sitting at a sidewalk café, munching *tortino di carciofi*, a baked artichoke pie, or nibbling at the almond biscuits that were a speciality of the ancient city, they contrasted the frantic globe-trotting of the past with the less demanding duties of a rural Parish priest.

After too much Chianti they would nervously admit to being racked with doubt about some of the Church's teachings. The recent Catechism brought out by the Pole as a benchmark of his Papacy came in for considerable discussion, much of it unflattering. Nevertheless, both men had acquired a tranquillity not to be found within the Vatican walls nor by fluttering from Embassy to Embassy like demented swallows. The vexed question of how a merciful God could allow so much suffering in His World remained, as ever, unresolved.

Sitting in the evening sun, they watched the roustabouts dismantle the sound stage of last night's concert from the fan-shaped square. Il Campo had hosted executions, plague, famine and horse races on its worn cobblestones for well over a thousand years. This was the first time, however, that the solid citizens of Siena had allowed it to be used for a rock concert. It had gone well, with no trouble to speak of, despite the enormous throng. Earlier in the day, there had been a protest against staging such an event on the hallowed cobblestones but it passed off quietly. Admittedly, the noise had been incredibly loud but they had expected that. Afterwards the crowds had dispersed quietly.

Father Jerry wondered anew as to how something like this would be received back in Brulagh, then brushed the worry from his mind. Agostini was haggling with a pedlar over the price of a ceramic tile and wanted him to mediate. When the deal was struck, Agostini handed him the tile. It depicted an hourglass of piercing blue set against a white backdrop.

'A souvenir, old friend,' he said gently. 'Don't wait so long to visit me the next time. Remember the sand in our hourglass is fast running out.'

Back in Brulagh, the welcome was not so cordial. Father Jerry was greeted by a furious Julia May. Her arms akimbo, she invoked the combined blessings of Mary the Mother of God and the lately deceased Padre Pio to give her strength to point out to her charge the error of his ways.

'Faith, I never thought the day would dawn when a priest of the Church would be seen, dead or alive, at a carry-on like that. A fine example you set for the rest of us, I must say, and our hearts broken from trying to put a stop to the cursed concert. I'll wager that His Grace was having forty fits when he saw yourself cocked up in that window. There you were, smiling and laughing down at the crowd of eejits leppin' and screamin' their heads off like they had a wasp down their trousers. How well you could take yourself off to a thing like that without troubling to call on Our Holy

Father the Pope to seek his blessing for the two of us, I don't know, but I can tell you one thing for sure – we're both going to need it if this rock concert comes off. While you were away, Maggie Flannery and myself got the full permission of the Bishop himself to do everything in our power to stop this work of the Devil. Haven't the pair of us been storming the Gates of Heaven with our prayers while you were off gallivanting around Italy? Not only that, but we got up a protest against it. This very day when the clown that's supposed to be organising the whole thing arrived, we had a demonstration outside the entrance to the Orchid Club. I'd say we put the fear of God into that Lady Aphra one, not to mention that oul' ram Flannery. You should have seen his face when he saw his own wife waving a placard at him. I thought he was going to drop dead on the spot from the shock with his face redder than any beetroot. Thanks be to God and His Blessed Mother, we put the fear of God into them. D'you know what I think, Father? 'Twouldn't surprise me one little bit if Mick Flannery had his eye on that brazen hussy . . .'

Whatever Mick Flannery and Aphra might have been up to in Julia May's fertile imagination was lost in the thin air as Father Jerry turned on his heel and started walking briskly away down the short drive of the Parochial House that led to the main street of Brulagh.

19

MULLARKEY EYED MAHONY, the Minister for Foreign Affairs, warily. It was rare indeed that Kevin Mahony entered the Taoiseach's office without a phalanx of secretaries and advisers. For one thing, he believed that it lent an air of ceremony to what might have otherwise been routine meetings. More importantly, it provided witnesses to what had been said. Mahony was a committee man to the bone, who told anyone prepared to listen that he preferred to work by consensus. In reality, he got his own way by a creative re-writing of the Minutes. Those who had fought him every inch of the way on a policy matter were astounded to discover later that they had supported Mahony's position without demur, according to the duly recorded Minutes of the meeting. It may have been the oldest trick in the political lexicon but it still worked. It was equally effective in the smoke-filled backrooms where political 'heaves' were plotted late into the night.

Mullarkey, however, had not survived the cut and thrust of political life without developing sensitive antennae. For some time now these had been twitching nervously. They picked up the telltale signs of a plot being hatched by Mahony, who had long aspired to the office of Taoiseach. He had the support of a *côterie* of well-heeled Dubliners who believed that anywhere outside the city limits was Indian territory. Examples quoted in support of this argument always included both Mullarkey and Mick Flannery. Of late they had been increasingly referred to as 'The Country and Western Band' – but not to their faces. Now the daily papers had picked up the phrase and were blaming the current crop of financial crises on the Country and Western School of Economics.

Rumour had it that when Mahony thought the time right, he would use Mick Flannery as the stalking horse to topple the Taoiseach, though how he would do so had yet to be revealed. It was not as if the two men were close; rather, they hated each other's guts. Flannery made no secret of the fact that he regarded the Minister for Foreign Affairs as being a cute hoor who slithered around delicate issues like the extradition affair because he hadn't the balls to confront Uncle Sam. In return, the Minister let it be known that Mick's presence in the European Parliament was an indignity that the country could well do without. He had leaked to his Press contacts the view that bulls in china shops conducted themselves with far greater decorum than the sporting legend from Brulagh. In private, he was more even scathing, referring to Mick as 'that rednecked ram from the arsehole of nowhere'. Hardly a solid base from which to launch a 'heave' against him, Mullarkey decided, even if both men's opinion of each other seemed fully justified.

Mahony droned on, outlining in considerable detail his exchange with the American Ambassador. For some reason Mahony seemed to attach greater importance to who should pay for the repairs to the Gaelic Palace rather than the inflexible approach by the State Department to the thorny and potentially explosive problem of extradition.

'I need hardly remind you, Taoiseach, that the Americans are not going to risk losing the Irish vote in an election year by sending our man back here to stand trial for murder. Every longhaired Leftie and closet Provo would march on the White House within minutes of such an announcement. Now the problem, as I see it, is that unless pressure is brought to bear on the State Department, it will be construed as weakness on the part of the Government . . .'

Mullarkey swore under his breath. A lengthy piece in yesterday's *Irish Times* had made that very point, quoting 'a senior Government official' as its source. Mullarkey had not the slightest doubt that the source for that, and much else that was damaging to him politically, came from the urbane ex-lawyer speaking in a low voice across the desk. It was all too obvious that the Minister was trying to distance himself from the extradition problem by suggesting that the charge of weakness would be laid at the door of the Government, i.e. Taoiseach Mullarkey, rather than where it belonged, in the lap of the Minister for Foreign Affairs. Mullarkey waited impatiently for the opportunity to lob this political hand-grenade back from whence it came as he tuned in once more to what Mahony was saying.

'. . . Despite the fact that both of you are from the same village, I have to advise you that Mick Flannery is a loose cannon. The image that he projects both at home and abroad is quite appalling. The man is a political dinosaur whose extinction could be hastened by the party officially distancing itself from him immediately.'

The Taoiseach's face was about as expressive as a cigar-store Indian's so Mahony pressed on.

'It took me an hour to persuade the British Ambassador that what the idiot said in New York about it being high time the troops got out of the North didn't reflect your Government's policy. Now Flannery has this crazy request lodged with my Department.'

For the first time Mullarkey brightened. It was always interesting to see what new rabbits Mick was going to pull out of the hat in a desperate bid to get re-elected. Already word of the Fireball Project had reached him and it smacked of vintage Flannery. As usual the EC were expected to cough up and the money could only be guaranteed if Michael J. Flannery remained in the corridors of power. Then – and only then – could the voters know for certain that the largesse from Brussels would not be hijacked by a gang of Mediterranean bandits.

The European Community was a well from which Mick had already drawn much water. One of these days, Mullarkey mused, it was going to run dry. Not yet though, it seemed. Mick had sent him a copy of a letter from no less a person than Sir Geoffrey Farmingdale, Assistant EC Commissioner for Fuel and Energy, and Permanent Chairman of its Fossil Fuel Conservation Committee. Wearing his FFCC hat, Sir Geoffrey stated without equivocation that substantial funds would be available in view of the favourable EIS report he had just read. The Environmental Impact Study had given a clean bill of health to the Fireball Project, with the recommendation that a Wildlife Preserve be established before the manufacturing plant came onstream.

A second document from the Commission of the European Communities in Brussels was from a Vice-President with responsibility for Structural Funds. The official document merely stated that Mick's application for funds from the Commission had been noted and would be discussed at the next meeting of the Finance

174

Committee. A handwritten note stapled to the letter was more informative. It read: *'Dear Mick, Don't worry. I guarantee you will get most of what you asked for the Fireball Project. You can quote me on that if you want. The FFCC will, however, require a deposit receipt from an Irish bank for the seed capital requirement of seventeen million dollars as proof that the project is going ahead. Regards, Franz.'*

Mullarkey laughed heartily at the very idea of anyone, least of all Mick Flannery, trying to borrow that kind of money. Nevertheless it had to be admitted that Mick had done his homework. The EIS report would spike the guns of those environmentalists who feared for the wildlife of the area. Money for the pipelines and roads was guaranteed, as was the establishment of a Wildlife Preserve. Plenty of jobs, and votes, in those. It certainly was preferable to covering Brulagh in six inches of coaldust. Now all the old fraud had to do was to find a crock of gold at the end of the rainbow. This time round, one thing was certain. If Mick didn't come up with the start-up money *before* the election, he could kiss goodbye to Europe.

Mullarkey turned his attention back to Mahony and inquired in as casual a voice as he could manage, 'What does he want?'

'A State Visit, no less. The Paramount Chief of Marabar is flying into Shannon next month and Mick Flannery wants him to be given a State Reception, complete with twenty-one gun salute!'

'Any idea why? I mean why Mick wants him to be given the red-carpet treatment?'

Mahony shrugged helplessly before replying in a disgusted voice, 'I just don't know, but you can be damn sure that it's connected in some way with his election campaign.'

Mullarkey nodded solemnly: it seemed the only explanation – though how in the name of God a Chief from Darkest Africa was going to help Mick remain in Europe was anyone's guess. The straw polls showed Mick in a neck-and-neck race for the last seat with the Farmers' Friend. Should Mick lose to that prophet of doom and gloom, McBride, it would be seen as a major setback for the Country and Western Band and, by association, for Pat Mullarkey. After all, the Farmers' Friend's campaign was based on attacking Mullarkey and his agricultural policies. Should he defeat Mick Flannery, it could provide just the impetus Mahony was seeking to launch the 'heave'. Mullarkey stroked his chin thoughtfully and listened to Mahony prattling on.

'Of course, it's completely out of the question. There's the expense, for one thing. We can't be expected to drag out the Army and yourself for every tinpot dictator that stops off in Shannon to buy his liquor duty free!'

Mullarkey continued to stroke his chin, carefully weighing up the pros and cons. He remembered a phrase from somewhere: 'Mine enemy's enemy is my friend'. Perhaps it was about time the mythical Country and Western Band started to get its act together. He treated Mahony to the bleakest of stares that indicated beyond doubt where the decision for a matter of such importance rested. It also signalled the end to the meeting.

'I'll think about it and let you know my decision on the matter in due course.'

The Army band struggled with as close an approximation to the National Anthem of Marabar as they could manage. They did so on the basis of a frantic rehearsal in an empty hangar earlier that morning. Without any sheet music, they had to learn the piece from a poor-quality sound tape that all too evidently left out the ending. This was amplified until the sound quality broke up. At that point the bandmaster allocated chunks to each section and told them to learn it off by heart while he hurriedly composed an ending. Afterwards, the consensus was that the ending was the best bit. This would have come as less of a surprise had the band been aware that the anthem had been composed on the back of a menu in Caesar's Palace by a guitarist friend of Freddie's. The National Anthem of Marabar was paid for with two plastic gaming chips worth fifty dollars, and a *piña colada*.

At times, the band almost drowned out the noise of the choppers buzzing furiously overhead like angry bees. Everyone connected with the State Visit was determined that it should go as smoothly as possible. The status of the airport as a compulsory stop-over for Transatlantic flights was under review. No cock-ups would be tolerated while the eyes of the world were upon them.

Arrangements for the State Visit of the Paramount Chief of Marabar had been completed in great haste. As well as the problem with the anthem, it transpired that not a single flag of the tiny African Republic of Marabar was to be found. Seamstresses had worked through the night running up the facsimiles that were now straining against the flagpoles, fluttering in the stiff breeze. A Guard of Honour would be inspected by Freddie and his father, after which they would adjourn for smoked salmon and Irish Coffee while the plane was being refuelled for its onward trip to New York. It was then that the AEF funding of the Fireball Project would be finalised.

Out on the tarmac, a breeze whipped at the peaked caps of the military band still struggling manfully to master the unfamiliar music. Behind them a tiered platform, bedecked in flowers, loomed large against the windswept sky that promised rain at any moment. On a smaller podium sat the dignitaries invited along to grace the occasion. Led by the Taoiseach and Mick Flannery, they were, in the main, elected members of local government and County Councils, with a sprinkling of sports personalities and well-heeled businessmen. A large cheering section from Brulagh had, due to the combined efforts of Pat Mullarkey and Mick, got themselves the best seats at the front, with a clear and un-interrupted view of the proceedings.

The official welcoming party included Pat Mullarkey and wife, Mick Flannery and wife, Luke and Aphra and the Bishop. The American and British Ambassadors had sent their regrets at being unable to attend due to prior engagements. Sir Geoffrey Farmingdale, however, had arrived to pledge support for the Fireball Project and confirm that its aims coincided with those of his Fossil Fuel Conservation Committee. All well and good, Mick reminded himself yet again as he watched the dot in the sky loom ever larger – but not worth two knobs of goats' droppings unless the start-up money for the whole damn thing came from Freddie and his father, the Paramount Chief.

Mick glanced sideways at Mullarkey who was also gazing skywards. The Taoiseach had just promised him that if the Fireball Project was funded, he would approve training schemes for the workers and subsidise the payroll with employment grants where possible. Welcome though it was, Mick wondered at this sudden change of heart.

Luke Divareli was also having a change of heart. Aphra had been working on him day and night. Her objective was to ensure that he didn't upset the applecart by going for Abe Linovitz the moment he came within striking distance. The two men had fallen out when it came to light that Abe had been selling bogus memberships in the Orchid Club and pocketing the proceeds. It was only when he relinquished his shareholding in the club that Abe was smuggled out of the country and far from the clutches of the US Treasury Department, who had shown a close interest in his activities.

The charges had been dropped against Abe only when Luke could not bring himself to testify against his erstwhile friend. That, however, didn't mean he wasn't going to knock his block off if he came within range. The best Aphra could manage in this respect was to extract a solemn promise from Luke that he would not confront Abe during the State Reception lest it damage the prospects for the Fireball Project.

The sleek Gulfstream touched down far out along the runway. The harsh screech of tyres indicated that it had been more of an arrival than a landing. In a few short moments, it would taxi close to where they were standing in the cold raw wind. The Paramount Chief would make his way along the red carpet, shaking hands with the line of Veeps assembled to greet him. The Taoiseach bit his lip as he wondered whether this colourful character from West Africa could really be a serious investor in the Fireball Project.

'. . . And so, without further ado, I now hand over to our esteemed Member of the European Parliament, Michael Flannery. I know that he, too, wants to welcome our distinguished visitors, the Paramount Chief of Marabar and the Right Honourable Alfred Emmanuel Okansu, on the occasion of their first – but I trust not their last – visit to our shores.'

Mullarkey sat down to a polite smattering of applause. He had milked the role of one Head of State welcoming another for all its worth – good for at least a thirty-second clip on TV, a dozen radio sound-bites and the front page of every newspaper in the country. Now the sooner he could get back to Dublin, the happier he would be. Mick Flannery was welcome to the remaining scraps of publicity. If the opinion polls were correct, he was going to need all the exposure he could get, with polling less than a week away.

He hoped Mick was going to keep it short. It was bad enough to have to wait around for an hour of aimless but obligatory chitchat. For him the talk would be punctuated by an endless succession of cups of tea. The rest of them would opt for the Irish Coffees in an attempt to get the blood circulating again after the Arctic cold outside. Mullarkey was proud of the fact that he had made it to the top without taking a drink. It was an example that Mick, even at this late stage in his career, would do well to follow. He had rarely seen the old reprobate looking worse. His complexion was deep purple and the smoker's cough that racked his portly frame sounded like a tractor failing to start on a frosty morning. Watching Mick grasp the microphone, he wondered if the rumour about him being caught *in flagrante* with Donnelly's wife were true. When would the old fool learn a bit of sense?

Gazing down at the VIPs and Press Corps, Mick waited for the applause to peter out. He had just overheard Freddie, fresh from inspecting the Guard of Honour with his father, confide to Abe that his nuts were stuck to his throat with the cold. Like the rest of his party he was draped in flowing robes, the traditional costume of the West African Republic. These were not unlike those worn by Maggie when praying with the Legion of Mary. Ideal as they were for Marabar – and the superheated cabin of the jet – they were quite unsuited to ths windswept platform, with its uninspiring vista of endless mudflats and ugly fuel-tanks.

Mick grasped the microphone even more tightly and shouted into it to make himself heard above the roar of the wind. He had been doing this from the back of a lorry outside church gates and in village squares for as long as he could remember.

'*A Cháirde, Céad Míle Fáilte!* For those of you not familiar with our native tongue, that means *"My friends, a hundred thousand welcomes!"* I promise I won't keep you out here for long. Still and all I have to say that it isn't every day of the week we get the chance to welcome a Head of State to this part of the country. Both of our sovereign nations have struggled free from under the heavy yoke of colonialism to emerge into the sunlight of freedom . . .' At this point, an unseasonable wind sent a wave of shivering through the audience, forcing him to abandon this promising vein of oratory in favour of: '. . . But that'll have to keep for another day. I just want to welcome the Paramount Chief and his son to our shores and hope that their stay, though short, will be pleasant and profitable.'

They stood to attention as the National Anthem of Marabar was churned out once more, this time punctuated by the boom of a twenty-one gun salute. After that it was time to call it a day and go indoors.

The band struck up a medley of Irish airs as the official party left the dais. Soon they were out of the public gaze in a comfortable lounge where waiters moved discreetly among them carrying trays of drinks and canapés. Mick was showing the Paramount Chief how to make an Irish Coffee while Freddie and Abe whispered urgently to each other in the middle of room.

Some distance away, Mullarkey and the Bishop sat on a couch, sipping tea and making small talk. In reality they were both straining to catch what the others were saying. It might have interested them to hear Freddie bringing Abe, who had been flying around the globe withdrawing AEF money out of various banks, up to date on developments in Marabar. There had been a demonstration in Charlesville the previous evening which the Imperial Guard had managed to quell. Some shops had been looted, a few heads broken and the mob had retreated to the old part of the city where the forces of law and order declined to follow them. It looked as though things were going rapidly downhill.

The Bishop tried in vain to catch Mick Flannery's eye. There were several matters that he wished to discuss with his old sparring partner, not least among them being the rock concert. He was not to know of the bog-slide that had forced its cancellation. Nor could he realise that his presence had prompted the Paramount Chief to tell Mick that the twin curses of Africa were the white ants and the White Fathers. In the hilarity that followed this, Mick gave up describing how to make Irish Coffees and started drinking them instead. In this he was joined by the Paramount Chief whose English seemed to improve with each glass that he drained. Mick was trying to explain the different grip for swinging a golf club and a hurling stick when an aide entered the room and tapped the Chief on the shoulder. They moved out of earshot, speaking urgently in their own language. Freddie was summoned to join them. There was further animated discussion, accompanied now by deep frowns and brows darkening with rage. At one point Freddie began to shout and wave his arms around but was hushed by the other two.

Abe sidled up to Mick and muttered out of the side of his mouth: 'It's my guess that the shit has just hit the fan!'

Before he had time to elaborate, he too was called over to join the discussion. This left Mick on his own until the Bishop beckoned him to join them on the large sofa.

The aide had brought a message from the pilot saying that permission to land anywhere in the United States of America had been refused. This had come to light only minutes ago, when the pilot filed his flight plan to New York in the usual manner. The reply to his 'please repeat message' spelled it out more clearly. The Paramount Chief was *persona non grata* with the US Immigration Authorities; accordingly, landing permission was refused.

For a mad moment, Abe thought that it might have something to do with Freddie's gambling debts, then dismissed the crazy idea even quicker than he had thought of it. He decided to call the meeting to order before Freddie became even more flustered.

'Lissen,' he told them, 'this is real serious. Do you figure it may have somethin' to do with the trouble at home?'

Freddie was first to offer an opinion. 'Could be, I suppose. The Americans want our neighbours to extend a submarine base lease for another five years and to let them build a satellite tracking station. I suppose . . .' he paused as the full implication of what he was saying struck him for the first time. 'Yes, I'm sure that's it! Just suppose for a minute those riots last night were planned to coincide with our leaving the country on a State Visit.'

Again there was a long pause while everyone tried to adjust to this latest development.

Meanwhile, over on the other side of the room, Mick sat down beside the Prelate.

'My wife tells me that you disapprove of the rock concert, Your Grace,' he said unctuously. 'Well then, you will be glad to hear that I've bowed to your wishes and cancelled it. I hope you're satisfied with that!'

With one ear cocked to the Bishop's thanks, Mick watched Mullarkey's expression as he was summonsed to take a phone-call. To judge by the expression on the Taoiseach's face, it was bad news.

'Hello, is that Taoiseach Mullarkey? Good of you to take my call, sir. Now I've got what you might call a situation here. I've just asked your Minister for Foreign Affairs to send those two guys from Marabar back home. He said he hadn't the authority to do so and suggested that I call you. Seems there's been a *coup* or something of that sort. Anyway, the new régime wants the Chief and his son to stand trial . . .'

Mullarkey broke in to inquire as to the nature of the charges, only to be greeted with a testy: 'How in tarnation do *I* know? The usual kinda thing, I guess — corruption, fraud, human rights offences and Christ alone knows what else. Seems they took most of the goddam Treasury with them before they left. Anyway, it's none of my business what they have — or haven't — done. What *is* my business is to make sure you get the message from us in the American Embassy loud and clear. Uncle Sam wants those guys outa there and packed off back to where they came from . . .'

This time there was a longer pause as Mullarkey pointed out that the Paramount Chief and Freddie were honoured guests of the State. At one stage the Ambassador tried interrupting with an irate: 'What in hell's blazes has that got to do with it?'

When this failed to stem the flow from the other end of the line, he lapsed into a sullen silence. With the receiver jammed against his ear, he listened with mounting fury to what Mullarkey had to say. Eventually he spluttered angrily, 'Sounds to me, Taoiseach, like you're trying to put an armlock on Uncle Sam. You know as well as I do that our President doesn't take kindly to that kinda thing.'

After a while, the flood of words from the other end eased somewhat and the Ambassador's scowl deepened. It was obvious that he had got little out of Mullarkey. In a voice shaking with anger he cut short further exchanges. 'Okay, Mister Mullarkey,' he shouted. 'I think I get the message. No deal unless we spring our guy first. Of course I'll certainly pass it on, but don't hold your breath 'cos I can promise you that the President won't hear of it. That guy serves his goddam sentence first and that's it! No horse-trading on that one, I promise. As for those Marabar guys down there with you, I know both the State Department and the President will be disappointed — *real* disappointed — that you can't see your way to oblige us in a small matter like this. Still, if that's the way you want it . . .' He hung up without finishing the sentence.

Mullarkey walked back to the middle of the floor and spoke in a voice that got the immediate attention of everyone in the room.

'Gentlemen, I have bad news. I'm afraid there has been a coup in Marabar . . .'

He paused while they reacted in different ways. Mick's 'Oh, sweet Jaysus!' was matched by Abe's 'Jeez – us!' Freddie and his father seemed less surprised than the others. Mullarkey told them what the American Ambassador had said about the State Department requesting that they be sent back home to stand trial. It was here that his account deviated somewhat from the truth.

'I told His Excellency the American Ambassador that we had extended you the courtesy of a State Reception and the very last thing in our minds would be to expel you and your party. At this he said that I might live to regret not complying with the express wishes of the State Department. Then he hung up on me.'

Mick chipped in. 'Don't pay any heed to that old shagger. Sure we all know he couldn't find his arse in the dark. What does he know about Marabar or our good friends here, for that matter?'

It struck Mullarkey that they were taking the news better than he could have hoped. Being unaware of their intention to quit Marabar forever, he attributed their calmness in the face of crisis to the anaesthetic properties of Irish Coffee. He glared at Mick before replying uneasily: 'Obviously I can't speak for the American Ambassador, except to remind you that whatever your private views of that gentleman might be, he *is* the legitimate Ambassador of our closest ally – and our most generous bene-factor. Any hint of sanctions against us by the State Department would cause massive outflows of funds with a disastrous effect on our currency. We would have to raise bank interest rates by several percentage points to protect our position.'

Another silence, this one much gloomier, descended on the small group. Abe eventually voiced what was on everybody's minds.

'If my friends here can't fly to the States and they don't want to go back home to get shot at, or be put on trial, what the hell *are* they going to do?'

Mullarkey seized the ball and ran with it. 'I didn't want to make matters worse by telling you this, but the Ambassador also said that the more obvious places – he called them bolt-holes – such as Spain, Switzerland and Mexico, have been warned not to offer the Paramount Chief, or his son, refuge.'

He paused for a moment to look straight at Freddie and the Chief before concluding in his sternest voice: 'Which seems to close off most of your options, gentlemen. I'm sure you will agree that all I can do in the circumstances is to offer my deepest sympathy.'

A stunned silence descended on the room after Mullarkey's grim condolences. It looked to Mick as though the little gobshite was throwing in the towel by yielding to pressure from the Yanks. So much for all his fine words about our being an Independent Sovereign State making our own way in the world! For Mullarkey to even consider sending these decent people back home was outrageous. They would be put up against a wall and shot, and with them would go his last chance of getting the Fireball Project off the ground. He strode across the room and took Mullarkey by the shoulder to steer him away from the others. When he spoke, Mick's voice was choking with anger.

'Ah Jaysus Pat, you're going to have to do a bit better than that! Surely to God you're not telling me that you're going to throw these dacent people out and they hardly arrived in the shaggin' country long enough to warm themselves?'

Mullarkey put on the hurt look of one who has been sorely wronged as he hotly denied the insinuation. 'Of *course* I'm not throwing them out – I wouldn't *dream* of doing such a thing! But we do have a problem on our hands, even if you refuse to see it. I didn't want to upset that pair any more than I had to, but you had better believe me when I say that the pressure from the State Department to expel them is far worse than I suggested – and it can only get worse. Of course . . .' Mullarkey's voice assumed a wistful tone as he looked questioningly at Mick '. . . the ideal solution from everyone's point of view would be for them to leave of their own accord.'

Mick snorted in disgust. 'Arrah, will you cop yourself on! They're hardly going to fly off out of here with nowhere to go. They could be arsing around the world from airport to airport for the rest of their born days. Jaysus, you wouldn't do that to a dog! What about the *céad míle fáilte* we're supposed to be famous for? A hundred thousand welcomes my arse! Listen carefully now to what I'm telling you and I swear to God it isn't one word of a lie. We'd only be making right eejits out of ourselves if we threw out these poor shaggers and we only just after giving them a State Reception and a twenty-one gun salute. You know as well as I do what the whole world and his wife will say about you. They'll say there was one reason and one reason only why a man like yourself would do such a thing. 'Twas because the Yanks twisted your arm and that cranky old divil up there in the American Embassy got out of the wrong side of bed this morning. What's more, Mahony and his friends will have the knives out for you. The dogs in the street know that his crowd are only waiting for the chance to give you the heave. Now, are you going to hand it to them on a plate by looking as though you're marching to the *Stars and Stripes Forever?*'

Though out of earshot, Abe and the visitors were impressed by the familiar, almost insolent way, in which Mick was haranguing his leader, the Taoiseach.

With an air of weary resignation, Mullarkey relented. 'Okay, so what would *you* do to solve the problem – just supposing for one second that you had the power to do so?'

'I'll tell you exactly what I'd do,' replied Mick vehemently. 'I'd lock the door and stay here till we worked something out. Don't forget, the Press and TV are outside waiting for a statement. When they get to hear of the coup, they'll be breaking down the shagging door to get an interview with the Chief. The way I see it, we've got about twenty minutes at most before all hell breaks loose round here. We'd better have something worked out before then, or we're going to look right eejits. Now you asked me my opinion of how to solve this thing, so here it is. The only thing you can do without getting egg all over your face is to offer them Political Asylum.'

Ignoring the appalled look on Mullarkey's face, Mick took a deep breath and pressed on doggedly.

'Of course, it's not as if they're poor bloody refugees without a penny to their name. Abe tells me they've money coming out their ears, and of course we'd be expecting something in return, if you get me . . .'

Mullarkey did not miss the switch to 'we' when the subject of money was introduced.

At the same moment, Freddie broke off from whispering urgently into his father's ear to inquire of Abe what he thought Mick might be doing.

'Reckon he's fighting your corner, son. That American Ambassador has plenty of clout round here . . .' He didn't think it necessary to relate how some time back, he himself had had to be smuggled out of Brulagh in the hold of a trawler to avoid being extradited back to the States. With that little misunderstanding long since cleared up, there was nothing to be gained by bringing the matter up again. 'And like the guy just said,' he concluded, 'there's nowhere else to hide. By the way, which of the Generals do you reckon it was, behind the coup?'

Freddie shrugged. 'Could be any one of half a dozen or so. Doesn't matter as far as we are concerned – one is as bad as the next. I hope you realise that there is no question of our going back, no matter what that Mullarkey fellow may think. Do you believe what he said about those other places being closed to us?'

'Yeah.' Abe frowned as he tried desperately to think of somewhere that might offer them a safe haven. 'I guess so. Seems to me like we might do a whole lot worse than stay where we are. Unless, of course, either of you has got a better idea?'

This was greeted with more helpless shrugs so Abe pressed on: 'Well, if that's the way of it, seems to me like we had better cut a deal with those two guys over there before they come up with a different answer.'

The Paramount Chief intervened before Freddie could object. 'There is much sense in what you say. You have been our friend for long enough now so we trust you to do the best you can. I presume we will have to pay for the privilege of staying in this wet and windy place?'

Abe nodded and was about to elaborate on this when Mick beckoned to him from across the room.

'The Taoiseach and myself have been trying to work out what we'll do with your friends. Like he said, the Yanks are kicking up bloody murder and threatening all sorts of trouble if we don't send them back to stand trial. Now we all know what'll happen if we do that, so we're racking our brains here to find some way round it. We were wondering if you had any ideas on the matter yourself?'

Without Mullarkey seeing it, he shot Abe a conspiratorial wink while awaiting his reply. Abe took his cue.

'My friends sure appreciate your concern for their safety. To send them back home would be to sentence 'em to death. As for going anywhere else, it sounds like that ain't an option either so I guess they'd kinda like to stay right here for a while until they see how things at home are going to pan out . . .'

Mullarkey cut in to tell him that the major powers had already recognised the new régime. Abe failed to stifle an oath.

'Jeez, that was quick! Looks like they had everything sewn up well beforehand. Just wanted 'em out of the way so there wouldn't be any serious opposition. Well then, I guess that clinches it – we just gotta stay here. Now, as I was saying to the Paramount Chief just a moment ago, this might be the right time to invest in your fine country. Mick was telling me earlier about this peat-pellet plant he's trying to get off the ground. The Alternative Energy Foundation is an independent body, only partly funded from the Chief's *private* assets, so no matter what anyone tells you, the new crowd in charge of Marabar have no claim on it whatsoever . . .'

Mullarkey again interrupted. 'Do you honestly expect anyone to believe that? I seem to remember you got up to some pretty complicated financial engineering while setting up the Orchid Club – so complicated that you left us, as I recall, without even saying goodbye.'

For a moment Abe looked taken aback but recovered well. 'This is completely different. AEF is registered in both New York and Geneva, not some Mickey Mouse Caribbean island. Its aims are solely to develop alternative fuels to oil and coal. Every cent it's got is as clean as a whistle. Get your own people to check it out if you don't believe me. This Fireball Project is just what we've been looking for. Now what I had thought we might do is this . . .'

20

THE PRESS CONFERENCE had been set up at very short notice. As Mick had predicted, the moment news of the coup hit the wire services, the reporters waiting for a routine briefing and photo-opportunity were suddenly baying for blood.

All of a sudden, the visitors and their welcome committee were snowed under by a blizzard of cables, phone messages and faxes all wanting the same thing; an exclusive interview with the ex-Ruler of Marabar. TV cameras were lugged into place in the large dining room that would serve as a Press Centre. The large contingent who had made the lengthy journey from Brulagh were invited along too, as something of particular interest to them was going to be announced.

Just before he walked out onto the platform to meet the press, Mullarkey was handed an urgent fax. It was from the American Embassy, Ballsbridge, Dublin 4. It read: *'Ignore previous request to send back party to Marabar. New régime do not, repeat not, want them back. The ban on their landing in the United States of America, however, still applies. End of message.'*

He crumpled it into a ball, thought for a second or two and then put it in his pocket. A smattering of polite applause greeted his entrance. Already seated at a long table – a microphone in front of each of them – were Mick Flannery, the Paramount Chief, Freddie and Abe. The Taoiseach cleared his throat, read out a short statement and asked for questions. The first was from the *Daily Telegraph*.

'Mr Taoiseach, you've just said that Ireland has offered Political Asylum to the Paramount Chief and his son. Does that mean they are going to remain in Ireland? And if so, for how long?'

Mullarkey shot his cuffs, cleared his throat again and fixed a glassy smile on his face.

'I confirm that they have been offered Political Asylum. I further confirm that they have accepted this offer. As to how long they will stay, that is for the Paramount Chief to answer, but as far as I and my Government are concerned, they can stay for as long as they like.'

Someone from the *Irish Press* had obviously kept his ear closer to the ground than his colleagues for he asked, 'Taoiseach, is there any truth in the rumour that the Paramount Chief is about to invest heavily in this country?'

Mullarkey put on his blandest expression and denied any knowledge of the matter. He did suggest that such questions might be better referred to the gentleman himself.

'Yes, it is quite true,' the Paramount Chief nodded and said very slowly in a deep bass voice. 'The investment comes from the Alternative Energy Foundation which my son and I set up some years ago. It is designed to wean countries like Ireland away from diminishing resources such as coal and oil. Together with our fund manager, Mr Abraham Linovitz, long before this we had already decided to invest in what is known as the Fireball Project. Our visit here was mainly to confirm this. The unfortunate developments in my home country have had no bearing whatsoever on this investment decision. I would like, at this stage, to thank your Taoiseach for extending the hand of friendship to me and my son, by offering us a safe haven when others . . .'

Here he frowned briefly before continuing as Mick watched admiringly at this effortless bending of the truth.

'. . . whom we had until today thought of as friends, turned us away. Thank you, gentlemen. Mr Linovitz will answer any further questions about the AEF, of which he is in charge. I have no more to say.'

With that, he switched off his microphone with an audible click and folded his arms across his chest. Several more frantic questions were yelped at him but he remained imperturbable, gazing fixedly at the ceiling as if in a trance.

The correspondents chose to ignore Abe for the moment, preferring to focus their attention on Mick. Hands waved in the air and voices screamed questions at him from every quarter. Cameras whirred and clicked, flashguns exploded and biros raced across notepads with the speed of light. Several reporters were talking directly to their editors on mobile phones. In this forest of hi-tech equipment, Mick suddenly caught a glimpse of Charley Halpin at the back of the room, one hand raised.

'Yes, Charley, what's your question?'

'Could you tell us, Mr Flannery, how much exactly the AEF are putting into the Fireball Project, how many jobs it will create and when will the factory come onstream?'

The sing-song voice caused those reporters unfamiliar with the Cork accent to snap their heads round in amazement. As for Mick, he beamed down at the tubby reporter much as an elderly headmaster might single out a prize pupil for special attention. Had he coached Charley beforehand, the man couldn't have come up with better questions. They gave Mick the chance he had been waiting for, and he didn't need to be asked twice. He took a deep breath, and drank in the scene before him of the serried ranks of the media, flanked on either side by the citizens of Brulagh. Many of them had come from the bar downstairs and this was now beginning to show as Mick started to speak. Before he had even got the first few words out, there were wild war-whoops and a lone voice shouting somewhat unsteadily, 'Good man yourself, Mick. You tell 'em!'

This Mick proceeded to do. AEF were investing around seventeen million dollars immediately in the Fireball Project. This was met with gasps of amazement and disbelief. Mullarkey remained impassive while Freddie and his father beamed from ear to ear. Abe just nodded solemnly in confirmation of the figure. More than two hundred jobs would be available within a month when the construction would begin under the direction of Derek Evans. His firm would fund phase two of the project. The EC and the Irish Government would also chip in with job-training grants and money for improving access roads *et cetera*. He expected the plant to come onstream within twelve months. It would employ thirty-eight people directly and only God alone knew how many in spin-off jobs. This was greeted by raucous cheering from the Brulagh contingent.

Someone raised the question of the impact on the environment. This allowed him to announce the establishment of a Wildlife Park to be funded by Sir Geoffrey Farmingdale's FFCC. This would protect the rare Greenland White-fronted Goose, a colony of which had taken up residence in part of Brulagh Bog. A cynic from a Dublin Daily inquired sweetly if Mick thought all this would help him get re-elected to the European Parliament. Amid the loudest-yet roars of encouragement from the crowd at the back, he confessed with a broad smile that he thought it would.

Charley had the honour of asking the last question. 'Mr Flannery, is the rock concert still going ahead?'

Mick shook his head. 'No, we've cancelled that. When His Grace the Bishop indicated that he didn't like the idea, we thought it better to cancel it!'

Aphra fought her way out of the packed room to find a telephone. When she finally found one free, she told Gally to be ready to receive the Paramount Chief and his son within hours. They would require the entire west wing for themselves for the foreseeable future. This, she reminded him testily, would more than compensate for the cancellation of The Howling Dogs' booking. Furthermore, the Nabob Suite was to be reserved for one Abraham Linovitz. Before Gally could protest, she hung up. It was, she reflected, going to be difficult enough selling Luke the idea of Abe being around without having to do likewise with her father.

When she got back to the Press Room, Abe was just finishing his spiel. He ended by stating bluntly that the only condition AEF attached to their seventeen-million-dollar investment was that Michael J. Flannery should remain in Europe to safeguard the interests of the Fireball Project. He then ended with a curt, 'No more questions, thank you!' and the Press Conference was over.

Soon afterwards, the Bentley bearing the crest of the Gallericks – two unicorns *rampant* under a banner bearing the legend *Nil Desperandum* – sped towards the Orchid Club. With Aphra driving, Abe and Luke shared the back seat. They had left the maximum space between themselves, opting to look at the passing scenery rather than at each other.

Some distance astern, a hurriedly leased limousine was gliding at a more sedate pace in the same direction. A glass partition separated the chauffeur from the Paramount Chief, Freddie and Mick Flannery. Mick had been holding forth on the difference between Irish pubs and those Freddie had frequented during his brief tenure at the London School of Economics. While the

Paramount Chief was staring out of the window, enthralled by the rain and the cloud-covered hills, Freddie suggested quietly that they might visit one before checking in at the Orchid Club.

'In the interests of research, of course. My father doesn't normally indulge.'

This came as news to Mick, who had personally seen the old guy lower at least four Irish Coffees without batting an eyelid. In fact, they were now taking their toll, for the Paramount Chief was suddenly becoming depressed at the drastic change in his circumstances. The view that presented itself through the rain-spattered window could not have been further removed from the sandy wastes and eternal blue skies of his homeland. In truth, the coup had not come as that much of a surprise. He knew full well that his enemies, in league with the superpowers, had long since decided that it was time for a change in Marabar.

He worried, though, about how he would cope with exile in a land so different from his own. It was some consolation that it appeared to be mainly agricultural, if one were to judge by the number of men with flat caps and shabby raincoats leaning over rusting gates and saluting his passing. The friendly respect shown by the ordinary people made quite an impression. Obviously Mick Flannery must be a man of power and influence when everyone saluted his passing. It was not until much later that he realised it was customary in Ireland to wave a greeting at friend and total stranger alike.

Out of the corner of his eye he examined his benefactor chatting easily with Freddie. Mick Flannery had a face that laughed easily yet he was no clown. Had he not singlehandedly persuaded the Prime Minister to grant Political Asylum against the clearly-expressed wishes of the American Ambassador? Would that his neighbours across the Marabar borders had been so courageous! A man such as this would make a better friend than an enemy, he decided, as he turned away from the window to listen to what the others were so earnestly saying.

When he found them discussing the relative merits of English and Irish pubs, he let his mind drift back to the time he had spent herding goats in the bush. It had prepared him for his future role in trying to persuade eight different tribes to unite and march in the same direction. On balance, he concluded, the goats had more sense and made for firmer friends. The palace and the riches that came much later had never been that important to him, though Freddie might not share this view. He watched as the purple hills changed colour when the watery sun chased rainclouds across the rolling hillsides, only to be swamped by yet another downpour. He wondered how long his tired bones could withstand such a wet, cold climate. He hoped that his newfound allies would not prove as fickle as the weather. Perhaps he should buy this big man's friendship before anyone else did . . . He would discuss the matter with Abe Linovitz, who was more familiar with the customs of this wet but welcoming island. Then, and only then, could he relax in this place they called the Orchid Club until such time as events back home took on a clearer pattern.

Grey walls consisting of stones placed on top of each other with nothing to bind them except their own weight, whizzed past his window. Not just by the roadside but right across the rolling landscape they divided the lush green pastures into a delicate patchwork of tiny squares. Some stretched arrow-straight across miles of undulating ground before climbing up the mountains, only to vanish in the mist that cloaked the brooding peaks like a shroud. He turned away from the window and asked: 'Why all the stone walls, Mr Flannery?'

'Mick – everyone calls me Mick round here. Except, of course, the shaggers who're looking for something off me. Now, about those walls. Well, it's really quite simple. Until the British arrived, we had open grazing. Everyone owned the land – or no one, if you prefer. The animals roamed as they wished, free as the air. Then the landlords came and fenced everything in. They changed the property laws so that each man had to have proper title to his own bit of land, no matter how small it was. When he died, 'twas left to his sons and so it had to be divided up again. They did that by putting up even more stone walls. After a few generations, as you can see for yourself, some of those fields are hardly big enough for a cow to stand in.'

The Chief digested this before commenting, 'I had quite forgotten your colonial past. Would the Lady Aphra be part of that?'

Mick nodded. 'Not that the Gallericks were the worst of them, to give them their due. Mostly they looked after their tenants, not like some of the other shaggers who left them to die during the famine.'

This came as a further surprise to the Chief. 'Oh I'm sorry, I was not aware that you had recently suffered a famine?'

Mick sought to correct the impression. 'Well, not *recently* – more like a hundred years ago. Even so, a lot of people died because of it. They've long memories round here, I promise you.'

'It seems, Mr Flan . . . sorry, Mick, that our two countries have more in common than I had first imagined. We too had famines on a regular basis until the drilling mud and later the Casino helped us manage things better. What you say about the walls interests me. In Marabar we also have common ownership. Until a few hours ago I owned the land but let the people farm it as they wished.'

He paused here to unleash a low chuckle. It was the first time he had smiled since the Press Conference. 'As long as they behaved themselves, of course. I'm told that you have an election coming up. Again that is something we do not yet have in Marabar. We thought them to be . . .' he paused for a moment, trying to find the correct word '. . . disruptive. Do you not find elections disruptive, Mick?'

'Damn right I do! Especially when it looks like I might lose. Anyway, let the last day be the hardest and never say die till you're dead, as we say round here. We're just coming into the village of Brulagh. I'll tell the driver to stop for a minute. I promised I'd show your son a real Irish pub. My own son runs this one and you won't find better the length and breadth of the island, even if I say so myself!'

Some miles ahead in the Bentley, small talk was at a premium. Luke was still trying to come to grips with the fact that not only was he expected to be civil to Abe Linovitz, but that now the little con artist would be occupying the best suite in the Orchid Club. The fact that the Club was now booked solid for the forseeable future could hardly compensate for sharing the same roof as the crook who had tried to swindle him. Abe had been gazing out the window, refreshing his memory as to what the countryside looked like. Aphra had been strangely silent, pretending to concentrate on driving, though stealing occasional glances into the mirror to see if there were any signs of a thaw in the distinctly cool relations betweent the pair in the back. Eventually Luke could contain himself no longer.

'Can you really get the go-ahead on this Fireball thing from the Paramount Chief?' he said, sounding doubtful in the extreme as he eyed the stocky little man from the Bronx. Out of deference to Aphra, he had resisted adding, 'Or is this just your usual line of bullshit?' Only she could have persuaded him to meet with the little scumbag, much less put him up for free in the Orchid Club. Definitely a case of feeding the hand that bit you, he concluded ruefully as he waited for a reply.

Abe paused, then forced a wounded expression on his chubby face as he rasped: 'Sure I can. Didn't Mick Flannery tell ya I'm the front man for the Alternative Energy Fund? Goddam it, Luke, I *am* the goddam AEF when it comes right down to it!'

'Hold it right there a moment.' Luke's voice was dangerously calm. 'Are you telling me that you are going to put up the money for the whole caboodle?'

'Yeah, I sure am. Flannery has fixed it with Brussels so that the money for the access roads and the pipelines will be okay. AEF will do the rest.'

This had a familiar ring to it, Luke decided, as he probed further. 'By "the rest", I suppose you mean putting up some clapped-out plant? Then when you've milked the whole goddam operation for every cent, you take the money and run. That your idea, huh? Just the sort of dirty lowdown scam you tried to pull on me, you asshole!'

Aphra shot her husband a look of alarm but to no effect. Abe took it remarkably well.

'Take it easy, ole buddy. If you want a fight, just ask the lady to stop the goddam car and we can settle it out on the road. But what's it gonna prove if we beat the daylights outa each other? Nuttin', that's what. Now as for this Fireball thing, I'm gonna tell it to you like it is. And I'm only goin' to say it once – and once only. If you don't believe it, then that's your tough shit 'cos it's goin' to happen whether you like or not . . .' Abe swallowed hard before continuing in a softer, more persuasive voice, 'We pay the wages, sign the contracts, erect the plant and bring it onstream. Everyone in the neighbourhood benefits from the spin-offs. I hear it's costin' one hundred thousand bucks to create a job round here these days. I can guarantee one hundred jobs for fifty-two weeks of the year until Hell freezes over. That's saving Pat Mullarkey's outfit ten million big ones right away. And in exchange for what? Just planning permission for a couple of lousy roads into a bog and a few pipes out of it that Brussels are gonna pay for anyway!'

Abe waited for Luke's reaction but none was forthcoming so he pressed on. 'Now whether you like it or not, I'm the guy that calls the shots on this Fireball thing. So it looks like we're goin' to be stuck with each other for quite a while. Now I guess you're still sore about that membership business, but before you go off at half-cock just remember this: when the smoke cleared away, you came out okay in the end. You got your goddam club built and I stayed outa jail, even if it cost me an arm and a leg to swing it. Whatever I did at the time was business, strictly business. There was nuttin' personal in it between you and me. So why don't we shake on it and forget about the past? It's all water under the fuckin' bridge anyway!'

Abe extended a pudgy hand which Luke reluctantly shook without saying anything. Then they sank into another silence, each man trying to adjust to their new relationship. Aphra, who had witnessed the reconciliation with apprehension, smiled to herself as she fought down a fresh bout of heartburn.

Back at the Orchid Club she had to dash around making sure that the west wing was ready for their distinguished guests. Meanwhile Abe had ensconced himself in the Nabob Suite and made complimentary remarks about its *décor*, which further improved relations with Luke. So much so, in fact, that some hours later they were sitting in the lobby, dredging up nuggets from the past when a black limo whispered up outside. It disgorged its occupants with some difficulty, after which Mick Flannery helped the Paramount Chief and Freddie to negotiate the steps that led up to the entrance. The unsteadiness of their gait indicated that their researches into native culture at the Brulagh Inn had taken rather longer than intended. This view was further reinforced by Freddie's singing *Galway Bay*, a performance he had yet to conclude when Mick slipped quietly away and gave the chauffeur an instruction in keeping with his surroundings.

'Home, James – and don't spare the horses!'

21

THEY WERE HUDDLED round the table, clutching steaming mugs to take the cold out of their hands. The tea was strong enough for an elephant to walk on without sinking. Steam rose from the wet overcoats draped over chairs close to the blazing Sellafield, making them look like sweating, exhausted nags in the unsaddling enclosure. The men in the kitchen were too exhausted to worry that the kitchen range spat venomous sparks from its flaming maw out on the tiled floor. It had been another fruitless foray into unfamiliar territory and Charley was voicing the opinion that most of it had been a waste of time.

'Jaysus, lads, we're gettin' nowhere. Half those shaggers we saw today are too lazy to get up off their arses to vote even if it stops raining. As for the rest of 'em, they've no notion of voting for Mick even if the sun was splitting the stones outside their door.'

Sean nodded. Charley was right, as usual. Mick Flannery's election campaign was going nowhere – fast. Despite his youth, Sean was a veteran of many campaigns. From the time he was in short pants he had traipsed after Charley and the band of stalwart canvassers who braved rain, sleet and dogs' abuse for the cause. They would explain away Mick's absence on the doorsteps by citing 'official duties'. Mick, they explained to friend and foe alike, put duty before personal gain at all times – even though he desperately needed their votes.

The reality was that Mick had always been more of a liability than an asset on a canvass. With hundreds of prospective voters to greet in the round of a day, invariably Mick would become engrossed in long conversations when all that was required was for him to press the flesh, intone, 'Sure you won't forget me on Polling Day' and move on to the next house. He was perfectly happy to talk forever about the price of milk or the prospects of the local hurling team. With the faithful of his own era, Mick was still a legend in his own lifetime. His four-in-a-row All Ireland medals had been enough to get him re-elected time and again, albeit by a diminishing margin. But not this time.

For one thing, the European constituency was much bigger, and many of the voters knew little and cared less about Michael J. Flannery. To make matters worse, interest in these elections was minimal, Brussels being regarded as just another stop for the European gravy train. Mick's campaign should have begun three months ago but, as usual, he had declined to bestir himself until the very last moment. Mullarkey had advised him to 'blitz' the big towns and cities, paying little or no attention to his old strongholds which were considered 'safe'.

It was this strategy that Charley was now disputing vigorously. The denizens of the crowded housing estates didn't give a tuppenny damn for Mick – or the Farmers' Friend for that matter. Any views they might have had about farming concerned the exorbitant price of milk on their doorsteps and the fact that farmers paid little or no tax. A candidate promising jobs to farmers' sons and daughters in the middle of a bog no one had heard of provoked a mixture of incredulity and scorn – not the stuff of which successful campaigns were made.

Mick joined them just as Charley was pounding the table and shouting that what they were doing was too little too late. It was all very well for bloody Pat Mullarkey and the backroom boys up in Dublin to tell them to concentrate on the big population centres. Did they know – here Charley caught Mick's eye for the first time but pressed on regardless – that Mullarkey and his party were going through a particularly bad patch? With unemployment set to scale new heights and rumours of a heave screaming out from every tabloid and TV in the nation, Mullarkey's honeymoon was well and truly over. He was suddenly being perceived as a bumbling country bumpkin. On the doorsteps, they were tarring Mick with the same brush. Most of his new electorate eked out a precarious existence in drab housing estates. This was a far cry from the familiar farms and villages where the voting preference of every family was an open secret. In this smaller fiefdom, Charley and Sean could gauge to within a few hundred votes how Mick would poll. Not so with this new and uncharted territory.

As he looked questioningly at his father, Sean knew in his heart that Charley was right. Without a doubt, this was the worst canvass ever. In the past, there had been many dire predictions of defeat but they had always managed to pull something out of the fire before Polling Day. Once it had been a pie-in-the-sky microchip factory. Before that, a state-of-the-art fish processing plant was to spring up by the yet-to-be-built new Brulagh pier. In the old constituency, a sufficient number of gullible voters swallowed each promise more outlandish than the last to ensure that Mick continued to stalk the corridors of power.

The current strategy was to claim that the vast wealth of the EC could only be directed towards this sprawling constituency if Michael J. Flannery – the man with the plan – were re-elected. This was a tactic that left much to be desired. Any of the other candidates could have justifiably claimed the same thing – especially the Farmers' Friend. Noel McBride had long since abandoned attacking the other two incumbents, who were odds-on certainties, in favour of criticising Mick's less-than-inspiring record of achievement. With the first two seats a foregone conclusion, the battle royal would be for the third – and last – seat. Although there were several other candidates for what was called 'the hind teat' seat, it was accepted that the struggle would be between Mick and the FF.

After inheriting the European seat from the late James O'Rourke, it had seemed to Mick as though his days of knocking on doors were over. Not that he had knocked on that many of them, preferring to leave such dreary tasks to his son Sean and the little group in shiny suits and white shirts that had been the nucleus of his support for the past three decades. For them it had been a labour of love – though when a relation needed a job in the Civil Service or a grant for an indoor toilet, they were rarely disappointed.

The European elections occurred every five years and were not subject to the fate of governments. All Mick had to do was to ensure that he was nominated by the party six months previously. He did this by engineering an unopposed nomination. Mullarkey had suggested that Mick spend the months between his nomination and the election in an intensive canvass of the vast constituency. He pointed out that the previous occupant of the seat, the deceased O'Rourke, had been a far more diligent servant of the public than Mick. Even then, he had experienced difficulty in retaining his seat. Needless to say, Mick had ignored this advice. He did not embark on serious electioneering until a fortnight before the 'off'.

Charley's high-pitched voice penetrated Sean's innermost thoughts. 'Them *townies* don't give a damn about farm prices or how many jobs Mick is going to get for Brulagh. Them boyos dance to a different tune altogether. Didn't you hear that woman today? She told us she wouldn't vote for Mullarkey's crowd if we knelt down and kissed her backside. I'm telling you here and now, lads, unless we think of something fast, we're up the creek without a paddle! As things stand, Mick here has as much chance of getting elected as I have of being made Pope!'

This outburst was followed by a long silence. No one disagreed with him, least of all Mick. He had just spent a happy hour dallying with Josephine Donnelly, whose husband was being released from dry dock that very evening. The return of Tom Donnelly, coinciding as it did with the last frantic days of the campaign, meant that it would be a long time before their next tryst. In those circumstances, he reminded himself with a chuckle, it was only natural that they should have sought to make the best of it. Though a deeply satisfying encounter, it was hardly the ideal preparation for devising a fresh strategy to snatch victory from what even his most fervent supporters were depicting as the jaws of defeat.

He examined the gloomy faces round the kitchen table. When no one seemed prepared to offer a contrary view to Charley's doomladen prophecy, Mick knew this was the last chance he might ever get to rally his demoralised troops. Lose this one, he told himself, and you'll spend the rest of your life tending to the vegetable garden and accompanying Maggie on her many and varied religious pilgrimages. He cleared his throat and tried to inject a note of confidence into what he was about to say.

'Well, if that's the case, Charley, then we'd better change our tactics and the sooner the better. Let's get back to basics – doing what we know best, I mean. You can't teach old dogs like us new tricks at this stage of our lives. To hell with the townies! As you say yourself, most of 'em aren't going to vote at all so what in the name of Jaysus are we wasting our time on 'em for? No matter what Mullarkey and those eejits with the computers try to tell us, this shaggin' election is no different from the others in one respect. It's still all about getting out the bloody vote. If we make that our goal, then the *fewer* of those townies that come out to vote, the better it suits us. As long as we get our crowd out in strength, of course. Remember what we used to tell 'em long ago? *Vote for Mick Flannery early – and often!* From now on, we're going to campaign like we did in the old days. My bet is that if we get enough of the old reliables out to vote, we'll beat the socks off the Farmers' Friend. Surely to God he must be getting the same response as we are when it comes right down to it. And I'll tell you something else. I'm going to get on the phone to Pat Mullarkey this minute and tell him to get his arse down here in double quick time unless he wants me to lose this election. He's no genius but he doesn't have to be one to realise that I could bring him down with me if we lose the seat. Now listen to me carefully because I won't say it again. With less than a week to go we've got to move heaven and earth to get out the old reliables on Voting Day.'

Heads nodded in agreement. Before they broke up, it was decided that the canvassers would divide into three groups, headed by Charley, Sean and Mick. Every household in his former constituency would be canvassed between them. Anyone showing signs of wavering would be visited again and again until their doubts were set at rest. They were all experienced enough to recognise the strategy for what it was – a desperate last throw of the dice. Even if they could get the old reliables out in strength, it would still require a tidal wave of apathy everywhere else for Mick to scrape in. Still, it was the only chance and everyone in the kitchen recognised it as such.

Two days later, Mick and a small group of canvassers found themselves outside Nora O'Brien's farmhouse high on the slopes of Mount Brulagh. They had parked the car in Johnny's farmyard and hopped over the ditch to canvass the widow: because of this, there had been no advance warning of their arrival.

When the door opened in response to some vigorous knocking, it was Sergeant Johnson who appeared on the doorstep. He was wearing nothing but a towel round his waist. The shaving cream on one side of his face bore testimony to the fact that he had been interrupted in his ablutions. He was trying hard to concoct some convincing excuse for his presence in the farmhouse, not to mention his state of *déshabillé* when his efforts were suddenly set at nought. Nora's voice rang out from behind an outhouse. 'Kevin darling, will you see what's banging on the door?'

When she appeared round the side of the house moments later, the unexpected sight of several men at her door made her drop the freshly laid eggs she had been retrieving from the henhouse. There ensued an embarrassed silence – one which Mick was in no hurry to end. Frozen as though in a *tableau*, everyone stared fixedly at the golden pool of egg yolks spreading slowly across the cobblestones. Each was afraid to make eye contact with another lest they might betray their innermost thoughts. Mick reflected happily that while the arm of the law was not in quite such a compromising position as he and Josephine had been, that night on the sofa in the Donnelly's apartment, it would do quite nicely until something better presented itself.

Just as it was beginning to feel like a long weekend in a Trappist monastery, the Sergeant recovered his powers of speech. 'You're a long way off your usual beat, Mr Flannery, if you don't mind my saying so.'

Mick was affability itself. 'I might say the same for yourself, Sergeant. At least I *know* what I'm doing here. Asking this good woman – and the Slatterys next door – for their Number One. But what about yourself? Surely you're not going to tell me that you're still looking for poteen after the last raid down by the lake? Doesn't the world and his wife know that every single drop of the craythur in the whole shaggin' country got buried in that mudslide a while back . . .'

His tone changed from ebullient to condescending as he concluded his remarks with a helpful, 'Even *you* must have heard about that by now.'

The Sergeant might have made a suitable reply but he was beaten to it by a short head. Nora had recovered both from the shock and the loss of her eggs. Instead of being annoyed, she was the very essence of civility.

'If that's what brought you all here, then you've had a wasted journey. God Himself knows that Mick Flannery always got our Number One in this house, even when my poor husband was alive.

Now that Kevin here has asked me to marry him, I'll see to it that you can count on his vote too!'

Short of Father Jerry reading out the Banns from the pulpit, there could have been no more public announcement of the Sergeant's matrimonial intentions. It was only then that she thought to explain his presence with: 'He was up here looking at the tyres on Johnny's tractor – something to do with poaching on the old Colonel's bit of a lake. But I told him not to be bothering his head about it. Johnny Slattery's the best neighbour anyone could have and he'd only be offended if Kevin . . .' at this point she took the Sergeant's hand and squeezed it affectionately before continuing '. . . went snooping around his place unknownst to him. Especially as we're all soon going to be the closest of neighbours.'

The hall was sparsely furnished. Tubular steel chairs with plyboard seats creaked and groaned as the count proceeded at a long trestle table in the middle of the floor. It was roped off from the general public, though the tallymen slipped in and out under the ropes with impunity. Those who counted the votes, and the tallymen, treated each other with easy familiarity. They were all seasoned performers in the endless circus of elections, even if the ringmaster on this occasion was new to the job. The candidates chainsmoked and pawed the ground uneasily like racing thoroughbreds sweating up in the paddock just before the 'off'. Despite their shared objectives, they kept very much to themselves. They were separated from each other by a solid phalanx of supporters clustering like pilot fish round a shark.

Moods varied from the smug confidence of the two candidates already home and dry to the forced gaiety of the no-hopers. These were the 'token' candidates who campaigned on local issues of pot-holed roads and dilapidated schools. Their race was run, for it was now clear that the struggle for the last seat would be between Mick Flannery and the Farmers' Friend. The tallymen swarmed like angry bees around the table where the sorting took place. They chewed on pencil stubs as they strained to catch a glimpse of each ballot paper being unfolded. Concentrating only on the Number One votes, they placed a tick opposite each candiate's name in their dog-eared notebooks.

In this way, they could often forecast the result before the official count had started. Prophets like these were invaluable to the Press and TV crews impatient to announce the result to the outside world. Not this time, however. Those with deadlines were reporting back to exasperated News Editors that the last seat, with some ballot boxes yet to be opened, was too close to call. With the tallymen of no use, the Returning Officer was proving even less helpful. The TV crew, knowing him to be new to the job, tried hard to persuade him to announce the winners of the first two seats there and then. That would provide a news bite for the six o'clock news. It would also give the Returning Officer his moment of glory on national TV. Their efforts were to no avail. He quoted from the rulebook to the effect that no announcement could be made until *all* the votes were counted and that was the end of the matter. Without another word he turned on his heel and made for the table where the sorting was still in progress. One of the sorters held up a ballot paper for him to inspect. All the names had a Number One after them. A barely legible scrawl at the end read '*as promised*'. He smiled thinly and placed it delicately, much as he might dispose of a long-dead rat, on the small pile reserved for spoilt votes.

The TV crew had withdrawn to a distant corner of the hall to lick their wounds and air their grievances. Who did that retired chalk-pusher of a schoolmaster think he was, anyway? It looked like the old bollocks expected them to hang around half the bloody night while he went through a never-ending series of counts and recounts to decide who got the last seat. When the crew realised that there was absolutely nothing they could do about it, they began to console each other that they were on overtime and entitled to generous Outside Broadcast expenses. That mollified them to the extent that had the wider implications of who won the last seat not been so important, the crew might have adjourned to the pub there and then.

Over the past week, Mullarkey had rolled up his sleeves and entered the fray on behalf of Mick Flannery. In a blitz of all the major centres, he had told the electorate that a vote for Flannery was a vote of confidence in the Government. The dissidents, led by Mahony, saw it that way too. Should Mick be defeated, it would be as much a kick in the arse for the Taoiseach as it would be for the dinosaur from Brulagh. If that should come to pass, it would be time to launch the 'heave'.

Those not directly involved in the struggle for the last seat found themselves impaled on the horns of a dilemma. For them the question was how long the proceedings were likely to take, rather than the final result. This was important because researches conducted earlier had shown that the nearest pub was a drab affair where the drink was suspect. The pint had a flat, sour tang to it and the whiskey tasted as though it had been laced with Johnny Slattery's poteen. Worse still, the bar-owner was a fanatical Mullarkey supporter. His premises were festooned with posters asserting that the Taoiseach's newfound disciple, Mick Flannery, was indeed 'the man with the plan'. If time permitted, those who doubted such an assertion would betake themselves to a more distant establishment where both the drink and the landlord's politics were more to their liking.

At the back of the hall, a large group of hefty men with ruddy faces and bulging waistcoats were roaring at each other in the same kind of voice they employed to summon the cows to the milking parlour from distant pastures. Strong farmers to a man, they clustered round a lanky figure in loose-fitting tweeds, sturdy brown brogues and a heavy flannel shirt fastened at the neck by a tie, loosely knotted and slightly askew. Thin strands of reddish hair were carefully plastered across his pate, drawing attention to, rather than concealing, his baldness. The gaunt features were those of an ascetic monk, possibly a hermit, whose high colour was acquired from time spent in the great outdoors rather than the confines of a snug. Indeed, Noel McBride, the real name of the Farmers' Friend, was a lifelong enemy of the demon drink. A drunken father, given to chastising his only child on the slightest pretext, had seen to that. McBride's belief that those who drank were, at best, misguided oafs should have been a serious drawback to his electoral prospects in a land so devoted to the consumption of alcohol.

That it did not tell against him was a tribute to his other qualities, not the least of these being a terrier-like determination in pursuit of his goals. An example of this was the gymkhana. What had started out as a small affair in aid of the local Pony Club had quickly grown into one of the major events on the equestrian calendar. McBride had accomplished this singlehandedly, and his falling out with Mick Flannery was part and parcel of the affair. He had invited Mick to officially open last year's three-day event – a glittering occasion with VIPs and sponsors in attendance. Mick had lunched well and not stinted himself in the Hospitality Tent. He began his speech with the observation that he had never liked horses, sharing Oscar Wilde's view that they were dangerous at either end and uncomfortable in the middle. He might have been forgiven for this *faux pas* were it not for his closing remarks.

'Now, ladies and gentlemen, it is both my privilege and pleasure to introduce you to the man who made all this possible, a man who I'm damn sure needs no introduction, Mister . . .'

Then Mick froze. The drink combined with the proximity of His Grace, the Bishop and the generous amount of leg being shown by Josephine in the front row had erased the name that needed no introduction completely from his memory. No amount of frantic searching could dredge it up as the audience looked on with a growing expectancy. After a pause that seemed like eternity, he leaned over to the Bishop seated next to him on the platform and whispered urgently, 'What's his name again?'

Unfortunately for Mick, the microphone picked up every syllable, providing the only laugh of an otherwise serious occasion. It also made a mortal enemy of Noel McBride, the Farmers' Friend.

Suddenly the Recording Officer's voice rasped over the Public Address System. It was his first public utterance and he wanted to get the attention of the various groups who continued to chatter noisily among themselves despite a few scattered appeals for silence from the body of the hall.

'Er . . . may I have your attention, please? The sorting will be completed shortly. After a five-minute break, the first count will begin. I would remind you all that only those people properly authorised to do so will be allowed to approach the table. I must insist that everyone else remain outside the ropes.'

Charley sidled up, a long sheet with names and ticks opposite them trailing behind him like a bridal train. He glanced briefly at a notebook to marshall his thoughts before delivering his report. He wore a worried frown that spread across his chubby face like a raincloud darkening the sunlit slopes of Mount Brulagh.

'Jaysus Mick, I don't like saying it but it don't look so good. There's only a few more boxes left to open and you're at least six hundred behind. The only thing in our favour is that one of 'em is the Brulagh box. Even so, if our own crowd don't come up trumps we're up Shit Creek without a paddle. It's hard to be sure at this stage but from what I can make out, even if every bloody one of 'em came out to vote for you, we could still be in trouble – unless, of course, the surplus from the first two seats is in our favour.'

As expected, the first two seats looked to have gone to the incumbents. The tallymen predicted a surplus of about three thousand votes to be distributed among the remaining candidates. After the first count, the no-hopers would be eliminated and their second preferences allocated to those contesting the last seat. Charley had calculated that neither of them would reach the quota so the final result could hinge on a single vote.

Mick digested this with apparent calm. Inside, however, he was shocked and frightened. In all the elections he had fought, there had never been one this close. He hadn't felt such an agonising knot in his stomach since the last hurling final in Croke Park.

Trailing by two points with only seconds to go, no one had given his team a ghost of a chance. And yet more by luck than skill, he had scored a goal in the dying seconds, to win by a single point! On that he had built a political career that spanned three decades. The question was, could he pull the rabbit out of the hat again? As his election agent, Charley understood the complicated workings of the proportional representation system better than most. If Charley said things were looking bad, then he was probably right. Mick tried hard to shake off the gloomy prospect of spending the rest of his life in Brulagh. Even if Maggie's humour were to improve dramatically, spending all his time at home still didn't bear thinking about.

He looked around for Sean, and spotted him at the fringe of the crowd watching the count from outside the ropes – a futile exercise as nothing further could be learned until the first count was completed. Mick used his eyes and a jerk of the head to semaphore that they should slip away quietly.

In the harsh light of the bar Sean saw just how much his father was suffering. Mick had aged twenty years in as many minutes. Around his eyes, crow's-feet stretched almost to his ears, and his ruddy complexion had taken on a dangerous hint of purple. Worst of all, he had the demeanour of one who had already conceded victory. This was the first time Sean had seen him like this. For as long as he could remember, his father's contests had been close. This was largely due to the benign neglect with which he treated his constituency. Yet he had always managed to get away with it somehow or other. Sadly, not this time – or so it seemed.

'Anne Marie, give us two pints and a ball of malt!'

The publican was in the hall, eagerly following the count that had just begun. With his daughter in charge, father and son were spared the ordeal of putting a brave face on what looked to be certain defeat. They took a sip and grimaced. The stout was not up to scratch. The head was flat and yellow, not the creamy froth that would leave rings inside the glass to mark its passing. Mick switched immediately to the large whiskey, leaving Sean to cope as best he could with the maverick pints. Apart from ordering the drink, neither had exchanged a word since they came in. It was only when they were seated at a table in a quiet corner of the bar that Mick said in a low voice that was directed as much to himself as to his son, 'Looks like the last hurrah for me this time. Charley's never wrong about these things, y'know . . .'

He looked towards the bar counter and called to the daughter of the house: 'Two more balls of malt, Anne Marie, like a good girl. No bird ever flew on one wing!' before dropping his voice to continue, 'Though I'd hoped that Fireball thing would do the trick. Anyway, I want to tell you what I had in mind – if I won, that is,' he added hastily.

Sean looked at him uneasily. Heart to heart talks had never featured much in their relationship up to now. Before he went to Liverpool years ago, he had advised his father to concentrate more on the younger voters – but to no avail. Apart from that, they had never discussed long-term strategies. Not that it would make much difference now, he reflected, because most of the youth had either emigrated in search of work or were too disillusioned to bother voting at all, especially for something as remote as a European election. He cleared his mind and tuned into what his father was saying.

'I didn't tell anyone this before now but I had made up my mind that this was going to be my last election,' Mick said heavily. 'I'm getting a bit long in the tooth for all this gadding about. Anyway,

I'd promised myself that if I got in for another five years, that would be it. In that time I had hoped to groom yourself for the job. I know that Pat Mullarkey tried to talk you into standing in the next General Election but that's only a mug's game compared to Europe. Fifty grand a year plus expenses is not to be sneezed at, y'know. Jenny could mind the pub while you'd be away and I can tell you one thing for sure . . .' he brightened visibly as he warmed to the theme '. . . it's a damn sight more fun than pulling pints behind a bar, even lousy ones like these.'

He waved a digusted hand at the half-full glasses and lapsed into an injured silence. After a while he unshipped a sigh that seemed to come straight from the heart as he admitted, 'I can tell you one thing, though, and it's the gospel truth. I'm going to miss it like hell. I wanted to be able to retire undefeated like that boxer fella . . .' neither of them could recall the name so he pressed on mournfully '. . . but it looks like that's not going to happen now.'

Another silence followed. Sean wanted to get out of this dreary place. The gloom was claustrophobic in its intensity, making his temples throb. It was worse than waiting in a Funeral Home for the corpse to be wheeled out. He had never seen his father so depressed and there wasn't a damn thing he could do about it. The sooner this bloody count was over, the better it would be for all of them. Then they could both get on with living the rest of their lives as best they could.

'I'll go back in and see how it's going,' Sean said hastily. 'Why don't you stay where you are. If there's anything new, I'll know where to find you.'

He left without waiting for a reply. Mick sat at the table, a lonely figure shrouded in his own misery. About ten minutes later, Charley Halpin burst through the door.

'Sean told me you were here. You're not going to believe this, but a few of the other tallymen got a look at how the transfers might work out. They say you're better than McBride by at least two to one. The main thing now is for the shagger not to reach the quota on the first count. If he doesn't – and I don't think he will – we could have him by the bollocks on the transfers.'

At this point he broke off to look at the unfinished pints. 'Jaysus, Mick, they look lousy. Does that little girl behind the counter know what she's doing at all? All the same, I'll risk a ball of malt . . .' he dropped his voice so that only Mick could hear '. . . though they tell me that the whiskey here isn't great either.' Whatever its quality, he lowered it in two quick gulps before dashing back to the count.

Sean came back again but not before Mick had drunk two more large ones to steady his nerves. To his disgust, they didn't seem to make him feel any better. He was afraid to raise the glass to his mouth while Sean was looking in case he noticed the shake in his hand. Charley's ray of hope was just that – no more and no less. Nevertheless, it was something to chew on. Now Sean had another piece to add to the jigsaw. The first two seats had been filled as expected. McBride was indeed almost 600 votes ahead but Charley and his tallymen reported that the Brulagh box, which they had seen at the sorting stage, should almost redress the balance.

It was now almost certain that McBride would not reach the quota – even with the distribution of the surplus from the two winners. That meant that the other no-hopers would be eliminated and their second preferences distributed between Mick and McBride, the Farmers' Friend. From here on in, they would be in uncharted territory. As Mick pointed out, anyone voting for the no-hopers had to be some sort of a headcase – seeing as how the dogs in the street knew that none of the shaggers had a snowball's chance in Hell of getting elected. It meant, however, that he was now in with a better chance than an hour ago. To celebrate this fact, when Sean went back to the count, Mick called for another drink and began to cheer up slightly.

The next twenty minutes passed quickly. At last the whiskey was calming him down. He had almost reached the point where it really didn't seem all that important whether he won or lost. Just then the bar filled with a group of noisy supporters. Within seconds Charley had pushed his way through them, his eyes blazing with excitement. He took the whiskey out of Mick's hand and swallowed it himself.

'You'll have no more of that till the speeches are over. Come into the hall with me this minute. The television men were inquiring where you had got to. Easy to see they don't know much about you or they'd have known damn well where to find you! Pull yourself together now, for Jaysus sake. You've just gone ahead by seventeen votes and the count is nearly over!'

22

CHARLEY HALPIN'S BY-LINE in the *Clarion*, 'Brulagh Notes', was longer than usual. References to whist-drives, the Annual General Meeting of the Gardening Club and a forthcoming Livestock Sale got short-shrift in favour of more pressing matters. The results of the European Elections were noted with barely concealed glee: '*Our own Michael J. Flannery triumphed by the narrowest of margins over the candidate of the recently formed United Farmers' Party. Close observers of the political scene attributed his victory to strong support from Brulagh, and the new factory to manufacture peat pellets. One hundred and eighty-three persons are currently employed in site preparation. In addition, a further seventy jobs have been saved at the Power Generating Station now that it will soon change from burning oil to peat pellets.*

The Paramount Chief of the Central African Republic of Marabar and his son are staying at the Orchid Club. So delighted are they with Brulagh and its climate that they have decided to extend their stay indefinitely. They declined to comment on affairs in their own country, where a new régime is experiencing difficulty in establishing itself. They will, however, be guests of honour at a banquet to be held in the Orchid Club on next Saturday night. At this function, which promises to be the social event of the year, a cheque for seventeen million dollars will be handed over to Mr Michael Flannery, our representative in the European Parliament. Among the distinguished guests expected to attend this glittering occasion is Mr Patrick Mullarkey, the Taoiseach and one-time resident of Brulagh. Despite the fact that the rock concert is no longer going ahead because of reasons outside the control of the organising committee, your correspondent believes that the manager of The Howling Dogs will also be among those present. Music for the occasion will be provided by the Brulagh Céili Band, with a bagpipe recital by Colonel Evelyn Thompson promising to be one of the highlights of the evening.'

Two flaming braziers lit the scene with a soft, flickering glow. They blazed steadily on either side of the carved limestone steps that led up to the front door. Six slender pillars supported the roof of the porch, modelled on a Grecian temple. It had been one of the Nabob's less happy embellishments, yet its stark grandeur persuaded Luke Divareli to retain it as the main entrance to the Orchid Club. Usually it was bathed in the harsh glare of concealed floodlamps. Tonight, however, these had been switched off in favour of the turf fires that were the traditional greeting for important guests and great occasions. When Mick Flannery brought home his fourth and last All-Ireland medal, every hilltop and crossroads for miles around blazed a salute. This time they would celebrate his re-election to Europe and the handing over of the cheque for the Fireball Project. A banquet had been arranged to welcome the Paramount Chief and Freddie for what looked to be an extended stay in Brulagh. Other distinguished guests were Sir Geoffrey Farmingdale, who that very day had approved plans for the Wildlife Preserve, and Julian Jagger, who had brought with him the promised stallion hounds.

At the last moment Pat Mullarkey sent his regrets. The Taoiseach cited pressure of business as his reason for not attending the festivities. However he did warmly congratulate Mick on his most recent success at the polls and welcomed the arrival of a new industry in Brulagh. The previous evening he had accepted Mahony's resignation and taken on the Foreign Affairs portfolio himself. This he would retain until a replacement could be found whose loyalty was not in question. Mick Flannery's narrow victory had, with hindsight, shown Mahony's attempted 'heave' to be a trifle premature. An overwhelming vote of confidence in Mullarkey by his parliamentary party proved that the Country and Western Band remained top of the charts, leaving the Minister for Foreign Affairs no option other than resignation. Having seen off one rival, Mullarkey preferred to remain at his desk to winkle out any other troublemakers.

Behind the scenes, there was another heave afoot. This was of a more local nature and concerned the Colonel and his bagpipes. After a heated argument amongst the members of the Céili Band during which a mass walk-out was threatened, a compromise was finally reached. The Colonel would act as a one-man band *outside* the banquet. He would take up position in front of the steps, though even then the Doc thought him rather too close for comfort. It fell to Mick to break the news to the Colonel. Summoning up every last ounce of diplomacy, he explained to the old warrior that it would help enormously if he were to play the part of Piper-in-Chief. It would be his responsibility, and his alone, to welcome the visitors in the traditional Irish fashion – by piping a welcome.

The Colonel blushed a deeper puce than usual and muttered in a voice choked with emotion, 'An honour, sir, to be of service.'

The conference area had been transformed into a huge banqueting hall, decked out in a startling array of flags and banners. These ranged from the flags of Marabar – soon to become collectors' items now that the African Republic was no more – through a wide selection of Irish Tricolours, to a banner that proudly proclaimed St Fintan to be the patron saint of the local GAA club. Some enthusiasts had gone so far as to stick up posters of a smiling, familiar face above the slogan *Michael J. Flannery – Your Number One in Europe! The Man with the Plan!* After some discussion, these were taken down again on the grounds that this was to be a social rather than a political occasion.

Mick was seated between his wife Maggie and Josephine Donnelly. It would not have surprised him in the least to learn that a giggling Aphra was responsible for such an arrangement. Since the cancellation of the concert, Maggie had been attributing the mudslide to Divine Intervention and had resumed diplomatic relations so that the atmosphere between husband and wife once more bordered on the cordial. As for Josephine, she could speak of little else but how life had improved since Tom had gone on the wagon. Mick cursed Josephine silently for choosing that topic of conversation. It was all too obvious that Maggie was much impressed by the banker's newfound temperance. Indeed, she may have had it in mind to recruit Donnelly into the Pioneer Total Abstinence Association for all Mick knew. He just wished she would stop elbowing him in the ribs to indicate that it was a course of action he himself might well adopt with results beneficial both to his health and their marriage.

Mick wondered how long Donnelly would remain 'dry'. Soon he would have to hand over the largest cheque ever drawn on the Brulagh Branch of The Allied Banks of Ireland. Surely the trauma of giving Mick seventeen million dollars rather than the back of his neck would be more than enough to drive him headlong back to the demon drink. Not just yet, however, for Donnelly was nursing a soda water and listening with a bored expression to Deaf Daphne and Abe Linovitz talking animatedly. The subject was not, as Mick had thought, the life and times of the White-fronted Goose. Rather it had to do with offshore investment opportunities – something very close to Abe's heart.

He had just discovered that the old broad had money coming out of her ears from some paintings she had sold. What's more, she now had a nice fat contract from The Audubon Society to paint a series on the wildlife of the area. Not, Abe reminded himself, that he had ever managed to find much wildlife around here. The women weren't much to look at and the bars never seemed to have enough ice. When he complained about the latter, one clown asked him, 'Where in the name of God do you think I'd get ice in the month of August?'

Daphne might be deaf as a stone but that didn't stop her from yackety-yacking thirteen to the dozen. Right now, well within earshot of Tom Donnelly, she was holding forth about bankers. Abe let the tidal wave of words wash over him as he attacked the soup.

'My late husband, bless his soul, told me time and time again never to have any dealings with the local bankers. He always said they were mostly silly little men with fat necks, bald heads and suits two sizes too small for them. Of course he was absolutely right. They don't even ride to hounds, for heaven's sake! Can you credit that? I'm absolutely blue in the face from asking Tom Donnelly here . . .'

She broke off here to point at him lest there should be any confusion about his identity. The banker stared gloomily into his soda water and sighed deeply without saying anything. Daphne picked up where she had left off.

'How can he expect to keep abreast of what's going on round

here if he doesn't even hunt with his clients! As for the interest he offers on deposit, it's nothing short of appalling. Now, you mentioned this island place where they seem to manage these things rather better . . .'

Donnelly excused himself and went in search of something with which he might enliven his drink. It was bad enough having to witness that wretched Flannery once more winning an election that he so richly deserved to lose, but to do so on plain soda water was more than flesh and blood could stand. As for that deaf old bag complaining about his bank, he might just survive the banquet if only he could find a bottle of vodka to help him while away the long watches of the night. Abstinence, he told himself, was all right for some, but men in stressful positions such as his needed a little relaxation every now and then.

Abe waited until Donnelly was well out of earshot before answering Daphne. He pushed aside the empty soup bowl and swallowed what was left of the mead in his goblet. It tasted worse than blackstrap molasses spiked with corn liquor. To make matters worse, it had an evil purple tinge that reminded him of Mick Flannery's complexion that time they had met by chance in Atlanta airport.

A lot had happened since that fateful meeting, what with Marabar going down the tubes and the Fireball Project about to take off. Another surprise had been how warmly Luke Divareli had accepted him, given the fraught circumstances of their last parting. He had lodged Abe in a nice suite, next to Freddie and his father. The Orchid Club looked to be a fine resort – if not as glitzy as the one they had originally planned, before Abe had had to leave Brulagh in such a hurry . . .

He checked again to make sure he had signed the cheque. The bearer bonds and cash in the plane had been deposited with Donnelly in the name of the Alternative Energy Foundation. Only Abe's signature would release the seventeen million dollars from this account. It had been agreed that in due course the Paramount Chief and Freddie would become non-executive Directors under the Chairmanship of Derek Evans. Now Abe turned to Daphne and set about explaining to her the great benefits to be gained from investing offshore. She became so engrossed in what the tubby New Yorker had to say that she completely forgot to take out to the Colonel the pink gin he had requested before they sat down to eat.

Outside on the gravel, the night air was filled with a caterwauling that caused the hounds in the kennels to curl up and whimper piteously. His cheeks bulging like a Botticelli angel, Colonel Evelyn Joshua Thompson was blowing the Scottish War Pipes for all he was worth. In a long and distinguished military career, he had never once deserted his post – not even under heavy fire. He had not the slightest intention of doing so now, despite the rain and chill breeze that snatched at his kilt. Nonetheless, he reflected sadly as he stamped his feet to keep warm, some attempt to victual the beleaguered garrison might have been made by those feasting within. Even a pink gin would have helped restore the circulation in his nether regions.

Arrangements to relieve him from his post were alarmingly vague even by Brulagh standards. The idea was that as soon as the guests were settled in their places, he would be called upon to pipe in the main course. This was to be one of the highlights of the banquet because Gally thought to lend a medieval tone to the proceedings by describing the various courses as 'removes'. Not content with leaving it at that, the daft bugger had concocted a menu wherein chicken soup was described as 'Capon Broth' and the permanent feature of the Orchid Club menu, roast venison, became 'Hind Flambeé'.

Wisely perhaps, no reference was made to the fact that it had been flamed with *poitin* that had gone, as Johnny put it, 'so wrong 'twould take the enamel offa your teeth before you had the time to spit it out!' Its powers of combustion, however, were in no way diminished. A trial run had proved that beyond any reasonable doubt. Gally had told him in the strictest confidence that the crisp outer skin of the 'hind' must have been close to one hundred per cent proof. Taken in conjunction with the mead, a *syllabub* of sorts devised by Harmon for the occasion, it was scarcely surprising that the diners had forgotten all about him.

What the Colonel did not know was that the mead consisted of honey, the remaining stocks of the low-grade port Harmon and his master had so much difficulty in disposing of and, last but not least, a generous measure of the 'pure drop'. It was poured out of earthenware jugs into similar goblets, not merely to lend further medieval colour to the festivities but rather to conceal its own – a vile shade of purple.

To be quite frank, he did feel a trifle ridiculous togged out in the full regalia of a piper, from the top of his furry black Busby down to the tips of the white, cutaway boots. Long stockings, supported by tartan garters complete with thistle-shaped rosettes, covered his battle-scarred legs. He nodded briskly to the late arrivals on their way into the banquet but he dared not take a break, however brief, from blowing. The effort to refill the airbag from scratch would have been more than any conversational gambit could possibly have been worth.

He continued to keep himself reasonably warm by stamping his feet in time to *Scotland the Brave*. Sadly his repertoire did not extend much beyond that. The truth of the matter was that he had thought to be part of the Céili Band where he could tootle away to his heart's content. Instead they had given him a solo spot and he didn't quite know whether to be flattered or insulted. The moon had begun to slip quietly behind a dark mass of cloud that threatened more rain. If that happened the blasted reeds would 'flatten' and give off a sour tone. Not that anyone would notice, since it was obvious that by now everyone who had been invited was already snug inside the Orchid Club.

How he longed for a drink. Even Harmon's purple witches' brew would be welcome at this stage. The moisture was already starting to bugger up the reeds. This made them sound even more strident than heretofore. Good piping, he never tired of telling anyone who would listen, depended on the tuning being absolutely spot on. This was because all four pipes must be blown at a steady rate of knots to give a sustained, wailing note. Already two of the reeds had gone flat in the soft drizzle that was threatening to turn into a downpour at any moment. The pity was that matters would in no way improve when they would eventually summon him inside. The sudden rise in temperature would, in all probability, make the stroppy little buggers sound much 'sharper'.

Inside, the dull roar of conversation had died down somewhat with the arrival of the first 'remove'. This allowed the noise of the 'Capon Broth' being slurped to act as a delicate counterpoint to the haunting strains of the Céili Band. When the last of the *poitín-*

incinerated venison had been cleared away, the Master of Ceremonies banged a spoon against his goblet to attract attention.

'Ladies and Gentlemen, I ask you to be upstanding – whatever that means – and raise your goblets in welcome to our guests.'

Mick Flannery's opening remarks were greeted by an outbreak of sustained cheering, accompanied by much quaffing of the mead.

'The toast is *'Slainte agus saol'* – health and long life to all of us. I don't intend keeping you long . . .'

This was greeted by the loudest cheer to date. Several voices cried aloud, 'Good man yourself!' and 'Get on with it!'

He waited for the hecklers to tire of their amusement, then continued unperturbed, 'But I could not allow an occasion like this to pass without thanking our Guests of Honour on your behalf for their generous investment in our new industry here in Brulagh. Sir Geoffrey Farmingdale has agreed to fund our Wildlife Preserve . . .'

A dapper diplomat with silver hair stood and bowed to the cheering crowd before speedily resuming his seat and letting Mick get on with it.

'. . . Then, of course, there is our own Taoiseach who cannot be with us tonight. He has promised all the help we need to get the Fireball Project up and running . . .'

This elicited more cheering, punctuated by a few indecipherable catcalls.

'And last but not least, our good friends, the Paramount Chief of Marabar and his son—'

Mick got no further. The diners rose from their seats, clapped their hands and roared 'Speech! Speech!' until Mick gestured at the Chief to speak. A few shouts of, 'Can't you stay quiet for Jaysus sake and give the man a chance to hear himself speak!' produced the first silence of the evening.

'My friends – I feel I can call you that after the welcome you have just given my son and me – I too will not detain you for long. I just wish to thank you for your hospitality in our time of need. The Alternative Energy Foundation is proud to be the major investor in your latest industry. In a moment I will call on Mr Donnelly to hand over the cheque. Just before he does so, however, my son and I have a more personal presentation to make. We have heard about the concert that had to be cancelled at the very last moment. We would like to help in some way to make up for that disappointment. Perhaps Mr Flannery, on behalf of the Leisure Centre that bears his name, would accept this personal cheque from us?'

As he thanked the Paramount Chief for this unexpected gesture, Mick glanced at the amount on the cheque. It was more than would have been cleared by even the most successful concert.

Suddenly it was time for the photo opportunity. Flashguns popped and cameras clicked as an unexpectedly cheerful Donnelly handed over the cheque to his sworn enemy. The banker had found a half-full bottle of Smirnoff. It was not until much later he would realise that it held Johnny's reject flambé juice rather than the vodka, *'prepared'* as its label insisted, *'under the formula and process of the successors to Pierre Smirnoff of Moscow, Purveyors to the Czars 1886–1917'*. As for Mick, he had quickly reverted to his role as Master of Ceremonies lest the grinning banker attempted to grace the occasion with a few words of his own.

'Before I ask you to drink the toast of welcome to our distinguished guests, I'd like to especially thank the Paramount Chief and his son, Freddie, for their generous and unexpected donation. I can promise them that the money will be well-spent on providing leisure facilities for the young and not-so-young. It is hardly necessary for the likes of me to assure them that they are welcome to remain here in our midst for as long as they wish!'

When the applause died down, he changed direction. 'Before I finish, I'd like to remind you that the mead we're drinking . . .' Gally shot Harmon a nervous glance but he need not have worried. Their secret was safe as Mick raised his goblet '. . . Was a very popular drink in the old days, especially with newly married couples. They believed that the honey in the mead made for virility and fertility. They drank this mead for one month after the wedding ceremony, hence the expression, "Honeymoon . . ."'

The rest was drowned out in guffaws and cries of disbelief. Aphra suddenly remembered the Colonel. Mick had asked her to bring him inside at least thirty minutes ago. On her way out, she passed close by the Doc. He plucked at her sleeve and whispered urgently. 'Your last tests came back this afternoon.'

Aphra had forgotten all about them, as well as the Colonel. It was a night for forgetting things, she concluded. Having been disappointed so often before, she had given up hope.

'So what did they say?' she asked irritably. 'Same as usual, I expect.'

The Doc examined the tips of his fingernails as though they held something of great interest before answering.

'Not this time. They were positive. You are two months' pregnant.'

She let out a whoop and dashed back across the crowded floor to tell Luke.

In the excitement, she again forgot about the Colonel. Any thoughts she might have had of keeping her news secret were doomed from the start. When she whispered some words into Luke's ear he leapt from his chair and shouted, 'You're WHAT? TWO months gone!!'

After that, the only person unaware of her condition was to be found outside in the rain. The Colonel stamped his feet yet again as he launched once more into *Scotland the Brave.*

AUG.   1994

BINCHY

FIREBALLS